I0823632

MURDER, LOCAL STYLE

Also by Leslie Karst

The Orchid Isle Mysteries

MOLTEN DEATH *
WATERS OF DESTRUCTION *

The Sally Solari Mysteries

DYING FOR A TASTE
A MEASURE OF MURDER
DEATH AL FRESCO
MURDER FROM SCRATCH
THE FRAGRANCE OF DEATH *
A SENSE FOR MURDER *

JUSTICE IS SERVED:
A TALE OF SCALLOPS, THE LAW,
AND COOKING FOR RBG

* *available from Severn House*

MURDER, LOCAL STYLE

Leslie Karst

SEVERN
HOUSE

First world edition published in Great Britain and the USA in 2026
by Severn House, an imprint of Canongate Books Ltd,
14 High Street, Edinburgh EH1 1TE.

severnhouse.com

Cover and jacket design by Piers Tilbury

British Library Cataloguing-in-Publication Data
A CIP catalogue record for this title is available from the British Library.

ISBN-13: 978-1-4483-1658-8 (cased)
ISBN-13: 978-1-4483-1951-0 (paper)
ISBN-13: 978-1-4483-1657-1 (e-book)

All Severn House titles are printed on acid-free paper.

Typeset by Palimpsest Book Production Ltd., Falkirk, Stirlingshire, Scotland.
Printed and bound in Great Britain by TJ Books, Padstow, Cornwall.

The manufacturer's authorised representative in the EU for product safety is Authorised Rep Compliance Ltd, 71 Lower Baggot Street, Dublin D02 P593 Ireland (arccompliance.com)

Praise for the Orchid Isle Mystery Series

"Immerse yourself in Hawaiian lore and savor the portrayal of the stunning landscapes while enjoying the entertaining mystery"
Kirkus Reviews on *Waters of Destruction*

"[An] entertaining cozy series launch.... Karst rewards armchair travelers without ignoring the thorny politics of Hawaiian tourism, and firmly grounds the core mystery in Valerie's emotional struggles. Readers will be hungry for the sequel"
Publishers Weekly on *Molten Death*

"Part murder mystery, part vividly evocative, colorful sketch of Hawaii . . . Armchair travelers and mystery aficionados alike will find it entertaining"
Booklist on *Molten Death*

"A gorgeous yet deadly setting, a tenacious amateur sleuth, and a real head-scratcher of a mystery. Will leave readers longing for their next trip to the Orchid Isle"
Jenn McKinlay, *New York Times* bestselling author, on *Molten Death*

"Leslie Karst's *Molten Death* transports the reader to the best that the Big Island can offer. You won't want to leave!"
Naomi Hirahara, *USA Today* bestselling author, on *Molten Death*

"With its compelling characters and engaging look at the culture and customs of the Big Island of Hawai'i, *Molten Death* is a delightfully immersive whodunnit. Fans of well-plotted, suspenseful mysteries with a foodie element will eat this one up!"
Kate Carlisle, *New York Times* bestselling author, on *Molten Death*

"Leslie Karst's passion and personal connection to Hawai'i shine on every page. She's created a heroine you'll adore and a mystery that's both touching and twisty. I loved it!"
Ellen Byron, *USA Today* bestselling author

To my Hilo neighbors, none of whom
(to my knowledge) are murderers

A note about grammar and language: I have used the spelling and punctuation routinely employed currently in the Hawaiian Islands. The ‘okina, or glottal stop [‘], as in the word “Hawai‘i,” is similar to the break between the syllables in “uh-oh.” A macron (kahakō in Hawaiian) over a vowel [ā] makes it slightly longer than other vowels. Note also that an internal “w” is sometimes pronounced as a “v”; thus “Hawai‘i” is often pronounced “Hah-*vai*-ee” by locals.

A glossary of Hawaiian and Pidgin (the creole spoken by many Hawaiian locals) words and phrases is included at the end of the book.

ONE

Paradise isn't always what it's cracked up to be.

Sure, Valerie Corbin knew she and her wife Kristen were supremely fortunate to now reside in the quaint, still-stuck-in-the-1970s town of Hilo on the magnificent Big Island of Hawai'i—home to lush jungles, fiery volcanoes, black sand beaches, and coral reefs teeming with eye-popping tropical fish.

But at this moment, all she could focus on was the bull terrier-spaniel mix next door barking so loudly that it almost—though not quite—drowned out the whine of the pneumatic tools its owner was using on a jacked-up truck, the parts of which were currently scattered all across his driveway.

Letting loose a few choice words regarding both dog and man, Valerie slammed shut the window above the kitchen sink, then returned to the stove to poke at her potatoes simmering in a pot of water. At the sound of the back door opening, she looked up to see Kristen and her nephew, Sean, come inside from the lānai, Valerie and Kristen's little white dog, Pua, trotting after them.

"We couldn't take the racket anymore," said Kristen, tossing her *Outside* magazine onto the counter. "Does he ever stop?"

"Who—Akoni or Larry?"

Kristen laughed. "Both, I guess. And yeah, I know the answer: rarely. Especially Akoni, with his constant yowling. Though I gotta say, it seems like Larry's been working on his vehicles a hell of a lot more of late. And I don't believe I've ever even seen that particular truck before. You think he's started repairing other people's vehicles, too?"

"Oh, God, I hope not. Though that would explain the increased frequency of the noise." Valerie switched off the heat under her potatoes, then turned to Kristen. "I wonder if it's legal to have a car repair business in this neighborhood. Maybe I should ask at tonight's meeting if anyone knows."

"Or maybe you could just talk to your neighbor about it," put in Sean, who'd taken a seat at the kitchen table and was busy typing something into his phone.

Valerie and Kristen exchanged glances, after which Valerie replied, "Maybe later. But first we should figure out where we stand on the issue."

Sean set down his phone with a shrug. "So what's this thing you're going to tonight, anyway?"

"It's the monthly meeting for the neighborhood orchid society," said Valerie, carrying the pot to the sink and dumping the steaming potatoes into a colander. "Shirley invited me—you know, the woman who lives at that house down the street with all those beautiful orchids in her tree ferns? I was admiring them the other day, and after we got talking, she invited me to come along tonight to see if I might be interested in joining. You wanna join me?"

Sean let loose his man bun, held in place by a wooden hair stick, and shook out his dirty-blond locks. "No can do; I'm working tonight at the hospital. It's my first time in the ER, which should be interesting."

Sean had come from Arkansas to do a three-month stint as a visiting nurse at the Hilo hospital and was now on his second week at the job—and at Valerie and Kristen's house, where he'd be staying for the duration of his time on-island. "I didn't know you were into orchids," he said in a lazy drawl, pulling his hair back from his face and retying the bun.

"I wasn't, not till we first got to Hilo. But they're so amazing and, I dunno . . . other-worldly."

"*Star Trek* flowers, I call them," said Kristen, and Valerie nodded.

"And they're so easy to grow here, so I'm thinking it might be fun to try it myself. Plus, it'd be a great way to get to know some of the folks in the neighborhood a little better."

"Like Larry?" asked Sean with a grin.

"Ha. I'm not so sure he's really the orchid type . . ."

* * *

Walking into the Buddhist hall for the orchid society meeting several hours later, however, Valerie saw that her assumption had been wrong. For one of the first people she saw was her next-door neighbor Larry, laughing and holding court with a trio of women.

She set her potato salad down on a table already loaded with delectable dishes—including ahi poke, Korean fried chicken, Spam musubi, seaweed salad, and the ubiquitous pot of steamed white rice—then looked about her. The hall was adorned with colorful banners, prayer flags, and silk wall hangings depicting lotus flowers, ginkgo trees, and Japanese characters, and upon side tables pushed up against the wall sat "lucky bamboo" plants and bonsai trees, along with several large candles and statues of the smiling Buddha.

Spying Shirley talking to an older man she recognized, Valerie crossed the room to join them.

"Ah, good, you came!" said Shirley, who then glanced around the room. "Is Kristen here, too?"

"No, 'fraid not. Orchids aren't really her thing. I mean, she likes to look at them, of course—who doesn't? But that's about as far as her interest goes." Valerie turned to Shirley's companion. "And you're Mr. Ikeda, yes? I'm Valerie Corbin. My wife and I bought that house down the street from you last fall. So pleased to finally officially make your acquaintance."

"Yes," he said with a slight bob of the head. "I know who you are."

Valerie smiled. "Right. The coconut wireless. I'm guessing there's not much that goes on in the neighborhood without most everyone hearing about it pretty quick."

"Mr. Ikeda is the president of the orchid society," said Shirley. "So he can tell you anything you need to know about our little club."

He bowed again, deeper this time. "But not right now, I'm afraid, as I believe it is time I check with the other board members to see about beginning the meeting. Nice to meet you, Ms. Corbin."

Valerie watched him walk over to a table at the far end of

the room, where several people had taken their seats and were shuffling through papers. One of the men turned to say something to the president as he walked by, but Mr. Ikeda merely shook his head without saying anything in return and took the empty seat in the middle of the table. "Not terribly outgoing, is he?" Valerie said to Shirley.

"Oh, that's just Uncle," she replied with a wave of the hand, using the term Valerie had learned was a common honorific employed in the islands. "He tends to keep to himself. I think he's far more comfortable with his orchids or with financial statements—he's a retired CPA—than with his fellow human beings. But he's a lovely man at heart. And he's put in hundreds of hours over the years serving as president of our society. Though I heard he's been thinking of stepping back from the society—something to do with his heath, I gather. Or maybe it's his wife's health; I'm not exactly sure. Here, shall we sit?"

Valerie followed Shirley over to the rows of folding chairs that had been set up in the hall just as Mr. Ikeda clapped his hands and called for everyone to come take their seats. Swiveling around, she saw there were about thirty people in attendance, mostly folks aged from around fifty to eighty, but with a smattering of youngsters, as well.

The first order of business was the reading and approval of the last meeting's minutes. This was followed by a summary of the year's ending financial statement by the society's treasurer, a tall, gangly gal who—judging by her barely audible voice and the way she stared fiercely down at her papers the entire time—was not too fond of public speaking. Or perhaps she was simply nervous because the president was no doubt far more experienced in financial matters than she?

But Mr. Ikeda seemed to approve fully, given his nods of approval as she read her report. "Okay, before we proceed," he said after turning to thank the shy treasurer, "I'd like to ask any newcomers this evening if you could please stand and introduce yourselves."

Valerie glanced at Shirley, who gestured for her to get up. "Aloha," she said with a smile and quick wave. "Some of you already know me—or more likely my dog, Pua—from our walks around the neighborhood. But for those who don't, I'm Valerie Corbin. My wife Kristen and I just moved here last September from Southern California. I'm a retired caterer—I worked for the TV and film industry back in L.A.—but I'm now bartending a couple nights a week at the Speckled Gecko, if you'd like to come down for an adult beverage and say hey." She started to sit, but then stopped. "Oh, and I should add that I've become a real fan of orchids since being here and hope I can learn more about these amazing flowers from all of you."

As she appeared to be the only first-timer, the president now moved on to the new business, the first of which was a lengthy discussion about the annual orchid sale to be held the following month in late February. Various members of the society—including those at the table—voiced emotional opinions about whether non-members should be allowed to participate in the sale, how they could ensure that members sold only orchids they'd propagated or hybridized themselves, what percentage the group should make on each individual's sale, and whether they should extend the event to three days, given its enormous popularity the previous year.

After close to twenty minutes, the conversation started to disintegrate into what Valerie would describe more as petty bickering than productive discussion. Mr. Ikeda eventually slapped a hand on the table and called for quiet.

"This isn't going anywhere," he said, "so I'm going to wrap it up. And I'm also going to pull rank as president and decree—since it's clear that you're incapable of coming to any kind of agreement—as follows: only members can sell their orchids at the sale, we'll stick with the previous fifteen percent for the society, and members need only affirm that they grew or hybridized their orchids in order to offer them for sale. As for whether or not to extend the event to three days, we can decide that at the next meeting once we have an idea of how many of us will be selling our plants."

A buzz of voices erupted at the conclusion of this declaration, many shouting "Hey, you can't do that!" and a few voicing their agreement with things like "Hear, hear!" and "You go, George."

With a scowl, the president stood up and clapped his hands. "That's enough. We're moving on."

He certainly seems to have an iron grip on the organization, thought Valerie.

There were a few more grumblings, but the crowd soon settled down, and Mr. Ikeda cleared his throat. "Okay. I know everyone's hungry and ready to attack that table full of 'ono kau kau, but we have one more important item to discuss: this weekend's benefit dinner. As some of you have likely already heard, Irene Souza had to leave suddenly for O'ahu this morning to tend to her mother, who's doing poorly. Since Irene was going to oversee the preparation of all the food for the benefit, we'll have to figure something else out, wikiwiki."

Shirley turned to Valerie with an elbow jab to her waist. "Hey, you could do it, yah? You said you were a caterer for all those movie folks. Dis should be easy-peasy compared to that."

"Uh . . ."

Others were now looking her way, including Mr. Ikeda, who held up his hands. "Now, no need to pressure our newcomer, Shirley," he said. "I'm sure we'll find someone to take care of it."

Valerie pushed her chair back and stood once more. "No, I'm happy to help out, if I can. You said it's this weekend—what day? 'Cause I'm working at the Gecko on Saturday night."

"No, it's Friday night, right here in this hall."

"So that would give me four days to prep. How many people do you expect?"

"Right now it's at fifty-five. There's bound to be a few more people signing up, but also some last-minute cancellations, so we're planning for around sixty."

Thinking back to the several hundred she used to routinely cater for at a pop, Valerie smiled. "That shouldn't be a problem."

"You are a lifesaver, Ms. Corbin." Mr. Ikeda clasped his hands together, and for the first time she saw him break into a broad smile. "Mahalo, from all of us."

This prompted applause from the room at large, which

Valerie acknowledged with an embarrassed smile as she sat back down.

"After the meeting," the president went on, "you should talk to Ms. Higa, who's been helping Irene with the preparations. She'll get you squared away about the menu and all." A woman in the front row with straight shoulder-length black hair and bangs turned around and waved at Valerie, who waved back.

Mr. Ikeda now asked if there was any other business to discuss and, after allowing a woman to make an announcement about the garage sale she'd be having the coming weekend, he called for a motion to adjourn the meeting.

Within two minutes, a long line was already snaking around the food table. Ms. Higa, Valerie observed, was at the very front. After waiting her turn, Valerie loaded her plate with curried beef and white rice, Spam musubi, slices of papaya, and a healthy serving of the potato salad she'd brought. She followed Shirley over to the table at which Ms. Higa sat, gleefully biting into a Korean chicken leg glistening with sweet-and-tangy glaze. Valerie guessed her age to be close to seventy, but the obviously dyed hair and pink Hello Kitty T-shirt she was sporting gave her the air of someone far younger.

"Aloha," the woman said after swallowing and wiping her mouth with a paper napkin. "I'm Emily. So nice to meet you. And thank you so very much for volunteering to help us out this weekend. As George Ikeda said, you truly are a lifesaver."

"Happy to be of help."

Emily was now digging enthusiastically into Valerie's creamy potato salad, flecked with carrot, cucumber, and peas. It was obvious she enjoyed her food. "Mmmmmm! This is so 'ono. I'd love the recipe. I wonder who made it."

"That would be me," said Valerie. "And I'm happy to give you the recipe. I got it from a friend who used to live in Japan. The secret is using Kewpie mayonnaise."

"Ah, yes, I taste it now. So much umami."

Valerie smiled. "Exactly. I could make it for the dinner this weekend, if you wanted."

But Emily shook her head as she once more wiped her

mouth. "The menu's already all planned, and a lot of the shopping has been done, too."

"Oh, okay. So what's on the menu?"

"I can't remember precisely, but I know there's an ahi tower for the first course and that dessert is a chocolate-mac nut tart with vanilla whipped cream. Oh, and we're using vanilla extract made by George Ikeda from his very own vanilla plants."

"Really? That's cool. And perfect for an orchid society dinner."

Emily laughed. "Yes, and he's been bragging about it for about six months, now. So, would you like to get together tomorrow to talk about the menu and shopping and all? If you come over to my house, I have a lot of the groceries there that Irene already bought for the dinner."

"Sounds good. What time?" Valerie picked up the block of musubi on her plate and examined its layers of sushi rice, teriyaki-brushed Spam, and toasted seaweed.

"As early as you want. I'm always up by six."

"It'll probably be more like eight or nine before I get there," said Valerie. "Even though I've been living in Hilo now for over four months, I still haven't gotten used to how early so many locals here get up and about."

"True," said Shirley, chiming in to the conversation. "But we go to sleep early, too. Now that my husband is gone—whose snoring you could probably hear a block away—I often fall asleep by nine."

"Well, I never had a husband to keep me awake with his snoring," Emily said with a laugh, "but I too tend to hit the hay by ten or so. Of course, the younger kids stay up later than us old folks."

"Well, I often stay up fairly late," said Valerie once she'd swallowed her bite of musubi. "Even though I suppose I definitely now count as 'old,' since I just turned sixty. But it's only because of my job at the Gecko. We don't close till eleven on weekends, and then I'm usually pretty wired when I get home from work, so on the mornings afterwards, I tend to sleep in a bit." Glancing across the room, she spied her neighbor, Larry, chowing down on what looked to be barbecued pork ribs. "When I can, that is. It's often kind of noisy in the mornings around our house."

"Oh?" Shirley followed Valerie's gaze, then turned back to face her, eyebrows raised.

"Yeah . . . I'm actually not really sure what to do about it, but maybe you two can give me some advice, since you've been in the neighborhood a lot longer than me."

"Sixty-seven years," proclaimed Emily. "I've only ever lived in that one house."

Shirley was nodding. "Sixty-eight years for me. My parents moved to the neighborhood when I was eleven."

"So maybe you can answer this question," said Valerie. "Is it legal for someone to repair other people's cars—you know, as a business—in our neighborhood? 'Cause my next-door neighbor starts up at about seven a.m. most days with his power tools, and we've noticed of late that he's been working on lots of vehicles that obviously aren't his. I'm wondering if there's an ordinance or zoning law that prohibits him from doing that—or at least prevents him from making such a racket so early in the morning. Oh, and don't even get me started about the dog he keeps chained up who whines and barks nonstop all day long."

Emily and Shirley exchanged a look, then both frowned.

"What?" asked Valerie.

"It's just that . . . well . . ." Shirley let out a sigh. "It's kind of the way it is here. People's dogs bark, the roosters crow, the coquís chirp—"

"And people like to work on their cars, mow their lawns, whack their weeds, and just, you know, live their lives," put in Emily. "I have no idea what the actual regulations are, but we don't tend to get involved in other people's business unless it's something really bad."

Valerie could feel the color rushing to her cheeks. "Oh, God, I must sound like an ugly haole, trying to force our Mainland customs on the local culture. I'm so sorry."

"Don't worry, dear," said Emily, patting her on the hand. "It always takes a while for malihinis to get used to the different way of life here. But you'll soon find that the aloha spirit far outweighs all the barking dogs and power tools."

"I do know that, and you're so right," Valerie said with a smile.

"But given what you've said," Emily went on with a laugh, "let's go ahead and make it ten o'clock for tomorrow morning."

TWO

Sean was in the kitchen when Valerie awoke the next morning, back in his same spot at the wooden table, phone in his hand.

"I'm surprised you're not in bed," she said, making a beeline for the coffee maker.

"I'm going there soon. But I wanted to decompress a bit, first." He took a long drink from the can of Big Swell IPA in front of him, then wiped his mouth with the back of his hand. "Oh, it turns out this woman I know from the hospital—she's the RN who's been showing me the ropes—is also a member of that orchid society. When I was talking to her this morning, she told me she was at the meeting last night."

"Oh, really? What's her name?"

"Tammy. And . . ." Sean stopped and cleared his throat. "Well, I'm kinda interested in her, actually, so when she told me about this benefit dinner they're hosting this weekend, I said I'd be up for going."

"How funny," said Valerie. "'Cause I actually offered to help out at that dinner. But I don't think I met Tammy. What's she look like?"

"Tall and thin, with long blond hair. But she had to leave the meeting early—before the dinner portion—in order to get to the hospital, so I doubt you'd have met her last night. Though you might recognize her, 'cause she lives up at the top of the street. I can introduce you on Friday."

"Good. Looking forward to it."

"Tammy's a potter in her spare time," Sean went on, clearly happy to talk about his new love interest. "You know, she works with ceramics, not that she's a pothead. Though she does wear a lot of tie-dye," he added with a chuckle. "And it can be pretty intense at the hospital, so it wouldn't surprise me if she smoked a little weed after work to chill. It was sure crazy last night.

There were so many admissions to the ER they had to set up gurneys in the hallway. And this was only a Monday. I can't even imagine what it must be like on the weekend."

"Well, I hope you have earplugs when you do turn in," said Valerie, pulling back the curtain to peer out the window at Larry's brown-and-white dog, Akoni, who was lunging on his chain and barking at something she couldn't see. "I swear he's gotten crazier over the past few weeks."

"Yeah, well, I'd bark too if I had to spend all my days chained up like he is."

Valerie nodded. "Truth. And I gotta say, it's one of my least favorite parts of the culture here on the Big Island—how a lot of folks treat their dogs." Leaning over, she gave Pua, who was lazing on her dog bed, a long stroke across her back.

"Doesn't the guy ever let him off the chain?" asked Sean.

"Not often. Only when he takes him hunting, I think."

"Poor thing."

"Poor *me*," said Kristen, coming into the kitchen from the lānai. "He started barking and howling at about five this morning, and I couldn't get back to sleep. Though you were out to the world."

Valerie shook her head. "That sucks."

"Yeah, well, it sucks enough that I finally went over this morning and talked to the guy. Not that it'll do any good, I'm sure."

"Wait. You talked to Larry?"

"I did. But don't worry—not about his cars, 'cause we don't know where we stand on that yet. I just asked him if he could take Akoni inside, or maybe put up a fence so he wouldn't be so territorial, being on that chain like he is."

Valerie put her head in her hands. "Oh, boy."

"What?"

"It's just a conversation I had last night with a couple of people from the neighborhood. I'd voiced the same opinion to them, that Larry was being obnoxious for making so much noise all the time, both him and his dog. And they basically implied that I was being an ugly haole—not that they actually came out and said that. But the sentiment was obvious. That

that's just the way it is here—with people working on cars, barking dogs, weed-whackers—and that I need to get used to it."

"Moving to the nuisance," said Sean, "like my lawyer friend back in Little Rock likes to say."

Kristen glared briefly at her nephew, then turned to Valerie. "Well, I don't care if it is 'how things are.' It's not humane to keep a dog chained up like that all day long, and it's not neighborly to continually wake up people with your noisy power tools at seven a.m." Stomping over to the coffee machine, she refilled her mug, topped it off with milk, then strode from the room.

"Well, there you are," said Valerie with a shrug.

Sean grinned. "That's my aunt. She's a pistol."

Two hours later, Valerie knocked on the screen door at Emily Higa's house, pen and spiral notebook in hand.

"Be right there!" her neighbor shouted out, and a moment later Emily appeared at the door, drying her hands on a palm-frond-print dish towel. "I was just doing the breakfast dishes so the kitchen wouldn't be a mess when you arrived. Come on in."

Valerie kicked off her rubber slippahs and stepped into the living room. The property from the outside had looked similar to Valerie and Kristen's house, but once indoors she could see it had undergone a substantial remodel. The canec ceilings and walls—made from a sugarcane byproduct and commonly used in 1930s plantation-style homes in Hawai'i—had been replaced with hardwood paneling, and the flooring was of slate-gray porcelain tile.

On the wall hung several paintings depicting tropical landscapes, and on a shelf sat a trio of delicate ceramic bowls with vibrant glazes in blue and green to match the framed artwork. "That's a Lloyd Sexton," Emily said, noticing Valerie gazing at a painting of a coconut grove with what looked to be Maunakea in the background. "A local artist who made good—he studied at the Slade School in London before returning to Hilo in the 1930s. That painting belonged to my parents."

"It's lovely," said Valerie.

With a nod, Emily led Valerie into the kitchen, which boasted granite countertops, a shiny stainless steel Sub-Zero fridge and dishwasher to match, and a gorgeous blond floor made from what looked to be bamboo. A far cry from Valerie's own kitchen with its original tile counters and linoleum floor, Kenmore fridge and stove, and no dishwasher. But even as she complimented Emily on her beautiful remodel, she was thinking how much she preferred the old-school feel of her own still-mostly-unaltered 1930s home.

"Here, I'll show you the menu for the dinner," said Emily, gesturing for Valerie to follow her into the dining room. They took seats next to each other at the large teakwood table, but then Emily stood up again quickly. "Oh, I haven't even offered you anything to eat or drink—how rude. Would you care for some coffee and banana bread? I just made the bread this morning."

"Sure, that sounds great."

Emily headed back to the kitchen. "Milk or sugar?"

"Just milk, thanks."

Once they were resettled, coffee and cake before them, Emily handed Valerie a sheet of paper with a list of the dishes for Friday night's benefit dinner:

ahi tower with avocado and wonton crisps
butter-shoyu chicken
Hawaiian-style fried rice
pohole salad
chocolate-mac nut tart with vanilla whipped cream

"What's pohole?" she asked.

"It's a kind of fern," said Emily. "It's also called hōʻiʻo here, but you probably know it by its Japanese name, 'warabi.'"

"Ah, right, I've had that salad—it's amazing. I'm pretty sure they use fiddlehead fern to make it. And butter-shoyu chicken—that's shoyu chicken, but with butter as well as soy sauce?"

"Correct. And in my opinion, the addition of butter to most any food item is always a good idea."

"Ha!" Valerie slapped a hand upon the table. "Agreed! But don't you think it might be a little . . ." She paused, searching for a word that wouldn't come across as too demeaning. ". . . *simple*? You know, for an elegant benefit dinner like this?"

Emily frowned.

Uh-oh. "I mean, it sounds truly delicious—especially with all that butter, an' all. But isn't shoyu chicken and fried rice something you'd typically get in a plate lunch, as opposed to a fancy restaurant?"

"Well, Irene and I thought they'd be perfect for the dinner, since everyone loves both dishes, they can be made in advance, and they're inexpensive—which George made clear was very important. He's what you might call . . . thrifty," said Emily with an affectionate smile. "And in any case," she said, gesturing toward the kitchen, "we've already done most of the shopping, so it's too late to change the menu at this point."

"Sure, I get it," said Valerie with what she hoped was an encouraging smile. "You're right—about all those things. And the ahi tower and dessert make for a fancy beginning and end, so it should all be great. Oh, and this banana bread is fantastic, by the way! What's your secret?"

"I add crushed pineapple to the batter," said Emily, standing and shoving back her chair. "Here, I'll show you the ingredients we've bought so far. They're out in the carport."

Her manner seemed to have cooled. Why on earth, Valerie chided herself as she followed Emily outside, hadn't she held her tongue about the menu?

Scooting around a pea-soup-green Kia Soul, they made their way to the back of the carport, where the food was stowed on a rack of metal shelves and in boxes on the floor: bags of rice, flour, and sugar; bottles of soy sauce, oil, sake, oyster sauce, and mirin; cans of Spam and pineapple; dried spices; and other dry goods such as macadamia nuts, dried cuttlefish and shrimp, cocoa powder, and semisweet chocolate.

"And in the deep freeze down in my basement is the chicken—six five-pound boxes of thighs." Emily consulted the list in her hand. "But we still need to buy the ahi, avocados, eggs, lup cheong—"

"Lup cheong?" Valerie interrupted.

"That's the Chinese sausage that goes in the rice." *Was that a rolling of her eyes?* "And we also need to buy the pohole—which we can get at the farmers market—vegetables for the salad and the fried rice, as well as the butter, cream cheese, ricotta, and whipping cream for the dessert. Oh, and you'll have to go get the vanilla from George Ikeda."

Valerie studied the ingredients lined up across the counter, then turned to Emily. "What about wine—or whatever beverages you're gonna have?"

"One of our members, Larry Kaimana, is handling all that, so we don't need to worry about it, thank goodness. He's bringing wines to pair with each course and also non-alcoholic drinks for people who don't want wine."

Larry? Could that be her neighbor—the one with the barking dog who worked 24/7 on his cars? He didn't seem the wine type, but then again, she hadn't thought him the orchid type, either. Valerie nodded. "Sounds good. So, is there a kitchen at the Buddhist hall?"

"Yes, and it has a four-burner stove and two ovens. Problem is, we don't have use of the hall until the afternoon of the dinner. So we were talking about making the tarts and cooking the chicken and rice at one of our own kitchens over the two days before the dinner, and then reheating things as needed at the hall's kitchen."

"You know," said Valerie, tapping a finger upon her upper lip, "it's possible we could use the Speckled Gecko kitchen, as long as we did it off-hours. Which would mean early morning, since they open for lunch at eleven."

Emily's face brightened. "That would be great. And as you know, I don't mind getting up early. So as long as you don't . . ."

"Lemme check with Nalani—the owner—tonight at work, and I'll get back to you. We could make the tarts Thursday morning and then do the rest on Friday. I'm sure there'd be room in the Gecko's walk-in fridge for all our food. And any last-minute prep we could do at the hall on Friday afternoon. Do you have recipes for the dishes you want to use?"

"Just for the tarts, the pohole, and the chicken. The ahi tower doesn't really need a recipe—"

"Right," said Valerie. "It's just a stack of chopped seasoned ahi, avo, and the wonton crisps."

"Uh-huh. And as for the fried rice," Emily went on, "Irene and I could do that in our sleep we've made it so many times, so we don't need a recipe."

"For sixty covers, though, it seems like it would be good to know the amounts—if only for the purpose of how much of the various ingredients we need to buy," said Valerie. "But that's okay," she quickly added in response to Emily's renewed furrowing of the brow. "I can just look at some recipes online to get an idea. So, when would you like to do the rest of the shopping? Or I could just do it by myself, if you wanted."

"No, I think it would be good for me to come along."

'Cause you don't trust me.

"I'm free any time tomorrow," Emily went on. "How about we say ten o'clock again? Oh, and by the way, I spoke with George, and we're prepared to pay you for your help with the dinner, though it's not much—a hundred and fifty dollars."

"Well, I don't know that that's necessary, but thank you—I appreciate it. And ten a.m. tomorrow works great." Valerie slapped her thighs. "I guess I should get going. I'll head on up to Mr. Ikeda's house now to see if he's home and I can get that vanilla."

Emily saw her out, and as Valerie walked back up the street, she shook her head. That certainly didn't go as she'd planned. Had she acted like an arrogant newcomer, or was Emily simply being overly sensitive to an outsider making comments about the local cuisine?

Well, no matter what, she'd do her best in the future to be more conscious of what she said to people—especially about things concerning Big Island customs and traditions.

Valerie walked past her own house and on to that of the orchid society president, admiring the large tree with glossy green leaves and a mixture of orange and white flowers in his front yard. As she started up the driveway, Valerie was hit by a pungent, sweet perfume from the tree's blossoms.

Mr. Ikeda was in his carport, which, unlike Emily's, was really more of a gardening shed than any place you'd store a car. "Aloha, Mr. Ikeda!" she called out, and he looked up from the box atop a rustic wooden table he'd been pawing through.

"Oh, hello, Ms. Corbin."

It was much cooler inside the carport, with a dank musty smell like that of a basement. Along the sides were shelves filled with potting soil, redwood bark, fertilizer, soil amendments, and the like; and on the back wall hung a pair of shovels, a rake, a weed-whacker, and a leaf blower, along with various hand tools such as trowels, cultivators, and pruning shears. All very neat and organized, she observed.

"I've come for that vanilla for the dessert Friday night. And please, you can call me Valerie."

He set down the roll of twine in his hand. "Ah, right," he said—not asking her to call him George, she couldn't help noticing. "Here, let me fetch it for you." But then he stopped. "Oh, but if you like, I could show you my vanilla plants first." The gleam in his eyes betrayed how eager he was to have someone come and admire his beloved plants.

"Sure, I'd love to see them."

Mr. Ikeda led Valerie around the side of the carport into the back yard, where rows of orchids sat on wooden benches, protected from the heavy rain and harsh tropical sun by black shade cloth strung overhead. "These are my Vandas," he said, indicating a section of orchids with long, leathery leaves that rose up on either side in two vertical rows—not unlike a pineapple, was Valerie's thought. Several of the Vanda orchids had buds, but none seemed to be currently flowering.

"Is this not the season for them to bloom?" she asked, looking about her and seeing that only a few of his orchids—and there must have been close to a hundred in total—had any color to them.

"Oh, they send out spikes year-round, but I bring them indoors or up onto the lānai once they're in bloom for my wife and I to enjoy. I'll have some of my best examples on display Friday night at the dinner, so you can see them then. Here." He led her over to another section, brushing away spider webs as he went, and leaned over to inspect a specimen with several stalks—spikes, she corrected herself—with buds about to open and one large flower. Its petals were a papery white, but it had a vibrant egg-yolk-colored center.

"Oooo . . . that's gorgeous," she exclaimed.

"Yes, and it's quite rare: a *Dendrobium bensoniae*. And unlike most orchids, it has a fragrance."

She leaned over to sniff the flower. "Wow. I get notes of chocolate."

"Very astute," he said with a smile, as if sizing her up anew. "I've actually been experimenting with hybridizing this particular orchid with another Dendrobium that has a pinkish hue—this one here, which unfortunately isn't in bloom." He pointed to a pot behind the white-and-yellow orchid. "The resulting progeny have both the yellow center and pink tips to their petals—very beautiful."

"Oh, will you show them to me?"

"They're right here," he said, indicating the two pots just down from the one in bloom. "They aren't blooming at the moment, but as you can see from their spikes, they should have flowers within a week or so. I'm hoping to enter them at our show next month."

Mr. Ikeda next led her to a series of vines strung along a wire trellis. None of these plants had flowers, either, but she could see several bunches of string-bean-type growths hanging down from the vines. "Are those what I think they are?"

"Yes, indeed. Vanilla pods. They're not ready quite yet, but I'll start harvesting them in the next couple weeks, once the tips start to turn yellow."

Unlike the other orchids Mr. Ikeda had shown her, which were all in individual black plastic pots, the vanilla plants were growing in a long wooden box full of mulch and bark. "Why are there bones in the soil?" Valerie asked, pointing to the skull of some tiny animal.

He chuckled. "Vanilla *planifolia* is quite fond of calcium, so my wife saves our chicken and pork bones for the plants. But I also throw in others I find in the yard when gardening, like that mongoose skull there."

"How long does it take to make the vanilla extract once the beans are harvested?"

"Ah." Mr. Ikeda's face grew serious. "It's a complicated process. The only spice more difficult to produce than vanilla is saffron. First, the flowers must be hand-pollinated, which is tricky, as once they open, there's only a four-hour window to do so. Then, if you're lucky enough to actually end up with fruit—the beans—there's a long and laborious curing process to transform them into what you see for sale in stores. And then after that, they have to sit in the alcohol—vodka usually—to infuse for at least six months and allow the flavor to be extracted from the beans. So from picking to finished product, it can take as long as ten months. Here, let's go get that vanilla for you for the dinner."

They returned to the carport/garden shed, where Mr. Ikeda removed a glass bottle from a shelf stocked with jars of jam, jelly, and other canned goods, and handed it to Valerie. She could see three vanilla beans through the dark liquid, and on a sticker affixed to the bottle was written "Vanilla—Orchid Soc. Dinner, 1/19."

"I made this exactly six months ago so it would be ready in time for the dinner," he said.

Valerie took the bottle from him. "Thanks. We certainly won't need all of it, but I can return the rest to you afterwards."

"If you want. But feel free to keep it if you like, as I've still got some I made last year for myself, and I don't use it too often. Neither I nor my wife do much baking."

"Well, that's very kind. I may very well take you up on it." She turned to look once again at the tree in his front yard. "By the way, the scent from those flowers is incredible. It's a pua kenikeni, right?"

"Yes, *Fagraea berteroana*. It's unusual in that it produces blooms year-round," Mr. Ikeda said in a professorial voice, clearly pleased to have one more chance to play the botanist for Valerie. "They use the blossoms for lei-making, and its Hawaiian name means 'ten-cent flower,' which I gather was the price of a single flower—quite a bit of money back in the day."

"Well, this specimen is absolutely beautiful—and obviously very happy where it is."

Mr. Ikeda flashed a sad smile. "I wish I could say that everyone agrees with you, but some of my mauka neighbors are unfortunately not of the same opinion. They want me to cut it down, or at least prune it back heavily, as it blocks their view of the ocean."

Valerie turned to gaze at the tree, which she guessed to be at least twenty feet high—taller than Mr. Ikeda's single-story plantation-style home. "Yeah, I guess I could see their point, especially if they used to have a view which is now gone."

He shook his head and turned to face his uphill neighbors' home. "No, they only moved in a few years ago, so they've never had much of an ocean view."

"Ah," said Valerie. "Moving to the nuisance is what my nephew says that's called. You know—coming to a new place and then complaining about things that were there long before you moved into the neighborhood?" *Like me and Kristen complaining about Larry*, she couldn't help adding to herself. "So how long have you and your wife lived here? It's a lovely property."

"My wife grew up in this house and I grew up one block over. We actually met in junior high school, but didn't start dating until I returned from the Mainland after college. And then when her parents had to go into assisted care, we decided to move into her old home. So that would make it about twenty-five years that I've lived in this house. Though sixty-eight years in the neighborhood, in case you're wondering about my age," he added with a chuckle.

"I bet the neighborhood's changed a lot since then," said Valerie, gesturing across the street to where the current tenants had planted a large vegetable garden in their front yard and painted the house in a rainbow of pastel colors that would have fit perfectly in an episode of *My Little Pony*.

He shrugged, but she could see the sadness in his eyes. "Yes, it has, indeed. So many of the families I grew up with are now gone, and the feel of the neighborhood is indeed quite different these days. But that's life, yah? You can't control who moves where, so you just need to accept the fact that nothing stays the same."

"Right." Valerie was tempted to apologize for being one of those people he couldn't control moving into his neighborhood, but instead merely thanked him for the vanilla and headed back down the street.

THREE

Two nights a week, Valerie tended bar at the Speckled Gecko, a restaurant down on the Hilo Bayfront serving a mix of Hawaiian, Asian, and Caribbean cuisine. After retiring from her job as caterer for the TV and film industry, she'd been training as a bartender to help out at her brother Charlie's hipster bistro in Venice Beach, but after he'd been killed in a car crash the previous winter, Valerie hadn't had the heart to return to Chez Charles.

And then she and Kristen had moved to Hilo. Which she didn't regret for a single moment. But it was hard picking up her life at the grand old age of sixty and coming to a place so very different from the Southern California culture in which she'd spent most of her life. Not only was she now an outsider—a haole, as locals referred to those not from the islands who were of European descent—but the only people on the Big Island she'd known at all well when they'd made their move had been Kristen's surfing buddy, Isaac, and his partner, Sachiko.

And so when Sachiko, who managed the front of the house at the Gecko, had asked her to come and bartend there, Valerie had been excited for the opportunity to create a new life—and perhaps even make some new friends—in this town she now called home.

Walking into the restaurant that Tuesday afternoon, Valerie greeted her co-workers as she headed through the indoor dining room and out to the bar. Sachiko was going over the reservation list at the hostess desk and Annie sat in the wait station inserting today's specials page into the menus. Outdoors, a deuce was finishing up their meal at the table next to the dolphin fountain, but other than that, the lānai was empty of customers.

Valerie got to work prepping the bar for the night's service:

restocking the well liquor, mixers, juices, beer, and wine, and then making sure there was enough clean glassware to get through the evening. That done, she headed for the kitchen to fetch lemons, limes, and oranges for garnishes.

Nalani, the Gecko owner and head chef, stood at the six-burner stove, tending to an enormous pan of sliced onions—not something Valerie thought of as generally being on the menu. "My, does that smell good," she said as she passed by. "Is it for a special tonight?"

"Uh-huh. Pork chops with an apple-cider-pineapple reduction, caramelized onions, and fried sage."

"Dang, girl. Can you save an order for me to have after work? Oh," Valerie said, stopping. "I have a question for you, if you've got a sec."

"Sure." Nalani set down her wooden spoon and turned from the stove. "What's up?"

"It's just that I volunteered to help cater a benefit dinner for my neighborhood orchid society this Friday night, and I was wondering if a couple of us could use the Gecko kitchen for some prep work on Thursday and Friday morning before the lunch service here. I promise we'd have it completely cleaned up and ready for you and Matt when you get in at ten."

"I don't see why not. You used to be a professional cook, yah?"

"Right. I was a caterer for the TV and film biz back in L.A. So I know my way around a kitchen—and more importantly in this instance, how to clean up afterwards."

Nalani smiled. "What'll you be cooking?"

Valerie gave her a run-down of the menu, and the chef nodded. "Sounds simple enough, so sure. Go ahead."

"And one more thing," said Valerie as Nalani turned back to her onions. "Would you have any problem with me asking Matt if he'd like to help? For money, of course."

"As long as it don' interfere with his work for da Gecko, I got no problem with that."

"Awesome. Thanks!"

* * *

The next morning, Valerie arrived at Emily's house right at ten. They walked out to the carport, and after one last look at the menu, the recipes, and what had already been purchased, they finalized their shopping list and headed off to the KTA grocery store.

"By the way," said Valerie as they pushed their shopping cart down the dairy aisle, "I asked the line cook at the Speckled Gecko if he'd be interested in helping out with the dinner prep on Friday morning, and he said yes. And don't worry; it won't cost you anything extra. I'm gonna give him the money you offered me, and I'll work for free. Happy to help out the orchid society."

"Well, that's awfully generous of him—and you." Emily compared prices between two brands of cream cheese, then placed six boxes of the cheaper one into their cart.

"Yeah, and in addition to the extra hands, it'll be good having someone familiar with the Gecko kitchen there to help. Plus, he's a great cook and a super nice guy."

"Does he like orchids?" asked Emily. "Because we're always looking for new blood."

"Well, you can ask him yourself tomorrow. Though I'm pretty sure he lives on the other side of town, so I'm not sure he'd be eligible for the group, would he?"

"We sometimes make exceptions, especially if the person has certain talents that are helpful to the society. Like being a good chef," she added with a laugh.

Over the next two mornings, they got the bulk of the cooking done for the dinner. On Thursday, Valerie and Emily baked the tarts—eight of them in total. Emily was hesitant when Valerie suggested adding dark rum to the recipe but eventually agreed when Valerie explained that it would help cut some of the sweetness and add depth to the rich dessert. Once the tarts were in the ovens, they got the Gecko's gigantic commercial rice cooker fired up so the rice could be chilled overnight before frying it up the next day.

Then on Friday, Matt showed up at seven a.m. to assist with the rest of the dishes. After some discussion, they decided that he would prep the ahi tower, Valerie the butter-shoyu chicken, and Emily both the pohole salad and the Hawaiian-style fried rice—since, as she'd boasted, she could do it in her sleep. Though Valerie did help with cutting all the veggies, Spam, and sausage for the rice before starting on her chicken.

As Valerie was chopping her way through a pile of carrots and onions, Matt came to her side. He'd finished cleaning and slicing the tuna, he said, and had a question about the rest of the composition of the ahi towers.

"It's just that it seems a little simple to me," he said, drawing a look from Emily, who was standing at the counter a few feet away, beating a bowl of eggs into a froth. "So I was wondering if, in addition to the avocado and wonton crisps, we could maybe add a layer of something piquant to add a bit of spark to the dish. A lemon mayonnaise was what I was thinking. We have all the ingredients for it here in the kitchen."

Valerie glanced over at Emily but couldn't tell if her frown was the result of disapproval or merely pondering this possible change to the appetizer. She hoped it was the latter, but the cook's use of the word "simple" was unfortunate, given Emily's reaction to that same word when Valerie had used it three days earlier to describe the proposed menu.

"Uh, that sounds like an interesting idea. What do you think, Emily?"

Emily set down her whisk and turned to face Matt, as if sizing him up. "Have you used it before in something similar, the lemon mayo?"

"Yeah. I made it here at the Gecko just a few weeks back to go in a poke bowl special made with ahi, furikake, papaya, and brown rice. It was so popular that we ended up running the special for three days."

"Maybe we should add papaya to the towers, too," said Valerie.

But this proved too much for Emily. "No," she said. "I'll go with the lemon mayonnaise, but the papaya would be too much. Let's leave it at that."

"Okay, you're the boss," said Matt with a grin. A grin, Valerie couldn't help but notice, that Emily did not return.

* * *

Valerie and Emily arrived at the Buddhist hall at four o'clock that afternoon, then lugged all the food from their cars into the hall: four hotel pans of already-baked butter-shoyu glazed chicken, several more of the pohole salad and fried rice, bowls of ahi marinating in sesame oil and soy sauce, two squirt bottles of lemon mayo, a box of avocados, bags of wonton crisps, the eight chocolate-macadamia nut tarts, and the cream, sugar, and vanilla for the dessert topping.

While Emily got to work slicing the avos for the ahi towers, Valerie saw to the whipped cream for the tart topping. After setting out the sugar, vanilla, and hand mixer she'd brought from home, she poured the cream into an enormous stainless-steel bowl they'd borrowed from the Gecko. At the sound of a man's voice, she looked up.

"Aloha! I'm here with da wine delivery."

As she'd suspected, the man at the door was indeed her neighbor, Larry, a big guy who, but for his age, could pass for a linebacker on the UH Hilo Vulcans football team. And as soon as she turned to face him, she could see something—surprise, distaste?—pass quickly over his face. She forced a broad smile. "Oh, hi, neighbor. I'm Valerie, in case you don't remember—helping out with the dinner tonight."

"Ah, dass right. I forgot you volunteered at da meeting to help out." He nodded, then glanced around the kitchen. "You know if dere's a dolly here I can use to bring all da boxes inside? I shoulda brought one but didn't tink to put it in da truck."

"I'll go look."

Valerie went in search of a dolly and, when she returned empty-handed, found Larry gazing hungrily at the tarts lined up on the counter. "Those look amazing," he said. "Can't wait for dessert tonight."

"Yeah, they're gonna be pretty tasty, I have to admit. But I'm sorry to say I found no dolly."

Emily, who'd gone to look for the hall caretaker, returned to the kitchen and shook her head. "No luck. But here, we can help you with the wine."

The three of them schlepped the boxes into the kitchen,

stowing the whites and the bottles of soda water in the fridge and setting the cases of red wine down in the corner. "The Chardonnay goes with da first course," Larry said, "the Pinot Noir for da mains, and da Prosecco is for dessert. I know most people would traditionally serve a white with da chicken, but I thought it would be nice to mix it up with a light red."

"So, where'd you learn about wine?" Valerie asked, and he shrugged.

"My dad was really into da whole wine thing, so I kinda had to pick it up. But I'm more of a beer and whisky kinda guy myself." He checked the time on his phone. "Anyway, I gotta jam. See you tonight." And with that, he took his leave.

Valerie watched him through the screen door as he climbed into his shiny red truck. This was not the Larry she'd thought she knew—he of the chained, barking dog and power tools. *I guess it goes to show you never can tell about folks*, she thought with a shake of the head as she returned to her whipped cream.

The dinner itself went surprisingly easily. The only hitch was beforehand, with the ahi towers: Emily and Irene clearly hadn't thought through the fact that they'd have to be individually constructed immediately before service, as there was no room for all of the plates in the hall's refrigerator. And with only the two cake rings they had at hand—also borrowed from the Gecko—it was a long and laborious process to make the fifty-eight stacks of ahi, mayo, avocado, and wonton crisps they needed. But even though the guests ended up being served their appetizer in waves, most everyone was thankfully a good sport about it. Though Valerie was a bit afraid the thirsty crowd would go through all the Chardonnay before the last of the towers were sent out to the dining room.

The rest was easy. Plates piled high with succulent glazed chicken, crispy fried rice, and savory fern salad were quickly ferried out to the guests, and during this course, Valerie was even able to scarf down a little of the food herself. "Oh, man," she moaned to Emily between bites. "This butter-shoyu chicken is to die for. My apologies for doubting its appropriateness for the dinner. And it goes perfectly with that rice."

Emily's knowing nod and smile said "I told you so" without having to speak it aloud.

The tarts had already been sliced and topped with dollops of vanilla whipped cream, and Valerie and Emily helped the volunteer wait staff plate them up and distribute the desserts to the crowd, which had grown more boisterous with each course and its accompanying wine.

That task completed, Valerie and Emily helped themselves to the last of a bottle of Prosecco and headed out to the dining room. Spying her wife and Sean at a table with two empty seats, Valerie led Emily that way.

"Ah, here's my aunt Valerie," Sean said, standing up. He gestured to the woman seated next to him. "This is Tammy Barker."

Valerie shook hands with Sean's new friend. "Very nice to meet you. And this is Emily, my cooking cohort for tonight's dinner."

"Yes, we know each other," said Emily with a nod toward Tammy. "Glad you could make it tonight."

"Ah, right. Of course—you're both members of the orchid society. Duh. But I don't believe you've yet met my nephew, Sean, or my wife, Kristen."

Sean and Kristen both shook hands with Emily, then Kristen held up her glass in salute. "Good job, the both of you—everything was simply delicious!"

"Thanks," said Emily. "But I'm glad it's over. Remind me next time there's a big dinner like this not to volunteer."

"Here, maybe this will help," Tammy said, shoving a slice of tart her way. "I'm lactose-intolerant, so I can't eat it."

"Nah, I'm trying to lose a few pounds." Emily patted her ample stomach. "You can have it, Valerie."

Valerie took a bite of the dessert, then set her fork down. "I'm actually not that hungry. Too hyped up, I guess. But I will have some more bubbly." Standing up, she started for the kitchen to fetch another bottle, but spying Mr. Ikeda and a tall, hefty guy talking by a display of orchids near the front door, she changed course toward them.

Wasn't that the same man Mr. Ikeda had ignored at the

orchid society meeting last Monday night when he'd tried to talk to the president? As she approached, she saw the tall guy shake a finger at Mr. Ikeda, then turn and stalk away, leaving the other staring after him.

Oops. It certainly didn't seem like a good time to chat with the president or admire his orchids. Turning on her heel, Valerie retreated to the kitchen, then returned to the table with a fresh bottle of Prosecco and poured herself a second glass.

Mr. Ikeda, she saw, had returned to his table and was chatting with a woman with styled gray hair as he ate his dessert. "Is that Mr. Ikeda's wife?" Valerie asked Emily.

With a frown, she followed Valerie's gaze. "Right. Sue is her name."

Valerie studied the two as they laughed at something George had just said, Mrs. Ikeda's face relaxing into a warm smile. Leaning over, she whispered something into her husband's ear, then gave him a soft kiss on the cheek.

So sweet. It was obvious they were still very much in love. Would she and Kristen, Valerie wondered, be as happy as these two appeared to be, thirty years on in their marriage? *If we live that long*, she added to herself with a wry smile.

Her musings were interrupted by the sight of the man who'd been talking with Mr. Ikeda sitting two tables over from the president and his wife. "Do you know who he is?" she asked Emily, pointing across the room. "The big guy with the red-and-yellow striped shirt."

Emily, who was still watching the happy couple, turned to see who she meant. "Oh, that's Don Ribeiro. He's one of the board members. And a bit of a pill, if you ask me," she added.

"Right. I remember him from the meeting last Monday. So what's he a pill about, if you don't mind my asking?" When Emily didn't immediately answer, Valerie leaned over and said in a hushed voice, "It's only that I just saw them arguing over by the orchid display. So I'm a little curious what the deal is . . ."

"I'm sure it's nothing," said Emily. "Just Don being Don. He's always complaining about something." Picking up her phone, she took a sip of Prosecco and proceeded to scroll through her texts.

"Got it." But as Valerie watched Don from across the room, she couldn't help but wonder if there was something more to it that Emily simply wasn't willing to share with this inquisitive haole.

FOUR

Roused by a harsh buzzing the next morning, Valerie sat up and grabbed for her phone atop the bedside dresser to try to switch it off before it awakened Kristen, as well. But then, seeing only Pua curled up beside her in bed, she remembered that her wife had said she was leaving early to go paddling.

The sound of the phone had awakened the dog, however, who now jumped up and began letting out urgent "time to get up!" yips.

"Hold on, sweets," said Valerie. "You gotta wait."

At the sound of this last word, Pua lay back down, but continued to keep a watchful eye on Valerie's every move.

Falling back onto the pillow, Valerie peered at her screen. The call—from a local 808 number she didn't recognize—was going to voicemail. *Now, who would be trying to get hold of me so early?* But then she checked the time and saw it was already eight twenty, not at all early by Hilo standards.

Rather than wait for the voicemail to finish recording, she punched the red callback number on her "recents." A woman's voice picked up.

"Hi. You just called? It's Valerie Corbin."

"Yeah, I did. It's Emily. I left a message—"

"Which I haven't listened to yet, actually."

"Oh, okay. Well, here's the thing. Several people from the benefit dinner have called this morning to tell me they spent the night sick."

Valerie sat back up. "Sick? You mean . . ."

"Vomiting, diarrhea. Food poisoning is what they're saying."

"Oh, no." Valerie put her head in her hands. This was a food service worker's worst nightmare.

"So, a couple of them want to talk to you. Is it okay if I give them your number?"

"I . . . I mean . . ." No way did Valerie want to have to deal with a bunch of sick—and likely angry—people right now. But how could she say no? "All right, I guess that's okay. Though I don't really know what I can do about it at this point. Beyond telling them to rest up and keep as hydrated as possible."

Within ten minutes she'd fielded six phone calls. Emily had clearly used this as a way to deflect them away from herself, Valerie realized. And she'd been right—most of the callers had not been friendly. "My wife was up all night puking her guts out because of *your* food!" was what one man screamed as soon as she took his call. And that wasn't even the worst of them.

She finally put her phone on mute and went to take a calming shower. But after toweling off, getting dressed, and heading out to the lānai with a cup of coffee, she reluctantly picked up her phone and saw that she had eight more messages.

Damn. With a sigh, she tapped her voicemail and put the phone to her ear. They all said basically the same thing: that sometime in the middle of the night, the caller had started experiencing severe abdominal pain, followed quickly by the symptoms that so often come with intestinal sickness.

But as she was listening to the sixth message, another call came in from Emily. "Don't tell me," Valerie said, taking the call. "Ten more people have reported getting sick."

"Worse than that. I just got a call from George Ikeda's wife Sue saying George has been taken to the emergency room."

"Oh, Lord. Is he going to be okay?"

"I sure hope so," said Emily, "but I'm worried for him; he's no spring chicken anymore."

Valerie had no idea what to say. She'd never in her life catered a meal where anyone had ever gotten sick, much less the dozens now calling in with their reports—and one in the ER.

"So . . ." Emily cleared her throat. "You have any idea what it might have been—that caused all this?"

"I don't. But given that it happened to so many people who all had the same meal, I'm guessing that's gotta be the cause.

You know, as opposed to something like the norovirus, which I'm pretty sure has an incubation period of at least a day or two. Here, lemme go through the menu: the ahi tower, which had tuna, avo, and lemon mayonnaise—"

"That's gotta be it!" Emily interrupted. "I saw Matt making the mayo with raw eggs. I bet they had salmonella or something."

"Maybe." But Valerie wasn't convinced this had to be the answer. People ate eggs all the time that hadn't been fully cooked—eggs over-easy, hollandaise sauce, aioli, chocolate mousse, eggnog and gin fizzes—and you rarely heard about them getting sick. And certainly not in the numbers they were hearing about now. "What about the avocado?" she asked. "Could the cutting board have had something on it that caused cross-contamination?"

"No way. I disinfected it with a bleach solution before slicing them."

"Oh, okay. Well, I'll ask Matt about the eggs—where they came from, and if they were pasteurized or not—and whether it could have been the ahi. But at this point, I'm not sure how we can know for sure what it is that got folks sick."

"Not the fried rice, that's for sure," said Emily. "Everything was fully cooked in that dish—and with no changes to the recipe at the last minute."

"Right." Valerie could hear what Emily left unsaid: that it had been she and Matt who'd decided to add the lemon mayonnaise to the ahi tower dish, and now look what had happened. "But it could also have been the chicken—that can have salmonella, too." But even as she said this, she knew that dish was an unlikely culprit, having been baked in the oven for close to an hour.

"And I ate both the chicken and the fried rice and I feel fine," said Emily.

"Yeah, me too. But neither of us had any of the ahi tower, right?"

"I didn't. And none of the dessert, either, because of my diet."

Could it have been the dessert? Valerie wondered. "All I had was like one bite of the tart," she said, then let out a long sigh. "I guess the next thing we need to do is find out from people what they did or didn't eat, to try to figure out what it was that made them sick. Though, as I said before, I'm not sure what good it will do at this point."

"Well, if nothing else, we'll know if we should throw out the leftover food that's sitting in my refrigerator."

"I think to be safe, none of it should be eaten, so go ahead and toss it all. Or, wait—maybe save a little of each dish, in case we can have it tested or something."

"Okay, will do. And I'll let you know if I get any updates on how George is doing."

As soon as Valerie heard the car pull into the driveway a half hour later, she ran outside. "Are you feeling okay?" she asked Kristen before she could even turn off the engine.

"What? Sure. A little sore from paddling—Tala wanted to go all the way down to Four Mile Beach before turning back—but other than that, I'm fine." Kristen climbed out of the driver's seat and started to reach for her bag of wet clothes, but then stopped upon seeing Valerie's expression. "Hey, what's going on?"

"A bunch of people got sick last night after eating our food at the banquet."

"Oh, no! That's awful." She frowned. "But I feel totally fine."

"Did you eat everything that was served last night?"

Kristen grabbed her bag and slammed the car door shut, pursing her lips as she thought back.

"There was the ahi tower," Valerie prompted, "the butter-shoyu chicken and fried rice, the fern salad, and the chocolate-mac nut tart."

"Sorry?" said Kristen as the whine of a pneumatic drill started up next door. "What were the last two things you said?"

"C'mon inside." With a shake of the head, Valerie huffed inside into the kitchen, followed by Kristen. "Damn. Does he ever stop? It's infuriating. Anyway, what I said was the ahi tower, the butter-shoyu chicken and fried rice, the fern salad, and the chocolate-mac nut tart."

"Right, I had all of those," said Kristen. "Oh, wait—except for the tart, which I was too full to eat after all that other food. So I wrapped it up in a couple napkins and took it home. I was about to have it right now for breakfast, as a matter of fact, after that brutal workout I just had."

"Uh . . . maybe you should hold off on that, given what happened. Though I'm thinking it maybe was the mayo in the ahi tower that's the culprit. It's possible some folks were just more sensitive to whatever it was than others, so the fact that you ate it without problem doesn't necessarily mean it was fine. But we need to find out what other people ate and didn't eat, to know for sure."

The ringing of Valerie's phone put a stop to their conversation. "I gotta get this," she said, and punched "accept." "Emily. What's the news?"

"Not good. Five more people have reported the same symptoms. But there does seem to be a pattern emerging. Only those who ate the dessert seem to have gotten sick."

"Huh. But the tart was fully cooked, and I don't see how there could have been any cross-contamination. Plus, if there had been, it would only have been for that particular tart—not all of them."

"What about the whipped cream?" asked Emily.

"I doubt it. If the cream had been off, I'd have smelled it. And besides, I tasted it as I added the sugar and vanilla after it was whipped, and it seemed fine."

"Well, I gotta go. I want to head up to the hospital to see how George is doing."

"Okay. Keep me posted. And do find out from anyone you talk to what exactly they ate and didn't eat."

As Valerie ended the call, she heard a noise behind her. Turning, she saw Sean come into the kitchen holding his stomach. She and Kristen followed him out to the lānai, where he gingerly took a seat on their new rattan floral-print couch and let out a low moan. Larry had thankfully turned off whatever power tool he'd been using earlier.

"Uh-oh," said Valerie. "Not you, too."

"Huh?"

"Are you having stomach issues?"

"That's an understatement. Though thank goodness it seems to be passing. No pun intended." His attempt at a smile came out as more of a grimace. "But what do you mean, 'not you, too'?"

Valerie and Kristen plopped down on the director's chairs across from him. "You're not the only one," said Valerie. "A whole bunch of people seem to have gotten sick after the dinner last night."

"Dang."

"Yeah, dang, indeed. But let me ask you this: Did you eat everything last night, or was there any dish you skipped?"

"I ate the *whole* thing, as they say. And it was all delicious—notwithstanding the night and morning that followed."

"You have any idea how Tammy is feeling this morning?"

Sean smiled again briefly, then shrugged. "We're unfortunately not that close yet that we text in the morning. But here." He reached into his shorts pocket for his phone. "I'll write her and ask."

Valerie gazed out at the garden as he typed. But not even the sight of her beloved yellow-and-red heliconia, pink ginger, and vibrant green monstera vines was enough to raise her spirits right now. *What the heck could have made all these people so sick?*

Sean set aside his phone and lay back on the couch, one arm thrown over his eyes, the other atop his stomach. Listening to the drone of a distant lawnmower, Valerie too closed her eyes and was close to nodding off when the ding of Sean's phone startled the both of them back to consciousness.

"It's Tammy," he said, peering at the device. "She says she's fine, and wonders if I'd like to come over to her studio today to see some of her pottery. *Uch.*" Leaning back once again, he shook his head. "Now what do I do? Tell her I'd love to come but I'd probably throw up if I got into a car? Super romantic, that."

But Valerie had already stopped listening. *Tammy didn't eat the tart either*, she recalled, *because she's lactose-intolerant*. She turned to Kristen. "So Larry doesn't appear to be feeling any ill-effects from the dinner last night. I wonder if he ate the dessert."

"I know he did," said Kristen. "He was two tables over from ours, and Sean and Tammy and I couldn't help checking him out as he inhaled the whole slice in like two ginormous bites. Tammy seemed especially disgusted by him," she added with a laugh. "It was pretty gross."

"Huh. So I wonder if that means it wasn't the dessert, after all."

That night at the Speckled Gecko, Valerie waited until the bar and kitchen had both slowed down before talking to Matt. Leaving Jun, the head bartender, to deal with the few remaining drink customers, she peered through the swinging door's small window into the kitchen. The cook was wiping down the stainless-steel counter, and it didn't look as though he had any active tickets left on the rail.

"Hey, Matt," she said, coming into the room.

He looked up and smiled. "Hey, Val. So how'd the dinner go last night?"

"Yeah, about that." She leaned against the counter and bit her lip. "Uh . . . not so well, actually. I mean, the dinner itself went fine, but there's been a problem afterwards."

He stopped his cleaning and gave her his full attention. "What kind of a problem?"

"A bunch of people got sick afterwards, and I'm worried it's some kind of foodborne illness."

"Do you know what caused it? Have you narrowed it down to any dish in particular?"

"No, but I'm guessing it was either the ahi tower or the dessert, since the other things were all fully cooked and then reheated before service. I assume you sanitized the cutting board before chopping up the ahi, right?"

"Of course. It's normal procedure."

"Okay, how about the mayo—did you by any chance use pasteurized eggs for it?"

Matt shook his head. "We just use regular old eggs here at the Gecko. I mean, not *old*—they're super fresh. And they're cage free. I don't think you can even get pasteurized eggs in Hilo—not the kind still in their shells, in any case. But I can't imagine it could have been that, anyway. Only like one in a thousand commercially produced eggs contains salmonella, so the chances are virtually nil that it could have been my mayo."

Valerie was typing a query into her phone. "It's actually more like one in twenty thousand, according to the CDC," she said after scanning the article that had come up. "So I guess you're off the hook."

"Off da hook for what?" Nalani stood at the swinging door, hands on hips.

"For food poisoning at that orchid society dinner last night," said Matt. "Though it wouldn't have been on me, in any case. She's the one who roped me into cooking for it."

And you're the one who suggested adding the homemade mayo to the ahi tower. But Valerie kept this to herself, instead turning to Nalani. "At this point, I'm thinking it was likely the dessert—the chocolate-mac nut tart with whipped cream."

"Which was prepared in my kitchen?" The Gecko owner did not look pleased.

"Uh . . . yeah. At least the tarts were. I made the whipped cream at the Buddhist hall."

"Well, we better hope it was da whipped cream, den, 'cause the last ting I need is for someone to blame my restaurant—or worse yet, sue us—because they wen' get sick." With a scowl directed at Valerie, she stalked over to the hot line and began emptying the remains of the mise en place inserts into plastic containers.

Matt, too, gave her a look before continuing with his cleaning of the counter, and Valerie took the hint and quickly headed back to the bar.

Pulling out her phone once more, she sent off a text to Emily telling her not to let anyone know they'd used the Gecko kitchen for the dinner's food prep. The thought of her being the cause of a lawsuit against the restaurant was something she didn't even want to consider.

But, Valerie couldn't help thinking, if it was in fact the whipped cream rather than the tart, although that would be good news for Matt, Nalani, and the Speckled Gecko, it would put the blame directly on *her*.

FIVE

The next morning, the news became far worse.

"George Ikeda passed away last night," said Emily in the voicemail she'd left for Valerie two hours earlier at seven fifteen. "I don't know any of the details, but I'm going over to see Sue right now, though I'm not sure she'll want any visitors—especially me." There was a pause, during which it sounded as if Emily might have been choking back tears. "Anyway, let's talk today. This is not good."

That's the understatement of the year, thought Valerie as she set her phone down on the kitchen counter.

No one else was up and about—Sean was still asleep, and Kristen had left a note saying she was going to coffee with her friend Diane. So Valerie had no one to talk to about this awful new development. Which was perhaps for the best. She needed time to let it all sink in.

Pouring herself a cup of coffee, she headed out to the lānai and dropped heavily onto the couch. It was a gray and rainy morning, which fit her mood. The water was streaming off the metal roof onto the lawn, where a pair of brown-and-yellow mynah birds squawked and splashed about in the puddles starting to form in the low-lying areas of the yard.

Did I just cause the death of Mr. Ikeda? He'd seemed so happy and full of life when he'd shown her his orchids and talked about making the vanilla extract just five days ago. And now he was . . . gone. Valerie bent forward, her head in her hands. *No, this can't be happening.*

A series of loud knocks followed immediately by the sharp yapping of Pua, who'd been asleep in the living room, caused Valerie to jump. Making her way to the front door, she spied her friend and neighbor Amy behind the screen. But Amy's face was tight, her mouth set. And rather than her normal shorts and tank top, she was dressed in khakis, a button-down shirt, and black leather Oxfords. A glint of metal peeked out from her waistband.

This was not a social call.

"Hey, girl," said Valerie, opening the door and motioning for Amy to come inside. "I'm guessing you heard the news about Mr. Ikeda?"

Her friend shook her head, then let out a sigh. "I did. So incredibly sad. He was a wonderful man."

"And I'm guessing you're here to talk to me about what happened." Amy was an officer with the Hawai'i County Police Department and had just two months earlier been promoted to detective.

"Uh-huh," said the cop. "But don't worry—it's just a matter of routine. Whenever there's an unusual death we have to interview people about it."

"And food poisoning is considered 'unusual'?"

"Well, even though he was elderly, it's not like dying from cancer or a stroke or something. It was brought on by an outside force."

Valerie swallowed. *And that "outside force" was me.* Did she need to be worried? Should she request that a lawyer be present for this interview? But then she shook it off. This was Amy, her friend. And of course the police needed to find out what happened. She had no reason to be worried.

"C'mon out to the lānai and we can talk," she said, and Amy followed her outside. "I'm surprised they asked you to talk to me," Valerie said once they were settled down. "Since we're friends, an' all."

"Well, as I said, this is just a routine interview—there's not even any case file that's been set up yet. Truth be told . . ." Amy lowered her voice and glanced about her, as if someone might be listening. "I wouldn't even be here, except that Mrs. Ikeda—who's apparently good friends with the chief—insisted we conduct an investigation. She's pretty upset by her husband's death. Not that she shouldn't be, of course. But anyway, when my boss found out you and I knew each other, he suggested I be the one to come talk to you."

"Ah. Yeah, that makes sense." But Valerie couldn't help

wondering if maybe the true reason was because as Amy's "friend," she might be willing to divulge more to her than she would to a detective who was a complete stranger.

Amy pulled out her phone. "You mind if I record this?"

"Uh . . . no, I guess that's okay."

"It's just 'cause I have no memory, and my note-taking kinda sucks. I can never decipher later what I wrote down," she added with a laugh. But then she frowned. "Sorry. I know this is serious. I guess I'm just a little nervous. It's weird having to interview you about all this."

"Well, let's get going and get it over with, then," said Valerie. "Why don't I just tell you what I know about what happened."

At Amy's nod of agreement, Valerie proceeded to recount all she could remember, from her volunteering to help with the dinner, through the shopping and prep work, to the dinner itself.

"So you think it was likely either the mayonnaise or the dessert that made people sick?" Amy asked when she was done.

"Yeah, those two make the most sense. I would've said it was definitely the dessert, as opposed to the mayo, since salmonella is really rare in fresh eggs. Except that bad dairy usually tastes off, and the dessert and whipped cream both seemed totally fine when I tried them."

Amy nodded. "And where'd you say you did the food prep?"

"Uh, I didn't say." So much for trying to leave the Gecko out the picture. "But we did a lot of it at the Speckled Gecko, and then finished up at the Buddhist hall right before the dinner."

"Okay."

"So, can you test foods for contamination in your lab to see what might have been the culprit?" Valerie asked.

"I doubt it. We only do simple things like urinalysis and blood tests for drugs and alcohol. And anything complicated like DNA we have to send out. As for food, I don't remember seeing anything like that ever tested at our Hilo station. But I'm not sure it's even worth testing for salmonella or e-coli or whatever, in any case."

"What if it's not just simple food poisoning?"

Amy frowned. "What? You have reason to believe it might have been intentional?"

"I don't know. It just seems weird that so many folks got sick. Given the menu we had and what I know about how it was prepared—the meticulous cleaning of the cutting boards and stuff like that—nothing makes any real sense as the cause of a foodborne bacteria or virus. But as I was telling you about all the food prep and everything, it hit me that maybe someone could have purposefully added something to one of the dishes."

"Okay," said Amy, slapping her hands upon her knees, "setting aside for a moment why anyone would want to do that, *how* could that have happened? You yourself said that only you and Emily were involved in the food prep—"

"And Matt, actually. He's one of the Gecko cooks, and he helped with the ahi towers."

"Right—and Matt, whom I'm assuming you don't suspect of poisoning the orchid society. So, when would anyone have had a chance to dump . . . whatever into the food before the dinner?"

Valerie thought back to the two days during which they'd cooked all the dishes for the benefit. Two times at the Gecko, when they'd been the only ones at the restaurant, and then at the Buddhist hall the afternoon of the dinner. And then she remembered coming back into the hall's kitchen after searching for a dolly.

"Larry—my neighbor," Valerie said in a hushed voice, pointing to the driveway next door where he could be heard talking to someone on his phone. "He dropped off the wine that afternoon and was alone in the hall's kitchen for several minutes while Emily and I went looking for a dolly for him to use."

"And why would he want to poison the orchid society members?"

"Maybe it was me he was trying to get at. Make everyone sick and I'd take the blame. I know he's not too happy with me and Kristen at the moment." Valerie stopped and stared out at a cardinal that had settled on the plumeria tree, its bright red plumage standing out against the gray sky. "But now that I think about it, anyone could have gotten to the ingredients for the dinner, actually, since they'd been stored for several days in Emily's carport, which isn't locked."

Amy was shaking her head. "I don't know. It all seems pretty far-fetched to me. And in any case, I doubt our lab could even do a test of mayonnaise or whipped cream. As I said, we mostly just test things like blood and urine—liquids."

"Liquids . . . Wait. I just thought of something. Be right back." Valerie jumped up and dashed into the kitchen, returning a minute later with a small glass bottle half-filled with a dark liquid. "How about this? It's alcohol-based."

Amy took the bottle and opened it to take a whiff. "Vanilla?"

"Uh-huh. And Mr. Ikeda made it himself. It's a mixture of vodka and vanilla beans, which sat in his shed for six months curing, or whatever you call the process. And his shed doesn't even have a door—it's wide open for anyone to get into. So what if someone tampered with that?" She nodded at the bottle in Amy's hand. "Could you test it to see?"

At Amy's dubious expression, Valerie went on. "It's just that nothing else makes much sense as the culprit. And look—it says it's vanilla for the orchid society dinner right on the bottle. And Mr. Ikeda was apparently bragging to everyone in the society about how the dessert for the benefit dinner was going to use his homemade vanilla. So if anyone wanted to poison the people at the dinner, they'd know this was a sure way to do it."

"Well, I guess I can take it down to the lab and see what they think," said Amy with a shrug. "But I can't guarantee anything. We don't even have any idea what to test it *for*."

The very next day, however, Valerie got a call from Amy. "You were right," her cop friend said. "It was the vanilla. I just saw the results of the various tests they did, and one came back positive for arsenic—and a really high level, for that matter."

"Ohmygod." Valerie sat down at the kitchen table and took a deep breath. "That means . . ."

"Yup. Someone clearly not only added it on purpose, but they meant business when they did so."

Valerie let out a stream of breath. Part of her was immensely relieved that it hadn't been food poisoning, and thus somehow her fault. But at the same time, the fact that someone had intentionally poisoned the vanilla was truly horrifying.

"I don't suppose you found any unusual fingerprints on the bottle?" she asked.

"I doubt we will, given all the people who handled it, but that's one of the reasons I'm calling. We need to get your prints, in order to rule them out. Did anyone else you know of handle the bottle, too?"

"Well, other than Mr. Ikeda, of course—and you—the only one I can think of is Emily Higa, who might have when we were unloading all the ingredients at the Buddhist hall the afternoon of the dinner."

"Right. I should get hers, too, then, just in case. I'll swing by and see if she's home and willing to give me her prints, and then come by to get yours afterwards. Will you be home for the next hour or so?"

"I'm not going anywhere today," said Valerie. "I'm just gonna lie down and stare at the wall and feel sorry for myself." But then she stopped. "Oh, God, that's completely insensitive, given what happened to poor Mr. Ikeda. I'm sorry. And yeah, don't worry. I'll be here when you come by."

Once they'd ended the call, Valerie headed out to the lānai and—as promised—lay down on the couch. But she didn't stare at the wall and mope. Instead, she considered what this new information meant. If there were high amounts of arsenic in that bottle of vanilla, then Amy was right: it had to have been intentional. And given where the bottle had been stored, almost anyone could have gained access to it.

But why? Why would anyone want to poison the orchid society members? And did they mean to actually kill people, or merely make them sick?

Pulling out her phone, Valerie typed in a query about arsenic, then scrolled past several articles from medical journals—which she could see contained far too much scientific jargon for her to understand—until she found one intended for a more general audience. Arsenic trioxide, she read, was most often found as a white powder that had no taste or smell. Symptoms of arsenic poisoning included gastrointestinal distress such as vomiting, abdominal pain, and diarrhea, and ingesting as little as 100 mg could be lethal.

She stopped reading. *Could anyone have ingested that much from the tiny amount of vanilla extract in each serving of whipped cream?* She wasn't sure what 100 mg of a powder would even look like, but it seemed unlikely. Then again, as far as she knew, everyone besides Mr. Ikeda had in fact recovered from their initial illness. But although the orchid society president was relatively old—in his late sixties, he'd said—he'd seemed perfectly healthy and spry on the occasions when she'd been around him. Could he have had some sort of medical condition which would account for his more serious—and deadly—reaction to the small amount of arsenic he must have consumed?

And then she remembered what Shirley had told her that night at the orchid society meeting—that George had been thinking of stepping back from the society. Some sort of health issue either he or his wife had, she'd said. *If it was George, could that have been the reason he'd died?*

Her thoughts were interrupted by Pua's high-pitched barking. "Aloha!" she heard Amy call out through the screen door.

Jumping up, Valerie invited her friend inside and into the kitchen, where Amy set her fingerprinting supplies on the table. "Is Kristen here?" Amy asked.

"Huh-uh. She's helping out a friend with a construction project, but should be back soon, if you need to talk to her."

"Nah, that's okay. I can talk to her later if I need to."

Once Valerie provided her prints—noting with surprise that there was no residual black ink on her fingers ("We got rid of that years ago," the cop told her)—she asked if Amy would like to stay for a cup of coffee, to which she readily agreed.

"I know it's only three p.m., but it's been a long day—I started at six forty-five this morning. But my watch ends at four, thank goodness, so you're my last call for the day. Might as well enjoy it."

They headed out to the lānai, followed by Pua, who had quickly detected the plate of goodies Valerie brought out to accompany their coffee. Taking a seat on the couch, Amy helped herself to one of the orange-tinged cookies, then let out a moan after biting into it and swallowing. "Ohmygod, these are like crack. Not that I've ever tried it," she added with a laugh. "But they're amazing—kind of like snickerdoodles with a kick. What's the secret red ingredient?"

"They're gochujang sugar cookies—you know, that fermented Korean chili paste that's all the rage these days? I kept reading about the recipe and decided I needed to try it for myself."

"Well, I for one approve, even if they are the new hipster fad."

They ate their cookies in silence for a bit, then Valerie turned to her friend. "So, how did Emily Higa take it, finding out about the arsenic? Or was she even home?"

"Yeah, she was there and, not surprisingly, shocked to learn about it. And from the look on her face, I think she might have been afraid I'd arrest her right on the spot because of her involvement in preparing the dessert," Amy added with a chuckle. "Anyway, I told her it was far too early to have any suspects at this point, but that she could help us solve the crime if she were willing to talk to me about what she knew. So she recounted everything she could remember—it pretty much matched everything you said, by the way. And she was happy to let me take her fingerprints."

Valerie grabbed a second cookie, broke a tiny part off for the ever-attentive Pua, then slowly ate the rest. "So," she asked, brushing the crumbs off her shorts, "do they know how come Mr. Ikeda ended up so bad off that he died from the arsenic, when all the other people affected just had bad GI problems but then recovered? Was it his old age? Though I gather he was only sixty-seven or so—not that much older than me. Or maybe he'd been poorly of late? I heard from my neighbor Shirley that he'd been thinking of stepping back from the orchid society because of some health condition that either he or his wife had."

Amy waited a moment before answering. "You know I can't talk about the case, right? I only told you what I did because you're the one who suspected the vanilla had been tampered with and gave me the bottle to test. Though now I'm wondering if I should have even let you know about the arsenic." But then she shrugged. "Oh, what the hell. Mrs. Ikeda has apparently been telling anyone who'll listen, and it's now all over the coconut wireless, so I guess I can tell you. It turns out her husband had preexisting liver problems, so his body simply couldn't process the toxin the same way a healthy young person could. And she also says he ate the whipped cream off her dessert since she's not a fan, which means he ended up ingesting twice the amount of arsenic as most everyone else. None of which lets the poisoner off the hook, of course. But it's super bad luck on Mr. Ikeda's part."

"No kidding," was all Valerie had to say to this.

Amy downed the rest of her coffee, then stretched her arms. "I should get going. I gotta get these prints to the lab and then write up a report before I go off my watch."

Valerie followed her indoors and back through the house. Sitting on the bench Valerie and Kristen had on their front porch, Amy pulled on the black leather shoes she'd left by the front door and cinched tight the laces. Standing up, she turned to face Valerie.

"I shouldn't have to say this, but given what I know about your propensity for wanting to investigate crimes, I need you to promise me that you won't go poking your nose into all this. There's clearly an unstable person out there, and I don't want you to be their next victim. Let the police handle it, okay?"

Valerie gave a small nod of assent, but this wasn't enough for Amy. "Okay?" she repeated.

"Got it. Okay."

"Right, then. See you later. And thanks for the cookies and coffee."

Watching Amy climb into her gray SUV, Valerie unhooked the two fingers she'd crossed behind her back. Childish, she knew. But she also knew that even though it was she who'd suggested the vanilla be tested, as the one who'd actually added the extract to the whipped cream, she had to be on any list of suspects the police were compiling.

And even ignoring that, Valerie mused as she let the screen door slam shut behind her, although it clearly wasn't her fault someone had added arsenic to the vanilla, she couldn't help but feel a little guilty that it was her dessert that had ended up poisoning poor Mr. Ikeda.

She owed it to the president to try to discover who had killed him.

SIX

Valerie almost collided with Sean as she turned away from the front door and started toward the kitchen. "Oh, sorry. I didn't realize you were up. Did we wake you?"

"Nah, I've been up for a while. And I have to admit I couldn't help hearing the end of your conversation just now. Single-wall construction and open windows, you know?" he added with a sheepish smile.

"Ah," said Valerie.

"So . . . what gives? What case was she talking about and why is she worried about you? Does it have something to do with that food poisoning?"

"You know Amy's a cop, right?"

He nodded. "Sure. She told me about making detective that first time we met. So is it a police thing now?"

Valerie followed Sean into the kitchen, and as he helped himself to coffee and doctored it with milk and sugar, she told him about Mr. Ikeda's death, and how she'd given the bottle of vanilla extract to Amy to have it tested for contaminants. "And I found out this morning that the test came back positive for arsenic."

"No way." Sean sat down at the kitchen table and shook his head. "Dude. No wonder I felt so lousy yesterday. We studied about arsenic in nursing school. Apparently it's pretty common in drinking water in some parts of the world—in rice, too, believe it or not—and that stuff's nasty. So, is everyone else who got sick okay?"

"As far as I know. I can't imagine that anyone ingested a super high quantity of arsenic—even though Amy said the levels in the vanilla were pretty darn high. But each serving of whipped cream would've had only a tiny amount. Mr. Ikeda just had the bad luck to have a preexisting liver problem, and he also ate two servings of the cream."

"That sucks."

"Yep," agreed Valerie.

"So I'm guessing because it was arsenic, they're now considering Mr. Ikeda's death a homicide."

"Uh-huh."

"And even though he had a preexisting condition which made him more susceptible to the toxin—an 'eggshell plaintiff' my lawyer buddy calls them—there's still as much liability as if he'd been strong as an ox."

"You're just a fountain of knowledge," said Valerie. "Too bad it's all bad news." Opening the refrigerator, she peered inside. "I wonder what I should bring to Isaac and Sachiko's tonight. Oh." She turned back to face her nephew. "They said to tell you you're welcome to come, too. Sachiko's cooking her mom's oyako donburi."

"I'd love to, but I'm seeing Tammy tonight. We both actually have the same night off, and she asked me up to her ceramics studio and then we're going out to dinner afterwards."

Valerie flashed a grin his way. "Oooooo . . . A first date! I hope it goes well."

"Yeah, well, I'm not even sure if she considers it a 'date.' But we'll see."

At five o'clock that evening, Valerie and Kristen knocked on their friends Isaac and Sachiko's door. Kristen had met Isaac surfing in Malibu some years back when he'd been in L.A. for a science fair, chaperoning some kids from the high school where he taught biology. But after Valerie and Kristen moved to Hilo the previous fall and Sachiko offered Valerie a job bartending at the Speckled Gecko, the four of them had now become close pals.

"We come bearing pupus and libations," Valerie called out, striding into the kitchen and setting down a bowl of edamame and bottle of sake. "My, does it smell good in here."

"That's the base for the oyakodon—onions simmering in a combo of dashi, sake, shoyu, and sugar."

"What else goes in it?" asked Valerie, peering into the saucepan on the stove.

"Basically just chicken, and then you drizzle in beaten eggs at the last minute. 'Oya' means parent and 'ko' means child—get it?" Sachiko said with a laugh. "And 'don,' short for 'donburi,' just means bowl, 'cause you serve it poured over steamed rice in a big bowl. But here." Sachiko gave the pan a quick stir, then switched off the heat. "I can finish it up real quick right before we eat. You two interested in a drink—beer, wine, cocktail? Oh, and Isaac mixed up a pitcher of white wine sangria if anyone's up for that."

"Sangria sounds refreshing," said Kristen. "I spent the day helping one of my paddling friends lay new flooring in her bathroom and I worked up quite the thirst."

Valerie nodded for Sachiko to pour her a glass, as well. "And I've been doing no physical labor whatsoever today, but I have had a stressful afternoon, so that sounds perfect."

They took their drinks and the pupus out to the lānai, where Isaac was hanging his board shorts over the railing to catch the last of the day's sun. "Sorry. I just got back from surfing aftah work. But I see you already got your drinks. Ho—and what's dis?" He peered into the bowl Valerie had in her hand and snagged one of the green pods. "Dass some 'ono edamame, sistah," he said, tossing the spent casing into the discard bowl Sachiko had set on the wicker table. "What's in it?"

"Sweet chili sauce, toasted sesame oil, furikake, and salt," Valerie said, taking a seat on the hibiscus-print couch.

"Delicious," agreed Sachiko, trying one of the beans. "So, what is it that made your afternoon so stressful?"

Valerie let out a moan. "It's that orchid society dinner."

"Oh, right. Nalani told me a bunch of people got food poisoning, and she's a little worried someone might sue the restaurant, since I gather some of the food was prepared there?"

"Uh-huh. But I think the Gecko's probably off the hook now, since it turns out it wasn't a foodborne illness, after all."

"Well, that's good . . . right?" Sachiko glanced from Valerie to Kristen, who both wore grim expressions.

"You tell her," said Kristen, "since I only found out less than an hour ago and know hardly any of the details."

"Found out what?" Sachiko asked, her voice rising in pitch.

Valerie took a large swallow of sangria before answering. "They found arsenic in the vanilla extract that was used in the whipped cream for the dessert."

"Arsenic?" said Sachiko and Isaac in unison.

"Yep, arsenic. And there was apparently quite a high level of it in the bottle."

Isaac was shaking his head. "How the hell could that happen? It's not like there's arsenic in the water here in Hawaiʻi. It would have had to be—"

"Intentional," Valerie finished.

Sachiko had now stood up and was pacing across the lānai. "Oh, God, this is all we need. Do they think someone at the Gecko added it to the bottle?"

"They don't think anything at this point. But I can't imagine that's where the cops are going with this. But . . ." Valerie paused, then took a deep breath before going on. "There's something else. Mr. Ikeda, the president of the orchid society, ended up in the ER after the dinner. And then I found out yesterday that he'd died."

This announcement was met by gasps from both Sachiko and Isaac. After a moment's silence, Sachiko sat back down. "That's awful," she said. "Was he old . . . or sick? I mean, since I'm assuming no one else . . ."

Valerie shook her head. "No, no one else has died—or even ended up in the hospital, as far as I know. And yeah, he was relatively old—in his late sixties. But more importantly, it turns out that not only did he have double the whipped cream everyone else did, but he also had a liver condition of some kind."

"Ah, so his body couldn't properly filter the toxin the same way a healthy person could," said Isaac.

As she often did when around local boy Issac, Valerie couldn't help but notice the way he flipped back and forth between Hawaiian Pidgin and Standard English, depending on whom he was talking to and the subject of the conversation. "Code-switching," she'd learned was the linguistic term for this. And this topic was clearly bringing out the biology teacher in him.

Pulling his phone from his shorts pocket, Isaac typed in a search, then nodded. "It says here that arsenic was widely used as a rodenticide until the 1970s. I bet tons of people around here still have it in their basements and garages, 'cause we got uku rats here in Hilo. Here, wait a sec," he said, jumping up and darting inside.

"So, what happens next?" asked Sachiko. "Are the police treating that guy's death as a possible murder?"

"I'm not privy to their thinking," Valerie said, "but Amy—my neighbor who just made detective; I think you've met her?"

"Yeah, I know who she is."

"Anyway, she implied as much. And they're certainly treating it as 'suspicious,' for sure."

"Shoots." Sachiko frowned as she took another sip of sangria, then turned as Isaac came back out onto the lānai, a small red-and-white metal container in his hand. "Found dis in our basement, along with a bunch of other stuffs left by the previous owners. 'Hot Foot Mouse and Rat Killer,'" he read from the label. "And check it out: the active ingredient is arsenic trioxide."

Valerie took the tin from him. "I don't see how this could have been used in the vanilla. I bet it would have a nasty taste."

"No, but it proves how common it is—da arsenic. Anyone who wanted to poison someone could-a gotten it from any number of garages or gardening sheds in Hilo."

Kristen frowned. "Do you suppose they were specifically targeting Mr. Ikeda?" she asked. "You know, because they knew he had liver problems and would therefore be more likely to have a bad reaction to the arsenic?"

"Maybe," said Valerie. She thought back to the president's carport, where she'd seen shelves of fertilizer and potting soil. Had there been any pesticides there? She couldn't remember. But then again, as Isaac had said, lots of people likely had pesticides containing arsenic in their gardening supplies, so the person could have simply brought some along with them to add to the vanilla.

Her thoughts were interrupted by Isaac. "Ho! I found something else here," he said, peering at his screen. "It says that you can develop a tolerance for arsenic, and there are even cases of people ingesting it on purpose to see how much they could eat without getting sick." He set the phone down. "Dass lōlō, brah."

"Right," said Kristen. "I read a mystery novel once where the murderer did that—ate a little arsenic every day to get a tolerance for it and then cooked a meal for himself and the guy he wanted to kill that had the poison in it. No one suspected him, because he'd purposefully eaten the same thing as his victim. Maybe that's what happened here."

"Which would mean it could have been anybody at the dinner, whether they ate the whipped cream or not," said Valerie with a sigh. But then she had another thought: "Wait. Mr. Ikeda told me the vanilla was made of vanilla beans soaked in vodka. What if whoever did it poisoned the vodka before Mr. Ikeda even used it to make the vanilla?"

"And what if it was one of them who did that—he or his wife?" said Isaac, excitement in his voice. "They could have sipped a little of the vodka over time to get a tolerance for it, and then when the vanilla was used in the whipped cream, they'd be immune to its effects."

"Except he clearly wasn't immune to it, given what happened," said Valerie. "And in any event, no way would George have even tried to build up a tolerance for arsenic. Not with that bad liver he had. Though I suppose his wife could have done so. But why would she want to poison the orchid society?"

"What if," said Sachiko in a low voice, "it was her husband she wanted to poison?"

Valerie shook her head. "I don't believe it. And if you'd seen how they were acting together at that benefit dinner—laughing and all affectionate—you wouldn't either."

"Looks can be deceiving," said Isaac. "You never know what goes on behind closed doors."

The next morning, Valerie waited until ten o'clock—by which time she figured Sue Ikeda would surely be up and about—then headed up the street bearing a lemon poundcake still warm from the oven. Walking up the Ikeda driveway, however, when she saw all the shades drawn in front of the house, she took a chance and quickly stepped into the carport.

It took a minute for her eyes to get used to the dim light inside, but once they had she took a good look at the shelves holding the gardening supplies she'd seen before. As she remembered, there were bags of redwood bark, potting soil, fertilizer, soil amendments, and the like. But then she saw that high above them on the top shelf—out of the reach of anyone without a step ladder—sat a row of insecticides and pesticides. Most were in new-looking containers, but one at the very end of the shelf looked to be decades old.

Glancing about her, she looked for something to stand on. A metal cage sat next to the shelving, but didn't look sturdy enough to bear her weight. But then she spied a wooden chair at the back of the carport. *That should work*. She set the cake aside, then climbed gingerly atop the chair, careful to place her feet on the edges lest its ancient seat collapse under her weight, and reached for the faded cardboard box.

"Rodenticide—Keep Out of Reach of Children" the label said. With an intake of breath, she turned it over and read the back of the container. But then she let out her breath again. The active ingredient was warfarin. Nasty enough, but not arsenic.

Part of her was disappointed, as it would have been so easy to simply blame Mrs. Ikeda for poisoning her husband. But mostly she was relieved. She didn't want to believe that the affection she'd witnessed between them the night of the benefit dinner had been simply a ruse on the part of Sue. She wanted to retain that image of the happy couple.

Valerie replaced the box, then stared at her hands. Had she gotten any of the poison on them? Noticing a rustic sink in the corner of the carport, she used a bar of soap she found on the counter and scoured her hands vigorously and dried them on her shorts. Then, with another glance at the still-closed shades, she retrieved her poundcake, walked up to the house, and very softly—lest the newly widowed woman was still in bed—knocked on the door.

There was no response for over a minute, and Valerie was

about to turn away when the door was opened by Sue Ikeda. The face of the laughing, joyful woman Valerie had seen just four days earlier was now gone, replaced by one with a slack jaw and tired, puffy eyes. She'd managed to apply pink lipstick, Valerie couldn't help noticing, but the bright color only served to set off the ashen pallor to her cheeks.

"Yes?" she said. "Can I help you?"

"I'm so sorry to disturb you, Mrs. Ikeda, but I'm Valerie Corbin from down the street." She pointed feebly downhill toward her home. "And, uh . . . I just wanted to come by and tell you how very sorry I am about Mr. Ikeda and to see if there's anything I can do for you. Oh, and I brought you this—it's a lemon poundcake made with Meyer lemons from a friend's tree."

A smile—though no doubt forced—brightened Mrs. Ikeda's face. "That's so sweet. Won't you come in for a bit? I was just about to brew a pot of tea, and we could have some of this along with it." Opening the screen door, she gestured for Valerie to step into the house.

It was dark inside with all the curtains drawn, and there was a stale, musty smell, as if no light or air had penetrated the room for some days. But then she led Valerie into the much brighter kitchen, which looked out onto the back yard and the area where Mr. Ikeda's orchids were grown.

"Here, sit," said Mrs. Ikeda. "And please—call me Sue. Mrs. Ikeda was my mother-in-law. Is Earl Grey all right with you? It's my favorite."

"Sure; it should go great with the lemon poundcake." Valerie settled into the breakfast nook in the corner of the room and watched as Sue spooned tea leaves into a flowered ceramic pot and poured in water from the kettle boiling on the stove. "I don't think we've actually met before," Sue said, leaving the tea to steep and joining Valerie at the small table, "but I've seen you walk your cute little dog up the street. Is it a whippet?"

"Pua's a poi dog, but I wouldn't be surprised if she had some whippet or Italian greyhound in her. As well as some terrier, too, given her feisty personality."

"Ah," said Sue, who then turned to stare out the window at

the rows of orchids under black shade cloth, her thumb tapping absently on the breakfast nook table.

"Do you have anyone to help you with all the orchids?" Valerie asked. "I mean, I don't know a whole lot about them, but I'd be happy to come and water the plants or do whatever's needed."

Sue smiled. "Thanks, but Don Ribeiro has offered to take care of them until I decide what I want to do with all of George's . . ." She trailed off, then blinked a few times and turned toward the window once again.

After a moment, seeing Sue's back moving up and down, Valerie realized she was crying. Standing up, she came to Sue's side and laid a hand upon her shoulder.

"I'm sorry," said Sue through her sobs.

"No need to be. I'm sorry I came by at such a bad time."

"No, no." Sue looked up and took Valerie's hand in hers. "I'm glad you did. I've just been sitting here all morning thinking about George, so it's good to have some company."

"Would you like to talk about him," Valerie asked, "or . . . rather not?"

Sue wiped her eyes with a tissue she took from the pocket of her pink-and-white mu'umu'u. "No, I'd like that, actually. But here, let's get the tea and cake." Standing up, she busied herself with slicing Valerie's cake and pouring milk into a small pitcher, using the activity to help compose herself once again. She set the cups and plates on the table along with the teapot, milk, and a bowl of sugar, and handed Valerie a cloth napkin, plate, and spoon.

"Shall I pour?" she asked.

"Please." Valerie waited quietly while Sue served their tea and handed them each a slice of the poundcake, not wanting to force the conversation—and unsure what she'd say, in any case.

After stirring milk into her cup, Sue took a small sip, leaving a smear of pink on the rim. "I know he wasn't a young man," she finally said, "and his health had not been good of late, but it was still a huge shock to have him go like that. So suddenly."

Valerie nodded. "I lost my brother about a year ago in a car accident, and it's still hard to believe he's gone. But I can't even imagine what it must be like to lose your husband like that—after so many years together. I'm truly sorry."

Sue cut a small piece of cake, then set the fork back down on her plate. "Did you have trouble sleeping after your brother died?" she asked.

"I did." Valerie was about to add that she still sometimes had a hard time falling asleep, even a year after Charlie's death. But realizing this would not help the grieving widow, she said instead, "I think it's only natural that nights are a difficult time for those who lose a loved one. Have you tried listening to something relaxing when you go to bed, like soothing music or comforting audiobooks?"

"No, but perhaps I should. Because all I do is lie there thinking about George—and wondering how on earth he could have died like that."

Valerie stared at the white and red ceramic "lucky cat" with its arm raised that sat upon Sue's kitchen counter—a figurine she'd often seen in the homes of Japanese-Hawaiians. *How to respond to this?*

"Did the police tell you exactly what it was that killed him?" she asked.

Sue shook her head. "Just that they think there was some kind of contaminant in the vanilla he made, and that it affected him so much worse than the others because of his bad liver. And also . . ." A tear had started down Sue's cheek, and she wiped it away impatiently. "I didn't want my whipped cream that night, so he ate mine as well as his, which means he ate double the amount as other people. So I can't help thinking I'm partly to blame for his death."

"No. That's not true. You couldn't have known. Whoever put . . . whatever it was into the vanilla is the only one to blame." *How would she react to this? Would any guilt show on her face?*

But Sue looked up at Valerie in what appeared to be genuine alarm. "They think it was intentional?"

Damn. Amy was going to have her hide for letting slip details of the case to Mrs. Ikeda. "As far as I know, they don't have any information yet except that it was something in the vanilla that made people sick."

"Wait." Sue's eyes had now grown even wider. "They don't think that *George* could have put something in the vanilla, do they?"

"I can't imagine they do. Why would he purposefully poison his own vanilla and then have second helpings of the whipped cream made specially with that vanilla? Unless, of course . . ."

Valerie paused when she saw Sue vigorously shaking her head. "If you're suggesting George may have committed suicide," she said, "nothing could be farther from the truth. He was very happy and content, and his religious beliefs would have prohibited it, in any case. Moreover, he would *never* have put other people at risk like that, even if for some reason he had decided to take his own life."

"No, you're right. I'm so sorry—I didn't mean to imply that at all." Valerie chewed her lip as she considered the mystery of the poisoned vanilla. "But this all does raise the question," she said after a bit, "of whether it was the vanilla—or maybe the *ingredients* of the vanilla extract—that had the . . . contaminant."

Sue sat back and frowned, then finally ate the piece of poundcake that she'd cut. After chewing thoughtfully and swallowing, she asked, "So what are the ingredients of vanilla?"

"Just vodka and vanilla beans, is what George told me. I don't suppose it would be easy to poison an actual vanilla bean, and the cops can test that if they want, since they still have the bottle of extract. But do you by any chance still have the bottle of vodka that he used for the extract?"

"Probably. Here, let's see." She walked across the kitchen and opened a cupboard underneath the counter, pulling out a tall, 1.75-liter bottle of Grey Goose vodka. "Looks like there's only a little left," said Sue, setting it on the breakfast nook table.

"You think this would have been the same bottle you had six months ago, or would you have gone through more than that since then?"

"Oh, heavens no. George doesn't—didn't drink, because of his liver problems, and although I do enjoy a cocktail from time to time, I don't drink vodka anymore."

"So when would have been the last time you might have had any of this?" asked Valerie, nodding toward the bottle.

"Around a year ago, I'd say. I used to drink vodka Martinis—George and I both enjoyed them. We were actually known as 'the Martini couple,' in fact, back in the day," she said with a laugh. "But after he got his diagnosis about his liver over a year ago, he had to stop drinking, and it was soon afterwards that I switched to gin for my Martinis."

"Oh?" said Valerie.

Sue blushed. "I never told George this, but I actually always preferred gin. But he so adored his vodka, and I loved having an 'us' cocktail—you know, something we both shared together—so I always had a vodka Martini along with him."

"Oh, how sweet! So, what about guests who'd come over," asked Valerie. "Would they have had any vodka?"

Sue shook her head. "We rarely entertain—entertained." She stopped and bit her lip before going on. "George wasn't terribly social—other than with the orchid society, of course—and he didn't like having people over. So if we wanted to see anyone, we'd go out with them to a restaurant."

Valerie inspected the bottle, which looked to be less than an eighth full. "Do you mind if I take this and give it to the police to test, so they can see if it's what might have contaminated the vanilla extract?"

"I don't see why not. Though I have to say the idea of someone waltzing into our home and pouring poison into one of our liquor bottles is pretty terrifying." Sue's shoulders shook in a quick shudder as she pushed the bottle toward Valerie. "But go ahead and have it tested. Whatever I can do to help find out what killed my George."

And now, thought Valerie, *all I have to do is figure out how to give the vodka bottle to Amy without her blowing her stack at me for sticking my nose into the case.*

SEVEN

Valerie walked back home with the vodka in a KTA grocery bag. "We don't want the neighbors getting the wrong idea about you," Sue had said with a sly grin, sliding the bottle into the brown paper bag. Valerie cared not a fig if anyone saw her carrying vodka down the street, but was happy that the bag would preserve any fingerprints that might be on the bottle.

Passing Larry Kaimana's house, she looked down his driveway and into his garage. His large red truck took up most of the space, but she could see shelving along the sides filled with what looked to be automotive equipment. She stopped for a moment, trying to detect anything that might be containers of pesticides, and was startled by a deep voice calling out, "What you lookin' at, sistah?"

It was Larry, whom she'd failed to notice at the side of his house watering an avocado sapling he'd recently planted.

"What? Nothing. I was just admiring your hibiscus." She pointed to the numerous pink blossoms that ran along the driveway between their homes. "It's gorgeous."

"Uh-huh," he said with a snort and turned back to his watering.

Valerie hurried indoors, then took the opportunity while her neighbor was busy tending his tree to head out to the back yard and peer through the hibiscus bush into his garage. From this angle it was hard to make out much, and all she could see was merely what she'd suspected: a variety of power tools and one of those heavy-duty metal cabinets with lots of drawers. But no gardening supplies or pesticides. If he had any, they had to be either in a part of the garage she couldn't see or perhaps in his basement.

Then, walking back indoors, she stared down at the brown paper bag sitting on her kitchen counter.

What to do? Should she call or text Amy to tell her about it? Take it down to the police station? And how was she going to explain the fact that she even had possession of the vodka in the first place?

"Whatcha doing? Looks like you're zoning out on a bag of groceries."

Valerie turned at the sound of her wife's voice. "Oh, hi. I'm just trying to figure out how to turn over a potentially vital piece of evidence to Amy without her going ballistic on me." She explained what the cop had said to her about not getting involved in the case and how she'd completely ignored the directive by going to talk to Sue Ikeda that morning.

"So what's this important evidence you got?" Kristen walked over and opened the bag.

"Don't touch it—it may have fingerprints!"

"No worries, Columbo," said Kristen, peering inside. "Vodka?"

"Yeah. Remember how we talked last night about how the arsenic could have been in the vodka before Mr. Ikeda used it to make the vanilla extract? Well, Mrs. Ikeda said I could take the vodka bottle to give to the cops to be tested. Which, by the way, points to it not being her, even if it does end up having arsenic in it—given how readily she agreed to have it tested."

Kristen leaned against the counter with a frown. "Don't you think it would have been better to just leave it at her house and tell the cops about it, rather than bringing it back here? You know, chain of custody and all that?"

"Now who's Columbo? But yeah, you're probably right." Valerie sat down at the kitchen table with a sigh. "I guess I just got a little too excited, is all. But at least Sue put it in a paper bag to protect any fingerprints that might be on it."

"Uh-huh."

"Anyway," Valerie went on, "I'm trying to decide how to tell Amy about the bottle and my idea. I'm thinking a half-truth is probably best. Simply tell her I paid a condolence call on Mrs. Ikeda, and she was reminiscing about George and his orchids and how he was so proud of his vanilla extract and then got to talking about how it was made."

"At which point *she* came up with the idea that the poison might be in the vodka?"

"Yeah, well . . ." Valerie shrugged. "I guess I can be vague about whose actual idea it was."

"Yep, she's sure to fall for that," said Kristen with a chuckle. "I'm gonna go out back and do the crossword while you wrestle with your conscience. Good luck with that."

"Thanks."

Valerie stared a while longer at the brown grocery bag, then, with a shake of the head, concluded that a simple phone call was for the best.

Amy was on her way to interview a witness in a car theft case and couldn't talk long, but it became immediately clear that she did not, in fact, "fall for it." The cop did tell Valerie, however, that she'd swing by within the hour to pick up the vodka bottle.

During which time Valerie fretted. Amy hadn't sounded exactly *angry* on the phone, but neither had she been her normal chatty self. So when her gray SUV finally pulled into the driveway, a blue police light mounted onto its roof, Valerie came outside with a smile and waved, steeling herself for a talking-to.

"At least you put it in a paper bag," said Amy when Valerie handed the vodka to her. "You see all those plastic evidence bags on TV—I guess so viewers can tell what's inside them—but law enforcement hardly ever uses plastic. It doesn't breathe and allows mold and other contaminants to build up, especially someplace as damp as Hilo."

Valerie wondered if this was her way of trying to ease the tension between the two friends. In any case, she was happy to roll with it. "Yeah, Sue's the one who put it in the bag. Maybe 'cause she's pals with the chief and so knows about cop stuff?"

"Maybe." Amy set the bag on her passenger seat, then turned to face Valerie. "Look, I get that you really want to help figure this all out—you seem to have it in your genes. And I can't stop you from talking to your neighbors when you want to. But just realize that one of those neighbors might be very dangerous. That arsenic didn't end up in that vanilla by accident, after all. And who knows what else that person might do if someone like you goes poking around their business. So *please*, be careful, yah?"

"I will—I promise."

"Right. I gotta go. I've got a call out in Wainaku to get to, but I'll drop this off at the lab on my way over there."

Valerie watched Amy drive off, then went to join Kristen on the lānai. Had she just been given permission to keep snooping around?

That night at the Speckled Gecko Valerie had plenty of time to think about the case and what Amy had said, since there wasn't much traffic at the bar. Tuesdays aren't generally a big night for most restaurants, and mid-January in Hilo is often slow in any case, since the high season for tourists in Hawai'i tends to die out between the new year and spring break.

As she waited on the three customers sitting on barstools and restocked the beer and wine fridge, Valerie mused about who could have put arsenic in the vanilla—or vodka—and *why*. Why would someone want to poison an entire room of people? Did they have some kind of grudge against the orchid society? Or perhaps the neighborhood? Or had they specifically targeted Mr. Ikeda, knowing of his liver problem?

She shook her head in frustration. It simply made no sense.

"Hard night?"

Valerie looked up from the dirty Martini she was stirring to see Amy, who'd taken a seat right in front of her at the bar. "Quite the opposite," she said, gesturing toward the near-empty outdoor dining room. "Which is allowing me time to obsess over who could have poisoned Mr. Ikeda and—perhaps more importantly—why."

"Well, I have some news on that front that likely won't make you too happy. The vodka tested negative for arsenic."

"Wow, that was fast. I thought it usually took a while for labs to do toxicology tests like that."

"Arsenic's easy to test for—especially if you know that's

what you're looking for. You can even get home kits to see if your drinking water has arsenic in it."

"Well, damn. So much for that theory."

"Could it have been in a previous bottle?" Amy asked.

"Not according to what Sue told me. George stopped drinking about a year ago because of his liver, and she doesn't drink vodka at all anymore. She says she switched to gin around the time that George stopped drinking—that she only had vodka in her Martinis because he did. And she also said they rarely entertain, so there's no way they would have gone through that much of that big bottle had it been bought after he made the vanilla six months ago."

"Assuming she's telling the truth," said the cop. "She could be lying about how much—or what—she drinks. Lots of people do."

Valerie shook her head. "Even if she is, in fact, secretly some kind of lush, I just don't see it being Mrs. Ikeda who killed George. The two of them truly seemed like they were in love at that orchid dinner, and you should have seen how upset she was about his death this morning when I talked to her. The whole vodka thing was just a long shot. But I gotta say it would have been so much simpler had it been that, since it was kept inside a locked house. Pretty much anyone could have put arsenic in the vanilla, which was just sitting there in that marked bottle out in the open-air carport."

"True," said Amy, "but they'd have to know it was there in the first place, which does limit the number of suspects."

Valerie grinned. "Are you actually helping me with my snooping?"

"No. You're helping *me* with my *official* investigation. Now how about a drink? It's been a long day."

Valerie fetched Amy the gin and tonic she requested, then went to check on the other two patrons at the bar, refilling their glasses of Chardonnay and entering an order of furikake fries for the duo into the POS. After filling herself a glass of water from the soda gun, she rejoined her friend.

"So how come you're not mad at me for, you know, 'snooping around' about the case? If anything, it almost seems like you're encouraging me."

"Oh, God, no," said Amy with a laugh. "It's just that I know you well enough by now to know nothing I say will stop you doing whatever it is you want to do."

Valerie smiled. "Truth."

Sean was still up, sitting in the living room watching late-night TV and eating a bowl of ramen, when Valerie got home from work that night.

"I didn't see you this morning," she said, helping herself to a beer from the fridge. Jimmy Fallon was doing his opening stand-up routine, but her nephew put the talk show host on mute as she plopped down next to him on the couch. "Does that mean . . .?"

"That I 'scored,' as I think you boomers like to say?" He let out a raw laugh, then stopped himself. "Oops—I guess we should try not to wake Kristen. But anyway," he went on more quietly, "naw, it's way too early for that, and I needed to get home for some beauty rest before my shift today at the hospital, in any case."

"Well, did you two have a good time—was it 'dope,' as I think you millennials like to say?"

"Ha!" Sean slapped his knee and nearly choked on his noodles. "That's so old-school—we say 'bussin',' these days. But yeah, we had a good time. And she invited me to hang out with her again at her ceramics studio this weekend for First Friday, so that seems like a good sign. Hey, you and Aunt Kristen should really come down and check it out. She and her studio-mates have some awesome works on display."

"Yeah, I've been meaning to get down to one of those—I just keep having other things come up. But I don't think Kristen and I have plans this Friday, so maybe."

At a sudden shriek from outside the living room window, they both started. "What the hell was that?" said Valerie. "It didn't even sound human."

"It's not." Sean stood up to peer out the window. The sound started up again, this time in duet with a second piercing yowl. "It's cats. I've been hearing them every few nights go at it in the early morning when I get home from my night shift. I'm not sure if they're fighting or . . ."

"Scoring?" Valerie said, causing the two of them to cover their mouths and stifle their laughter.

As the wailing subsided, Sean sat back down and reached for the can of IPA on the side table. "So, did you find out anything else about that guy's death?"

"Not really. Just that the arsenic wasn't in the bottle of vodka he used to make that vanilla extract, which means someone must have put it into the vanilla after he got it going."

"Which was when?"

"Six months ago," said Valerie.

"Oh."

"Yeah. A long time for anyone to have come along and dumped poison into it, especially since it was sitting the entire time in an unlocked carport with 'Vanilla for Orchid Society Dinner' written right on the bottle."

"Huh." Sean took another sip of beer and stared at the woman in tight black slacks singing on the TV screen. As the sound was off, Valerie couldn't tell what the style of music was but guessed it to be hip-hop from the dance moves that accompanied the song.

"Oh, by the way," said Sean, turning toward Valerie. "I talked to your neighbor Larry this evening."

"You did?"

"Or, I should say, he talked to me. I'd let Pua out into the front yard to do her business and sniff around when I got home from work, and he came over and started haranguing me about her being off-leash, and how he's found dog poop in his yard that he's sure is hers."

Valerie leaned back on the couch. "Great, that's all we need. You do use a dog bag, right?"

"Of course. I got the feeling he just wanted a reason to gripe about you and Aunt Kristen, 'cause of how she'd complained to him about *his* dog. Oh, and he also seemed upset that you'd been 'scoping out,' as he put it, what was in his garage. I gather he had some tools stolen recently, so he's paranoid about anyone appearing to have an interest in his stuff."

"Well, he's actually right about that thing, 'cause I was

scoping it out. But I wasn't checking out his tools—I was trying to see if he might have any pesticides in his garage."

"Like ones containing arsenic?"

"You got it. But I couldn't see anything other than automotive equipment. Though I'm sure he does have garden supplies somewhere. I mean, his yard always looks really nice, and we know he's into orchids, since he's a member of the society."

Sean sat forward. "So you think *he* might have been the one to poison the vanilla? Why would he do that?"

"I've been thinking about it, and maybe it was about *me*, not the others in the orchid society. I know Larry's got a chip on his shoulder about Kristen and me, so what if he was trying to get me in trouble for making everyone sick? I was, after all, the one in charge of the food for the dinner."

"But it doesn't make any sense that he'd do that—risk the health of everyone at the dinner just to get at you."

"Hey, people do lots of crazy things," said Valerie. "And it wouldn't have been any big deal if Mr. Ikeda hadn't had a bad liver and hadn't eaten two servings of the whipped cream. It would have just been a case of garden-variety food poisoning as far as anyone knew, and the cops would never have gotten involved."

"But your name would have been mud," said Sean.

"Yup."

EIGHT

The next morning, Valerie and Kristen were lying in bed talking, an unusual occurrence, given their different schedules. Kristen was generally up with the sun, whereas Valerie tended to sleep in, especially after a late night working at the Gecko.

But Valerie enjoyed the mornings when they did laze around together. It seemed so decadent after all those years as a working stiff. Plus, she always found it to be kind of romantic—like something out of a Nancy Meyers movie—lying in bed and telling each other about their previous night's dreams and what their plans were for the day.

"I had this weird dream about Amy," said Valerie, stroking the still-snoozing Pua curled up between them.

"Was it X-rated?" asked Kristen with a Groucho-style eye waggle.

"No." Valerie swatted her wife on the arm, causing Pua to let out a growl of annoyance. "She's half my age. And besides, how could I dream about another when I have *you*?" she added, planting a kiss on Kristen's cheek.

"I'm getting mixed messages here," said Kristen with a laugh. "But let's go with the second one over the first. So what was this weird dream about?"

Valerie rolled onto her back and stared at the ceiling fan spinning slowly above them as the coquí frogs sang outside their window. "We were back in L.A., and Amy had just been promoted to head homicide detective there and came to our house to arrest me."

"For murder?"

"No, for interfering in an important case—something about a woman who killed her husband by bashing him on the head with a potted plant." Valerie frowned, trying to remember the details of her dream. "Ohmygod—I just remembered. It was an orchid she used. Man, talk about real life intertwining with your dreams."

"Well, at least yours was an exciting one. The only dream I can remember from last night was me trying unsuccessfully to fix a leaky sink—both boring and frustrating at the same time. So, do you suspect Mr. Ikeda's wife of killing him—is that why you dreamed about it?"

Valerie shook her head. "No, not really. I mean, in some ways she is the obvious suspect, but I just don't see her doing it. Oh, and that vodka tested negative for arsenic, by the way. Amy came by the bar last night and told me. And get this." Plumping up her pillow against the headboard, she sat up and turned to face Kristen. "Not only is Amy not going to arrest me for interfering in this case like in my dream, but it actually seems as if she's encouraging me. She does keep telling me to be careful, but at the same time, I swear she seems actually glad I'm snooping around."

"Weird."

"Yeah, totally. Maybe she thinks I might actually discover something that she, as a cop, can't. You know, since folks'll talk to a friend or neighbor in a way they never would to a police officer?"

"True. And you do seem to have a knack for it."

Valerie swung her legs over the side of the bed. "Yeah, but I think I need to take a break from it all and try to relax. I'm sure that dream was my brain telling me to chill out for a bit."

"So you wanna do something fun today?" asked Kristen. "I don't have any plans, and it looks like a nice day—the forecast is for no rain till the afternoon. I was thinking we could maybe walk down to Coconut Island with the pooch and then stop for lunch on the way home at that new sushi place on Kam Avenue. I saw the other day that it has an outdoor area where dogs are allowed."

"Sure, that sounds great—I could use the exercise. And we can pick up some veggies for dinner at the farmers market."

An hour later, after fortifying themselves with coffee and Hawaiian sweet bread toast slathered with butter and papaya jelly, the threesome set off down the hill toward the ocean. Pua pranced about in excitement at this outing with the entire pack—small that it was.

They made their way down Haili Street, past the cream-and-pink Spanish baroque-style St. Joseph's Church—which always reminded Valerie of a fancy confection from a French patisserie—and onto Kamehameha Avenue. Only a few people were about, mostly tourists off the cruise ship checking out the gift shops, restaurants, and paddling stores along the historic Bayfront. Several, Valerie was pleased to see, were checking out the menu posted in the Speckled Gecko window with great interest.

But once they reached the farmers market, this being Wednesday—one of the market's big days—the activity level greatly increased, its vendors calling out to the early morning shoppers filling their bags with Japanese eggplant, taro root, rainbow papayas, and buttery-rich Sharwil avocados.

Crossing the street, they walked by the Moʻoheau bandstand and onto the low-lying floodplain fronting the ocean—now a grassy expanse dedicated to soccer fields. Once they reached the canoe beach with all the hālau for the paddling clubs, Kristen stopped on the black sand to scan the bay.

"Looks like Becca took Tala out in her new OC-2," she said, pointing to an outrigger canoe in the distance with two forms paddling steadily toward the shore. "Her husband bought it for her for Christmas. Pretty sweet." She turned to Valerie. "Hey, maybe we should get one."

"I dunno . . . it looks pretty big. Where would we keep it? And for that matter, how would we transport it down to the beach? It seems like you'd need a truck for that kind of thing."

"Yeah, you're right," said Kristen, continuing on down the beach. "But maybe someday—if I end up really getting into this paddling thing."

They walked on, past the small boat harbor, the Suisan fish market, and the Liliʻuokalani Gardens, and over the footbridge to Mokuola, aka Coconut Island, where they sat for a bit at the picnic table looking back at little Hilo town. The two fourteen thousand-foot mountains were out in all their glory,

Mauna Loa to the left and Maunakea to the right, her observatories sparkling in the sun.

Valerie poured water from her bottle into her palm for Pua to lap and then took a long drink from the bottle for herself. Watching the dog settle down in the shade under the table, Valerie was reminded of her conversation with her nephew the night before.

"Oh, I forgot to tell you," she said to Kristen. "Larry came over yesterday when Sean was out in the front yard with Pua to complain about us. He thinks we haven't been cleaning up after Pua—which I know isn't true—and he also accused me of 'scoping out' his garage. I guess he had some tools stolen recently, so he's apparently gotten paranoid about anyone seeming to take an interest in his stuff."

Kristen snorted. "I'm sure it's just payback for me talking to him about Akoni last week."

"Yeah, well, I was in fact checking out his garage, and he saw me doing it. I was trying to see if he had any pesticides in there."

"You think *Larry* might have poisoned the vanilla? Why would he want to do that?"

"To get at me," said Valerie, "since I'm the one who would have been blamed if they'd thought it was just food poisoning. Which I know is both unrealistic and a bit narcissistic at the same time. But I swear he's had it out for us ever since we bought the house. I get the feeling he doesn't like haoles all that much—at least not when they move in next door to him."

"And kvetch about his dog," added Kristen. "Sorry 'bout that."

After stuffing themselves with tuna and avocado rolls, gyoza, grilled hamachi cheek, and sticky rice, Valerie and Kristen made their way back home. It was now quite warm—in the mid-eighties—and they'd already walked about five miles, so they kept to the shady side of the street as they trudged uphill.

Once at the base of their block, Pua—who'd been moving increasingly slowly—perked up and trotted eagerly ahead, her home now in sight. Then, without warning she leapt forward, and Valerie, surprised by the action, lost her grip on the leash. A ginger cat missing part of its right ear darted across the road, and Pua chased after it like a tiny Greyhound in pursuit of its prey.

"Pua, no!" Valerie cried out, but the dog paid no heed and began racing around and around the banana grove in which the cat had taken refuge.

Kristen ran over and waited for Pua to complete a circuit, then grabbed onto the dragging leash as she flew by.

"Thank goodness there wasn't a car coming," Valerie said once Kristen had led the dog back across the street. "And what's up with all these cats in the neighborhood, anyway? Does that one belong to anyone you know?"

"They're feral," a voice called out, and Valerie turned to see Emily standing on her front porch surveying the chase. "Someone must be feeding them," she said, "because their numbers have been increasing in the last year or so."

"That's not good," said Kristen. "I've read about how much damage they can cause here in the islands—that they're the number one killer of native birds."

"And they've been making a racket in our front yard, fighting or whatever. Did you hear them going at it last night?" Valerie asked Kristen.

"Huh-uh. I was dead to the world."

"Well, they've also been making a mess of my flower garden." Emily indicated the bed of impatiens next to her front porch. "They've taken it over as their own personal cat box."

"Ugh," said Valerie. "That stinks."

"It does indeed," said Emily, betraying anger in her tone. "Some of us have been trying to trap them so we can take them down to the pound and have them neutered, but until we figure out who's feeding the cats, it's gonna be hard to solve the problem."

Coming down the steps, she crossed the lawn to join them. "I was actually meaning to come see you to find out if you've heard anything else about what happened. You know . . . with the arsenic? It's so awful that, and on so many levels. I still can't believe George is gone." She took a deep breath and pinched her nose, then let out a slow breath. "I so miss him."

"You knew him a long time?" Kristen asked.

Emily nodded. "Since kindergarten," she said, pointing downhill toward the elementary school several blocks away. "We used to play jacks together on this very driveway."

"I'm so sorry." Valerie laid a hand upon her shoulder, then quickly removed it, not sure if they were close enough to merit such an intimate gesture. "But, to answer your question, I don't think anyone knows much yet. I do know that the vodka Sue gave me from her liquor cabinet came back negative for arsenic, which means it's likely that the vanilla was poisoned after it had been made—you know, as opposed to someone putting arsenic in the vodka beforehand."

"Ah," said Emily, her eyes still focused on the driveway where she and George used to play as kids.

"So the question is," Valerie went on, "who would have put arsenic in the vanilla and *why*?"

Emily shook her head. "I can't imagine who would do that. Why would anyone want to hurt George?"

"Well, we don't actually know it was him they were after. But we do know it was likely someone in the orchid society who did it—someone who knew he was making the vanilla and knew where it was being stored all those months."

This concept appeared to take Emily aback. "One of our group?" she said, finally turning back toward Valerie and Kristen. "That's a horrible thought."

"I know, but it makes the most sense. So I've been thinking about who in the orchid society might have some kind of vendetta against George—or maybe against other members of the group—and I remembered what you'd said about Don Ribeiro being a 'pill.' What exactly did you mean by that? If you're willing to say, that is . . ."

"Oh . . ." Emily watched as Pua—tired of all this standing about—plopped down and stretched out on the cool grass. "I guess I can tell you, since George is no longer here to protest. He's the one who didn't want us to gossip about the whole thing—though Don sure loved to talk about it. The thing is,

Don had accused George of stealing some of the hybrids that he—Don, that is—had been working on for almost ten years."

"Stealing—you mean the actual plants?"

"Uh-huh. Don says that George snuck into his greenhouse last year and took the plants—I guess there were two of them—and then George claimed them as his own hybrids."

"Wait, George showed me those when I was at his house," said Valerie. "And one of the parent orchids—isn't that what you call them? It was white with a yellow center, and he said he'd crossed it with a pink one and the resulting hybrid was light pink with a yellow center. Though neither of the progeny were blooming at the time."

Emily was nodding her head. "Right. That's the one—a hybrid of two Dendrobiums. But Don claims that he's the one who developed the hybrid, not George. And he's pretty darn angry about the whole thing."

"Wow." Valerie chewed her lip as she considered this new information. "I wonder if that's what the two of them were arguing about at the dinner," she said after a bit. "So do you believe him—Don?"

"Not really. I don't think anyone in the group does, to tell you the truth, because Don's not nearly the accomplished orchid grower that George is. Was." Emily paused and glanced again toward her driveway. "You see," she went on after a bit, "hybridizing is really quite an art and takes an incredible amount of meticulous and specialized work—not to mention patience. First you cross-pollinate the parent flowers, and then you have to germinate the seeds and wait for the flowers to mature into blooming size, which can take seven years—or even longer. And because of how genetics works, no seedling will be exactly the same, so you have to propagate as many as you can, in order to get the result you're after."

"Mendel and his peas," said Kristen.

Emily looked her way. "Huh?"

"Nothing. I just remember studying in high school biology about how this German monk bred sweet peas to study how their traits were passed down, and I gather that was the beginning of modern genetics."

"Ah, right. I think I studied him, too. Anyway, this is all probably a lot more than you wanted to know about hybridizing orchids, but my point is that Don has only been growing orchids for about ten years total, whereas George did it for more like forty. So I'd be truly surprised if George would want to steal orchids from Don—or if Don could have even successfully hybridized any that someone would *want* to steal."

"Yeah, makes sense," said Valerie. "But did you know that Don's the one who's offered to take care of George's orchids until Sue decides what to do with them all?"

Emily's eyes grew large. "Really? Now, that's interesting."

"I know," said Valerie. "You think there's any way he might have gone so far as to poison George over all this—either out of anger, or as a way to take those hybrids for himself?"

"I . . . I don't know." Emily frowned as she turned to look up the street where a gardener was mowing the lawn at the Ikeda house. "I mean, I know I said he was a pill, but to intentionally kill someone? That seems a step too far—even for Don."

NINE

On Thursday morning, Valerie went grocery shopping, one of her favorite tasks in her new town. She loved pushing her cart up and down the aisles, examining the wealth of items on display that she'd be hard-pressed to find at her local grocery store back on the Mainland: frozen mahi mahi fillets, pickled plums, liliko'i butter, locally-made poi, and guava-flavored Hawaiian sweet bread—not to mention a host of Hello Kitty and other Sanrio wares, including umbrellas, hand bags, and even steering wheel covers.

Today, however, she was disappointed to see that the dairy section was almost completely depleted. A few lonely cartons of milk sat next to several tubs of sour cream and yogurt, but the pickin's were slim—a not uncommon occurrence in a town dependent on supplies coming from Honolulu after a long journey across the Pacific Ocean. She'd have to wait till her next shopping trip to buy the cottage cheese she'd been looking forward to having for lunch that day.

But all was not lost. In addition to her weekly grocery needs, Valerie was hoping to find inspiration for that evening's dinner and was therefore pleased to see they had hekka-style chicken on sale. She'd recently read an article online about this dish, a Hawaiian-Japanese take on sukiyaki that originated in the late nineteenth century on the sugar plantations of old Hawai'i. The traditional version called for a whole chicken chopped up into rough chunks, bone and all (the "hekka" cut of the bird), which was stir-fried with various vegetables and glass or cellophane noodles—known locally as "long rice"—and finished with a sweet-and-salty sauce of sugar, shoyu, and sake.

Selecting a package of the chopped chicken, she headed to the produce section where she snagged some carrots, onions, mushrooms, ginger, garlic, and a head of mizuna—an Asian green similar to baby mustard greens. She then pulled up the recipe for Chicken Hekka on her phone and, after consulting the ingredient list, headed off for cans of bamboo shoots and baby corn, as well as a package of glass noodles.

Once home, Valerie deposited her purchases on the kitchen counter and in the fridge. Then, succumbing to Pua's sharp yips and scolding eyes, she took her out for a walk. As they headed up the street, Valerie saw that Sue was in her front yard talking to a man in khaki shorts and a red T-shirt. She had on the same pink-and-white mu'umu'u as two days before, accented by the same lipstick that set off the bright colors of the dress.

Not wanting to interrupt them, Valerie stopped and let the dog sniff around the trunk of a coconut palm, glancing surreptitiously at the pair from behind the tree.

After a bit, the man gave Sue an awkward hug, then headed down the driveway, around the side of the carport, and into the back yard. Valerie continued on up the street and called out hello as Sue turned to go back indoors.

"Was that Don Ribeiro?" she asked, crossing over to Sue's side of the street.

"Yes. He's come to check on George's plants—you know, water and feed them, or whatever it is they need. Good thing, too, since I know practically nothing about orchids. They'd probably all die if I were to try to care for them."

"Right," said Valerie, wondering if she should tell her what she'd learned about Don's interest in George's orchids.

"Oh, by the way," Sue said, interrupting Valerie's musings, "that policewoman—Amy, who lives down the street—came by this morning. She said the vodka I gave you didn't have any contaminants in it, so she wanted to return the bottle to me. But she did ask to take the vanilla I had in my cupboard so they could test that, as well." A quick shiver passed over her body. "I have to say the idea that I've been using poisoned vanilla in my cakes and cookies for the past six months is not pleasant—not that I bake all that often."

"No, I can imagine it wouldn't be. Did she tell you what sort of contaminant they're looking for?"

"She did." Sue shivered again. "She said it was arsenic."

"Yikes," said Valerie, doing her best to act surprised. Though it wasn't difficult to do so, as the whole thing was pretty darn alarming—not to mention creepy.

"How could someone intentionally put arsenic into something they knew an entire room of people would be eating?" Sue asked, voicing Valerie's thoughts.

"I have no idea. Whoever it was must have had an incredible grudge against . . . I don't know, the orchid society at large? Or maybe someone in particular?" She let that last sentence hang, in order to see if Sue had anything to say in response.

When all she did was shake her head, however, Valerie decided to take the plunge and ask what it was she really wanted to know. "So, I was wondering if George ever said anything to you about Don . . ."

"What about Don?"

"Uh, well, I heard that he'd been accusing George of stealing some hybrid orchids that he—Don—had propagated."

Sue's jaw went rigid. "Who's been saying that?"

"Emily told me. But I gather from her that Don's been saying the same thing to others in the orchid society, as well."

"Well, George never mentioned it to me," said Sue. "Nor would he ever do such a thing. And I'm appalled that anyone would even think it possible."

Valerie held up her hands, palms out. "I totally agree. It doesn't correspond with anything I've ever heard about George. The only reason I bring it up is because it makes me wonder if that has anything to do with Don's volunteering so quickly to take care of George's orchids. Because whether Don's simply mistaken or is outright lying about the whole thing, it does seem a bit suspicious that all of a sudden he now has complete access to George's collection."

"Wait. Do you think he might have *killed* my George to get his orchids?" Sue's jaw had become slack, and confusion showed in her eyes.

"No, no, that's not what I'm saying. Though . . . I suppose it's possible . . ."

Both Valerie and Sue turned to look down the driveway where Don had gone minutes earlier.

"But no matter what," said Valerie, "you might want to keep an eye on him when he leaves to make sure he doesn't take any of George's orchids with him."

Sue turned back to face Valerie. "Should I be afraid of him?"

"I don't think so. We don't really know anything at this point. It could have been any number of people who tampered with that vanilla. Which brings me to another thing. Do you know anything about a couple up the street who were angry about that big tree in your front yard blocking their view?"

"The Souzas? Yes, George did tell me about that. They wanted him to cut it down, or at least prune it back significantly. But that tree was his pride and joy. He planted it in honor of his mother, who made lei from pua kenikeni blossoms as a young girl to sell at the port to visitors who'd come in on the cruise ships."

"Wait. You mean Irene Souza—the one who was originally going to prepare the dinner for the orchid benefit?"

"Was she?" asked Sue. "I hadn't heard that. But yes, Irene and her husband, Hugo. They moved to the neighborhood about four years ago from somewhere down in Puna—HPP, I'm thinking. When they bought the house, the tree wasn't as big as it is now, and I guess they had a view of the ocean from their living room. But as it grew taller, they started to complain to George, telling him he needed to keep it at the height it had been when they moved in." Sue laughed. "But anyone familiar with those trees knows they grow like weeds. And no way was George going to cut his 'ha ha' tree, as he called it—you know, for 'mom' in Japanese. He was very adamant about it."

"But they were both in the orchid society, Irene and George, so was that a problem?"

Sue shrugged. "Probably. But there's always discord of some kind or another in groups like that, isn't there?"

"No doubt," said Valerie. *But enough to kill someone over?*

And besides, Valerie mused as she and Pua continued on their walk, *Irene wasn't even in town the week of the orchid society dinner.* But then she stopped, startling the dog, who'd been trotting several paces ahead of her.

That wouldn't have prevented Irene from being the culprit. If anything, it would make it an even better crime, since she wouldn't have even been around when it had occurred. And she certainly knew the vanilla would be used in the whipped cream: she'd been the one who'd planned the menu in the first place.

Could Irene's supposedly "sick mother" have been merely a ploy to get her out of town for the dinner prep and the event itself?

Pua tugged on the leash, anxious to get moving again. With a shake of the head, Valerie followed after the little dog. This was crazy thinking—that someone would intentionally poison an entire group of people because one of them let his tree block their view.

But then again, the fact that *anyone* in the orchid society had seen fit to poison the rest of the group was pretty darn crazy. Who could have done such a thing?

Valerie and Pua made their way to the top of Halai hill, an ancient pu'u formed by an eruption that occurred some ten thousand years ago—the oldest dirt in Hilo, Kristen had told Valerie, since anything older had since been covered by more recent lava flows from Mauna Loa.

Gazing out across Hilo Bay, she could see waves crashing over the breakwater. A barge riding low in the water made its way into port loaded down by a stack of brown and blue shipping containers. *Good.* Maybe one of those containers included pallets of cottage cheese and milk.

"C'mon, let's head on home," she said to Pua, who'd settled down on a patch of grass after the short but steep climb up the hill.

As they approached Larry Kaimana's house, Valerie saw her neighbor open the passenger door of his big red truck and let Akoni jump inside. He then climbed in himself, pulled out of the driveway, and sped down the street.

"Right. Now's the time," she said to Pua. Hustling the dog into her own house, she came back outside, glanced up and down the street, and walked quickly down Larry's driveway to his garage. He'd left the door ajar, so she knew he wouldn't be gone for long. She had to hurry.

Slipping inside, she took in her surroundings. Sure enough, on the side of the garage nearest her house sat shelves of gardening supplies. She stepped closer to examine the items on the top shelf, below a pegboard hung with trowels, clippers, and other tools. Redwood bark, gypsum, orchid food, sphagnum moss . . .

And then she saw it: "Rat Poison." Glancing about her once again, she read the label: "brodifacoum" was the active ingredient. She had no idea what that was, but it certainly wasn't arsenic. There was an older, far more faded box behind it, however.

Setting down the first box, Valerie took down the other. This one merely said "POISON" in large block letters, with a drawing of a dead rat, its eyes bulging out dramatically like in an old cartoon.

And underneath was the single word: "arsenic."

She pulled out her phone and switched on the flashlight to examine the box more closely. In smaller print it provided a detailed warning about the toxicity of the contents, which in addition to arsenic trioxide, included sodium carbonate and lime. There was also an antidote listed: "After an emetic, give sweet oil, butter, or milk, and hydrated oxide of iron."

With a shiver, Valerie opened the container and—taking care to hold her breath—shined the light inside. The box was about a quarter full and, as she'd read online about arsenic, the contents appeared to be a white powder, similar to ground chalk.

Ohmygod.

After taking a photo of the box and its contents, she quickly replaced it and the other box. Then, checking first to make sure no one was about, she slipped outside and dashed back down Larry's driveway, across her lawn, and up to her own front porch.

Which is where Kristen found her a minute later. "What the heck are you doing?" her wife asked. "Pua was acting really weird, whining and scratching at the front door, and now I find you out here panting like you just ran a marathon?"

"I just found a box of arsenic in Larry's garage."

"You went in Larry's garage?"

"Yeah, but that's not the point. The point is, I found *arsenic* in there." Spying Larry's truck come racing back up the street, Valerie scooted Pua back inside from the porch and retreated there herself. "I saw him drive off with Akoni, so I figured I had at least a couple of minutes to snoop around his garage. And I hit the jackpot. Here, check it out." She held out her phone for Kristen to examine the photos she'd taken.

"Dude. Isaac was right. That box looks like it's fifty years old."

"Older, I'm sure," said Valerie. "They didn't outlaw arsenic in pesticides till the seventies, but this looks like it's gotta be from the fifties or sixties. Check out that retro drawing of the dead rat."

Kristen grimaced. "Yuck. Though kinda cool, at the same time."

"But I'm guessing arsenic doesn't ever go bad, you know, lose its potency—"

"It's an element, a heavy metal," said Kristen with a roll of the eyes, "so of course it never goes bad."

"Right. Well, I guess I better go wash my hands."

TEN

Every first Friday of the month, downtown Hilo is home to an art and cultural event in its historic downtown, with shops, art galleries, and museums open late, many offering free food and drink, as well as live music, hula, and other entertainment. On this "First Friday," as the occasion is known, the weather was typical for February—which meant rain.

And lots of it. By six o'clock that evening when Valerie and Kristen made their way downtown, their back yard gauge was up to three-and-a-half inches since the morning. And although the rain had now tapered off to a mere drizzle, it showed no sign of stopping.

But that didn't dissuade the crowds. This was Hilo, after all, the rainiest city in the United States, so folks didn't blink at "a little wet." And as the pair made their way down Kamehameha Avenue, they had to fight through a steady stream of people laughing gaily as they splashed across the flooded streets in their rubber slippahs. Some protected their shorts and aloha shirts with umbrellas, but most simply darted quickly to the cover of the Old West-style awnings that ran the length of the blocks along the Bayfront.

Stopping at a storefront with windows displaying enormous photographs of flowing and fountaining lava, Valerie and Kristen walked inside, where about a dozen people were milling about, accepting cups of hot cider and ginger cookies as they gazed at dramatic scenes of the volcano in all her glory.

"I'm not sure I could handle one of these in our house," said Valerie as they inspected a photo of a fissure spouting forth a sheet of lava the color of yellow-hot metal smelted in a blast furnace.

"Too close to what we witnessed up close and personal last year," agreed Kristen. "But hey, this one is pretty nice." She gestured toward a framed print of spattering lava that had formed the shape of a heart. "Kind of sweet, actually."

Valerie shook her head. "Yeah . . . but I don't think I'm ready for any lava pictures just yet."

They continued down the street, admiring a window with silk-screened shirts depicting monstera leaves, sea turtles, and tropical fish, then moving on to a shop displaying stringed instruments.

"Maybe you should buy a ukulele and learn to play," Valerie said to Kristen, who laughed.

"Oof. I haven't played guitar in years, so my callouses are long gone." But then she smiled. "It would be fun, though. And the fingering's the same as for the guitar, even if it's minus two strings and in a different key. Here, let's go in."

Kristen examined the various ukuleles hanging on a wall and then—after a nod of approval from the shop clerk—took one down and gave it an experimental strum. "What kind of wood is it?" she asked. "Maple?"

"The neck is maple, but the body is rosewood. And I have a few made from koa, if you'd like to check them out." The man nodded at a row of instruments with a burnished wood grain of red and gold.

"Beautiful," said Kristen. "But way out of my price range. And I'm just looking right now, in any case. But I may be back. Thanks!"

Once outside, they resumed their stroll down the block. "Oh, here's Tammy's studio," said Valerie, stopping at a sign that read "Mo'o Ceramics." As soon as they walked in, Sean jumped up from a chair he'd been lounging in along the back wall of the studio.

"Yay! Here's my aunts!!" He gave them each a hug and kiss on the cheek, then led the pair over to a table where Tammy stood chatting with a man and a woman.

The potter greeted them with a bright smile. "So glad you could make it. Help yourself to some refreshments, if you like." On the table sat plates of cheese and crackers, chips and salsa, and bottles of wine.

"Don't mind if I do," said Valerie, pouring herself a glass

of Merlot. “Nice place you got here. How many of you are there in the studio?”

“Right now we’re seven, including these talented artists here, Kimo and Doris.” Valerie and Kristen introduced themselves, and then the two other potters excused themselves to go talk to a group who’d just walked in the door. “We’ve had as many as ten at a time in the studio,” Tammy went on, “though it can get crowded if that many are all here at the same time. We only have two wheels, and as you can see, there’s not a ton of space.”

Valerie took in the worktable in the center of the room, which had room for maybe six people. Right now, two young girls were seated there, working with clay. One had crafted what looked to be a gecko and the other was rolling cylinders of brown clay and forming them into spirals. “So, what exactly is a moʻo?” Valerie asked, turning back to Tammy. “You know, the name of your studio? It’s a kind of lizard, right?”

“Well, some people translate it simply as ‘lizard.’ But in Hawaiian lore, the moʻo were actually shapeshifter deities, able to appear as both beautiful women and as dragons who protected bodies of fresh water—you know, like waterfalls and the ancient fish ponds where the Hawaiians cultivated fish for food.”

“Ah, hence all the lizards—or dragons, rather—around the studio.” Kristen nodded toward the stylized paintings of reptiles on the walls, some with wings, others with long tails and spots all over their bodies.

“And check *these* out,” said Valerie, walking over to the collection of wares on display in the window. Among the hand-thrown bowls, mugs, and plates were two ceramic dragons with fierce expressions standing about two feet tall. One was deep crimson with black-edged scales, the other cobalt and teal, and both spouted orange and yellow flames from their mouths.

She sucked in her breath. “Wow, those are amazing. Are they yours?”

“I wish, but no. They were made by one of the founders of the studio who no longer works with ceramics. But luckily she lets us keep them here in the window. They're for sale—as is all the artwork here—but I'm actually hoping no one buys them, since they tend to bring people into the store."

Valerie leaned over to read the price tags on the dragons: $975 each. "Ouch. Too steep for me. So, can we see some of your work?"

"Those two bowls are Tammy's," said Sean, pointing to the window display. "The ones with—what d'ya call it? Craze?"

Tammy smiled. "Close. Crazing is when it's unintentional, but I did this on purpose, so it's called a 'crackle' glaze. But there's not really much difference between the two. I use a high feldspar glaze to encourage the crackling, then rub colorants into the crack lines to heighten the effect. But they're just art pieces; you wouldn't want to use those bowls for dinner ware, as the crackling makes them pretty weak."

"Well, they're very cool," said Valerie. "Way too pretty to eat out of."

"And these are also mine," said Tammy, leading the trio over to a set of shelves along the side of the shop. "That set of mugs at the top. They're raku, which is an ancient Japanese method where you take the pieces out of the kiln while they're still red hot and let them cool in the open air. But I use what's called the American method, which means you fire at a really high temperature, then pull them out hot and put them in an open-air container with some kind of combustible material, which acts as a reduction chamber. For those I used newspaper, but lots of people like to use organic materials like leaves or straw."

"The iridescent colors are super trippy," said Kristen. "All the different blues and that burnt orange. What kind of glaze did you use—cobalt?"

Tammy turned to look at Kristen. "You know about glazes?"

"My mom was a potter, so I know a little. But I'm certainly no expert."

"Well, you're partly right—I got those colors from a combination of cobalt and copper. Here, you want to check out some of the awesome glazes we have here?"

She was clearly pleased to have an interested audience, so Valerie said, "Sure, why not?"

Behind the two potters' wheels at the back of the studio was a low shelf on which sat a row of white plastic tubs with names scrawled on them in Sharpie pen: oatmeal, eggshell, matte white, tenmoku, peacock blue, celadon, shino, kaki, toasted arsenic . . .

"Wait," said Valerie, "you use arsenic in your glazes?"

Tammy's body jerked and she turned to Valerie, her eyes showing . . . confusion? Surprise? Valerie couldn't tell.

"What?" Tammy said, then shook her head with a laugh, her shoulders relaxing. "Oh, right. I use that glaze so much that I don't really think about the name anymore—it's one of our favorites, actually. It gives you this cool blue that kind of floats on top of a dark red made with iron oxide. But that's just its name; there's no actual arsenic in it."

"Ah, well, that's good," said Valerie. But she was curious about the potter's reaction to hearing the word. *Did Sean tell Tammy about the arsenic in the whipped cream?*

At that moment a gaggle of people came into the studio, shaking off their umbrellas and leaving them in a stand just inside the front door. "I better go chat them up—potential customers," said Tammy with a grin, then strode across the floor toward the newcomers.

By this point the place was pretty crowded. And with all the chitchat in addition to the rain now pounding on the metal roof, it was loud inside, as well. Sean and Kristen had returned to the pupu table and were munching on chips and sipping from their cups of wine. But Valerie wanted to check out the other ceramics on display, so she slowly made her way around the room, admiring the studio's collection of mugs, vases, pitchers, and objets d'art.

She was checking out a set of food and water bowls with colorful paw prints painted along their edges when her eye was caught by an open cupboard in the back corner of the room. Curious, she walked over to check out the various tools for crafting pottery that sat upon the shelves. There were wooden shaping tools, sponges, several items that looked like dental instruments, and one with wooden dowels on either end of a length of wire—for cutting hunks of clay, no doubt. Underneath were several sieves, whisks, paintbrushes, a stack of thick rubber gloves, a digital scale, and an expensive-looking respirator.

Above the tools sat labeled bags, boxes, and plastic bottles of what she figured must be glaze ingredients: Cobalt, Soda Feldspar, Silica, Frit 3124, Quartz, Copper, Cadmium, Zinc Oxide, and Kaolin. And then at the far end, she spied a white plastic container reminiscent of a drug or supplement bottle and gasped. Did that say what she thought it did?

She leaned in closer. It did: the word "ARSENIC" was clearly printed on the label.

Glancing about her, Valerie looked to see if anyone was looking, then pulled out her phone, snapped a photo of the bottle, and quickly stepped away from the cupboard.

How could they leave something as dangerous as arsenic just sitting there in an open cupboard like that?

Returning to the dog and cat bowls, she kept an eye on the corner of the room and watched as Doris left the group she'd been talking to by the front door and made her way to the cupboard. She set down a glass bottle containing what looked to be a red powder, then closed the door and secured it with a lock. *Ah*, so she'd just opened it to show something to those people.

But still, why on earth would a pottery studio have arsenic on hand?

Which is what she said to Kristen as soon as they left the studio and continued on their way down Kam Avenue.

"Why didn't you just ask Tammy?" said Kristen.

"Because of how she reacted when I asked about that glaze—you know, the baked arsenic?"

"Toasted arsenic, I believe is its name."

"Whatever. The point is, it seemed like she flinched when I asked about it, almost as if she felt, I dunno . . . scared? Guilty?"

Kristen stopped so suddenly in the middle of the sidewalk that several people following closely behind almost ran into her, then muttered as they passed by. Oblivious, she turned to Valerie, hands on her hips.

"Are you saying you think *Tammy* might have killed George Ikeda?"

This elicited a shocked look from a man coming out of the gift shop they stood in front of.

"No!" hissed Valerie. "And maybe we should try to keep our voices down."

"Then what *are* you saying?" Kristen did not, Valerie couldn't help noticing, make any attempt to lower her voice.

"I'm saying that, A, it seems awful strange to me that a pottery studio would have a bottle of arsenic on hand, and B, that Tammy acted kind of weird—or sensitive or whatever—when I asked about that glaze. So I certainly wasn't going to ask her why she had arsenic in that cupboard. I mean, doesn't it seem a bit odd that when we talked about the glaze she didn't at that point say, 'Oh, but we actually do have arsenic here; we use it for X'? Wouldn't most people mention that if the topic of arsenic had come up?"

"Maybe they simply don't want to go advertising that fact to the general public, since it's such a dangerous thing to have on hand. And as for why it's there, I bet it's used in glazes or something. Here . . ."

Kristen stepped to the side of the sidewalk and leaned against the wall of the gift shop as she typed a query into her phone. After scrolling through several entries, she said, "Aha! Check it out. It says here that arsenic trioxide acts as an opacifier in pottery glazes by creating a fine matrix of bubbles that impede light passage."

"Huh," said Valerie. "I'm kind of surprised they allow its use. But then again, I saw other pretty toxic stuff in that cabinet, too. I think cobalt and cadmium are heavy metals, aren't they?"

After another minute perusing her phone, Kristen nodded. "Yup, they are. And it also says in this article that glaze colorants that are known to be human carcinogens include arsenic, beryllium, cadmium, chromium, cobalt, nickel, and vanadium. Yikes. Pretty darn toxic, as you say."

"Which is why they have that fancy respirator and all those heavy-duty rubber gloves I saw—not to mention the lock on the cabinet. I had no idea working with glazes and ceramics could be so dangerous." Valerie shook her head. "But, still . . ."

"What?"

"Don't you think it's a weird coincidence that Tammy—who's a member of the orchid society and who was at that benefit dinner—has arsenic in the cupboard of her studio?"

ELEVEN

Back home that night as they were getting ready for bed, Valerie once again brought up the question of the arsenic at the Mo'o Ceramics studio. Kristen had asked that they drop the subject earlier, and instead simply enjoy their night out rather than spend the evening worrying about who might have killed Mr. Ikeda.

Valerie, nevertheless, had continued to brood on the issue as they made their way down the Bayfront checking out the paddling store—which was offering free onigiri rice balls stuffed with pickled plums as a come-on—and the various other merchants along the downtown shopping district. So distracted was she with her musings that she'd failed to notice Sachiko waving as she and Kristen passed by the Speckled Gecko.

But Kristen did, and stopped at the restaurant's front door, outside of which a crowd of people were milling about. "Hey, girl. Pretty busy, eh?"

"Yah. First Friday's always a good night for us."

"Dang," said Valerie, shaking off her thoughts and coming to a halt next to Kristen. "Had I known, I would have offered to help out at the bar."

Sachiko smiled. "That's sweet of you, but Jun's got it handled. And he's got Kai helping out, as well. But I'll see you tomorrow night." She checked the wait list in her hands and called out a name, then led the party of four indoors to get seated.

Valerie and Kristen next made their way past the farmers market, which had only a few vendors left at this late hour, then turned right and headed back up the hill toward their neighborhood—Valerie returning once more to her ruminations about that arsenic at Tammy's studio and nodding absently as Kristen talked about a beautiful koa paddle she'd seen at the paddling store.

As soon as they got home, Valerie followed Kristen into the

bedroom and waited as she changed into her night clothes—an oversized Tito's Tacos T-shirt—giving her wife the same look that Pua did when waiting for her dinner.

"Okay, fine, spill," said Kristen, plopping down onto the bed and patting the covers for the dog to jump up next to her. "I know it'll kill you to keep it inside any longer. No pun intended," she added with a wry smile. "So you really think Tammy could have killed Mr. Ikeda?"

"I don't know." Valerie let out a stream of breath and leaned against the wall, too amped up to sit down just yet. "It does seem a little far-fetched . . ."

"Well, who are your other suspects? I know there's Larry, for one—especially now that we know he's got arsenic in his garage. Though you'd think if you poisoned someone with something, you'd make sure to dispose of it afterwards, wouldn't you?"

"Maybe not. How would you dispose of such a thing? You can't put it in the garbage or flush it down the toilet. I mean, you technically *could*, but it would be a really bad idea. Which is probably why so many people still have containers of it around after all these years. And besides, it's not as if you could trace the arsenic to a specific bottle."

Kristen scratched Pua under the ear as she thought a moment, then frowned. "And also, remember how I told you I watched him practically inhale his slice of tart at that dinner? You wouldn't eat it if you knew it had arsenic in it."

"He is a big guy," said Valerie, "so maybe he knew it wouldn't affect him like it would someone way smaller, like me. Oh, wait. Remember what Isaac found online when we were there for dinner Monday night? About how people can develop a tolerance for arsenic? Maybe Larry did that—intentionally ingested small amounts for a while before the dinner. Or maybe he eats a lot of rice, which gave him a tolerance. Given his size, he wouldn't even have had to develop much of a tolerance to be immune to small amounts of arsenic, I bet."

"Maybe." Kristen stared for a moment at the shadows of ti leaves slapping against the window in the rain behind the curtains. "So, what about your other suspects?"

"Well, there's Don, the guy who accused Mr. Ikeda of stealing his orchid hybrids. Did I tell you he's now taking care of George's orchids until Sue decides what to do with them?"

"Now, that's a red flag," said Kristen. "And a motive."

"Yep. And there's also Irene Souza and her husband, who were mad at George because he wouldn't prune his tree that blocks their view of the bay. Irene's the one who originally came up with the menu for the benefit dinner, but then supposedly had to go to Honolulu because of her sick mother." Valerie finally grew tired of standing and sat down next to her wife.

"Supposedly?"

"Well, it was a rather convenient excuse for not being there when the actual poisoning occurred."

Kristen let out a laugh. "Oh, boy, now you're truly sounding like a TV detective. But do you really think she'd kill someone over a blocked view?"

"I know, it does sound unlikely. But people can get pretty hot under the collar about stuff like that. And maybe George was a total jerk about it, you know, taunting her or something?"

"Doesn't sound much like Mr. Ikeda," said Kristen.

Valerie nodded reluctant agreement. "No, you're right. Which brings us back to Tammy."

"But she certainly has no reason to want to do him harm—or to harm anyone else, for that matter. Unless you know something I don't."

"No. It's just 'cause of that arsenic I saw—and the fact that she's a member of the orchid society. So maybe there is something we don't know about. You think we should tell the cops about the arsenic at her studio?" At the sudden thumping of Pua's tail upon the mattress, Valerie looked up to see Sean standing in the doorway to their bedroom. "Oh, hi. I didn't hear you come in."

"Yeah, obviously not." Her nephew did not look happy.

"We were just talking about—"

"Tammy," he said. "I heard. And I can't even believe you'd think something like that about her." With a scowl, he turned and stalked down the hall to his bedroom, slamming the door behind him.

"Oops," said Valerie.

But Kristen's only response was to stand up with a shake of the head. "I'm gonna go brush my teeth," she said, and headed for the bathroom.

Valerie let out a sigh. "Well, that sucks," she said to Pua.

Sean was gone when Valerie rose the next morning. But she knew he wasn't supposed to start work till ten, and he generally liked to hang around and drink coffee before heading off to the hospital. *Not a good sign.*

"Did you talk to Sean before he left the house?" she asked Kristen, who was out on the lānai staring at something on her laptop.

Kristen closed the computer and set it on the wicker coffee table. "I did. And he's pretty upset by what he heard last night. I think he needed some time to process it before talking to you."

"Great." Valerie set down her coffee, then plopped down onto the floral-print couch. "And now I suppose he's going to go tell Tammy, and I'll be persona non grata for the both of them."

"I doubt it. He said he didn't want Tammy to know what you said—that it was too . . . 'mean and creepy' I believe were the words he used."

Valerie lay back against the sofa and stared up at the metal roof, where a bright green gecko was making its upside-down way across a wooden beam in search of some breakfast. "Not sure that's any better," she said. "So do you think the same thing—that I'm mean and creepy?"

"He wasn't talking about you, personally—it was what you were suggesting about Tammy. And, well . . ." Kristen let out a sigh. "I gotta say I do think maybe this whole investigation thing is getting a bit out of hand. I mean, when it starts to affect our family like that . . ."

The gecko was now directly above Valerie, and she watched as it stopped, opened its mouth several times as if tasting the air, then continued on its way.

What she was tempted to say to Kristen in response was, "Don't you think someone maybe trying to poison all of us with arsenic affects our family a lot more than my commenting on the fact that I saw some at Tammy's studio?" But she held her tongue. The last thing she wanted right now was an argument.

Instead, she said, "Yeah, I get it. That's not good. I'll talk to Sean and try to make it right with him."

This seemed to satisfy Kristen, who nodded, then went back to whatever she'd been reading on her computer. Valerie, however, was too unsettled by the conversation to chill on the lānai just yet, so she decided to take Pua for a walk in the hopes of shaking off her unease.

Letting the dog lead the way, she wandered down the street as Pua sniffed at the hāpuʻu ferns in Shirley's yard, then followed a scent to a pile of trash bags sitting on the side of the road waiting for pickup.

"No, not for dogs," Valerie said as Pua began to paw at one of the bags and pulled her away from the enticing smell.

As she passed by Emily's house, she spied her neighbor sitting on the front porch, a mug of coffee in hand. Waving, Valerie was about to continue on her way down the block, but when Emily called out her name, she turned and walked up the driveway instead.

"Aloha," Emily said. "Nice to have the sun back after yesterday's downpour."

"For this one, especially," said Valerie with a nod toward Pua. "She absolutely detests going out in the rain to do her business. You'd think she came from someplace like Palm Springs rather than Hilo, given how much she hates the wet."

Emily let the dog sniff her hand, then scratched her under the chin. "Well, I wouldn't want to have to go outside in the rain for that, either, so I get it." She turned to Valerie. "Can I get you a cup of coffee?"

"In exchange for hearing if I've learned anything new about . . . you know what?" At Emily's embarrassed smile—proving true her hunch about why Emily wanted to chat—Valerie laughed and said, "Sure, I'd love some coffee. And I actually do have some new intel, though I don't know how important it is." *And it'll be good to bounce it off someone else, since I don't think my wife wants to hear anything about the case right about now*, was her unspoken thought.

"Great." Emily stood and held open the door. "Come on in—the both of you."

Valerie, with Pua trotting happily behind, followed her to the kitchen, where she poured a cup of coffee for Valerie, then led them into the dining room where they'd sat before when talking about the menu for the benefit dinner.

"So I've learned several things over the past few days," said Valerie after blowing on her coffee and taking a sip. "First, as you know, the vodka from Sue's house tested negative for arsenic, but Amy took the vanilla that was in her kitchen—which George also made—to test, so we'll see what happens with that. Second, when I was talking to Sue on . . . Thursday, I think it was? Right, the day before yesterday, she told me George had never mentioned to her what Don's been saying about him stealing those hybrids. Which is kind of interesting. Though I get how he might not want to talk about it with her, especially since she doesn't seem much interested in orchids or orchid growing."

Emily nodded. "Yeah, I don't think it means a whole lot that he didn't tell her. But how did she react when you did?"

"Surprised. And angry that anyone would accuse George of that. But she also asked me if she should be frightened of Don, since he's now at her house a lot, taking care of the orchids."

"What'd you tell her?" asked Emily.

"That I didn't think so. I mean, it's not as if we know anything for certain about him at this point."

"Agreed." Emily glanced out the window, which faced up the street toward the Ikeda house. "I think Don is wrong—or even outright lying—about those orchids, but I can't see him being actually *dangerous*."

"Well, I sure hope we're right about that," said Valerie. "Anyway, I also asked Sue about Irene Souza."

"Irene? What's she got to do with any of this?"

"She and her husband are apparently pretty upset about that tree in the Ikedas' front yard that's blocking their view."

"Wait," said Emily. "Are you suggesting they might have poisoned the vanilla because of a *tree*?"

"Okay, so it does sound pretty extreme. But what if it wasn't just that? What if George and the Souzas had been having an ongoing dispute. He did seem upset by all the new people moving into the neighborhood and changing its ambiance, or dynamic, or whatever. Maybe his refusing to prune his tree was just the last straw for them."

"But Irene wasn't even in town the day of the . . ." Emily trailed off with a frown. "Oh. I guess that doesn't much matter, does it?"

"Right. And she could even have planned to be away for just that reason, so she wouldn't be considered a suspect. How well do you know her? Does she by any chance have a hot temper?"

"I don't know her very well, as they only moved to the neighborhood a few years ago, but I've never seen anything to suggest she has a temper." Emily shook her head. "No, I don't believe it of her—or Hugo. That seems too far-fetched."

"Okay, then, how about Larry Kaimana? I know he's got a big chip on his shoulder about me and Kristen 'cause, well, we complained about his dog barking and howling all the time." *Or Kristen has been*, she was tempted to amend when Emily gave her a look she read as, "I told you not to be such a haole," then shook her head once more.

As Emily opened her mouth to speak, Valerie held up a hand. "But that's not all," she said. "I found arsenic in Larry's garage."

"Huh." Emily drank some coffee, then shrugged. "Well, I bet lots of people have it around. I wouldn't be surprised if I even had some, since it used to be a pretty common rat killer back in the day. And I certainly haven't cleaned out my garage since my parents passed away."

"Yeah . . ." Valerie was tempted to tell her about the arsenic she'd seen at the Moʻo Ceramics studio but held back. If word got out that she'd been spreading that information around, it would spell bad news for her relationship with her nephew—not to mention her wife.

Draining her cup, Valerie pushed back her chair. "I guess I

should get going. Pua's probably ready for the rest of her walk." Upon hearing this word, the dog jumped up and let out a high-pitched yip. "See?" said Valerie with a laugh. "But thanks for the coffee. And for letting me brainstorm with you."

"Any time you want to talk about it, I'm here," said Emily. "I'd love nothing more than to help catch whoever's responsible for George's death."

The three made their way back through the house toward the front door, and as they passed through the living room, Valerie commented on the ceramic bowls she'd seen the first time she'd come over.

"They're lovely. May I?" she said, reaching out toward one. At Emily's nod, she carefully removed it from the shelf and then drew in a breath as she saw the design painted on the inside of the piece: a blue-and-teal dragon with orange flames shooting from its fierce mouth. "Did you buy these at the Moʻo Ceramics studio? 'Cause this dragon looks a lot like some amazing sculptures I saw there last night."

"No, I didn't buy them there," Emily said. Then, after a beat, she added: "But I did *make* them there. As I did those two moʻo sculptures you saw."

"Wow." Valerie looked up from the bowl to Emily's smiling face, seeing her in a brand-new light—not as the elderly and slightly persnickety neighbor she thought she knew, but as a talented artist who could create magnificent fantastical beasts such as those dragons at Tammy's studio.

No, she realized as these thoughts passed through her mind. *Emily's* studio. For hadn't Tammy said that the person who made the dragon sculptures was one of its founders?

"Do you still work there at the studio?" Valerie asked, already knowing the answer.

Emily let out a sigh. "Alas, no. I had to quit ceramics over a year ago because the clay started giving me nasty rashes. I don't know if it was an allergy to mold in the clay we sourced or simply that it was drying out my hands—and heaven knows I've been suffering from horribly dry skin far more as I age—but I finally had to give it up." As Emily stared at the bowl she held, Valerie could detect the longing and sadness in her eyes.

"Well, Tammy seems to miss you there," said Valerie. "And I know she's thankful that some of your pieces are still on display at the studio. So, did you two first meet in the orchid society, or at the ceramics studio?"

"At the studio. She joined four years back and then, after hearing me go on and on about orchids all the time, finally decided to come to one of our meetings. I think she's been a part of the society for, what . . . two years now? So how do you know Tammy? Other than her being at the dinner that night, that is."

"She and my nephew, Sean—you met him that night at the table with Tammy and my wife—are dating. Or at least 'seeing' each other. I'm not sure what they call it these days."

Emily laughed. "Hanging out? I think that's what my sister's grandson says about the woman he's been seeing recently. But I can never keep up with the current slang."

"Well, you seem pretty hip to me," said Valerie with a nod at the SpongeBob SquarePants T-shirt peeking out from beneath Emily's white cotton blouse. "Anyway, at Sean's urging we went down to the Moʻo studio last night for First Friday to check it out. It was really cool—lots of beautiful pieces there."

"Yeah," said Emily with a sigh. "There are. I do miss it."

TWELVE

As Valerie and Pua made their way downhill, Valerie pondered what she'd just learned.

What a small town Hilo was. She loved how everyone seemed to know one another. It wasn't particularly surprising to discover that Emily had been one of the founders of the studio that Sean's new girlfriend was a part of. But these sorts of connections certainly added to the charm of her newly adopted residence.

Walking past the Lyman Museum, the morning sun casting elegant shadows of slender fan palms upon its creamy stucco walls, she wondered just how well Emily knew Tammy. The two hadn't seemed especially close that night at the benefit dinner, though it looked as if they were on perfectly friendly terms. But did Emily resent the fact that Tammy was still able to work with ceramics, while she'd been forced to give up what was obviously one of her great passions in life?

And then she had a thought that made her stop in her tracks: Could *Emily* have taken some of the arsenic from the Moʻo studio? Although she no longer worked with ceramics there, she clearly still had a connection to the place, given that her sculptures were on sale there. And none of the other members of the studio would think anything of it if one of the founders came around to hang out.

But this once more raised the fundamental question of *why*? Why would Emily want to harm members of the orchid society? And if she did do it, who would she have been intending to harm? Certainly not Mr. Ikeda, given her obvious distress at his death.

At the corner with the gas station, Valerie stopped and waited for the green light as Pua investigated the smells at the bottom of the pole. *If Emily were for some reason resentful of Tammy, she could have been the target*, she mused.

Or it could have been me. Emily had been rather peeved at her that morning they'd discussed the menu for the dinner, and then again when she and Matt had suggested changing up the ingredients of the ahi tower. Could she have tampered with the vanilla to make Valerie—who'd been in charge of the dessert—take the blame for food poisoning? A prank gone very very wrong?

But as the light changed and she tugged Pua away from the light pole, she shook her head with a snort. These were ridiculous thoughts. Who was she going to suspect next—Sean? Or Kristen?

A sudden burst of loud, high-pitched *bangs* made Valerie flinch, and she turned quickly to make sure Pua hadn't been spooked by the sound. But the dog seemed not the least bit concerned and was busy investigating a to-go container someone had left on the ground.

What could have made such a noise?

And then she remembered. *Right.* Today was the celebration of the Lunar New Year—she'd read about it in the paper the day before. Turning right onto Kam Avenue, Valerie was hit by the acrid smell of sulfur along with a rhythmic cadence of beating gongs and drums. At the far end of the block stood a crowd of people enveloped in a cloud of gray smoke, in the center of which two large pink-and-red forms were moving about.

The dragon dance!

With another glance at Pua to make sure she was still okay, Valerie led the dog down the street so she could watch the show. The dragons were made up of two men each under an elaborate costume, the one in front holding up the beast's head and some poor sucker at the rear who had to stay bent over the entire time. The dragon heads were bouncing back and forth in time to the percussion, and whenever someone approached holding a small red envelope, the large mouth would open to accept the offering. It was considered good luck, Valerie had read in the newspaper article, to "feed" the dragons with cash stuffed into the traditional red envelopes.

Another round of firecrackers made her jump, and a group

of little kids squealed in delight, dancing away from the string of red paper cylinders exploding on the asphalt.

To her amazement, Pua calmly took this all in as if it were a normal day-to-day event. Valerie knew the dog wasn't deaf. Perhaps her previous owners had been firecracker fanatics, and she'd simply become inured to the sound? She'd been pretty darn calm on New Year's Eve, come to think of it, when their normally peaceful street had erupted into a virtual war zone for the night.

Smiling, she returned her attention to the two dragons, who were now engaged in an elaborate dance, their backs arching and bending as they moved in wide circles through the ever-growing crowd.

A man dressed in a red-and-white costume offered her one of the red envelopes, which she accepted. Might as well take part in the tradition. Reaching into her pocket, she pulled out her wallet, extracted a five-dollar bill, and slid it into the envelope.

The pink dragon, observing this activity, approached her and opened wide its enormous mouth. She reached inside, and her offering was grasped by a human hand, reminding her of a snake springing suddenly from an undersea cavern.

Laughing, she clapped her hands as the dragon continued its dance, turning circles around a trio of girls dressed in black-and-gold Year of the Pig T-shirts. Valerie pulled out her phone and was about to snap a photo of the dragon when a sharp tug on Pua's leash caused her to step back several paces.

She'd just turned to her left to see what the dog was doing when there was a burst of light followed immediately by an ear-splitting explosion almost at her feet. Valerie jumped back even farther, but not quickly enough to avoid being hit by some of the debris from whatever had detonated.

Dropping Pua's leash, she reached down to her calves, hurriedly brushing off the still burning cinders that had been ejected by the blast. Several people ran to her aid, offering water from their drinking bottles, which she gratefully poured over her stinging legs.

"Are you okay?" one asked.

Valerie stood back up. "Yeah, I'm sure I'll be fine. I just need to get home and ice them a bit, I think. Did you see who lit that firecracker?"

They all shook their heads. "I stay watching da dragon," said a young girl, and the others nodded agreement.

"And dat was no regular firecracker," a man peering down at the explosion site added. "Mo' like one M-150, I'd say." He kicked at the smoldering remains and shook his head in disgust. "Yah, dass what it was, aurite. You one lucky sistah it no go off right underneat' you. Now what buggah wanna go an' set off one of dem down here wit' so many people around?"

But Valerie was staring at the smoking ash and torn red paper tube—which were precisely where she'd been standing before being pulled away by Pua.

Had someone tossed it at her feet on purpose?

She shivered, then glanced around to take in the faces of the crowd along the Bayfront. No one she recognized. She turned to Pua to thank the dog for saving her from . . . what? Maiming? Or worse? But then she realized that this time, the dog *had* reacted to the blast and was staring up at Valerie, her little body shaking in fear. "Oh, poor thing," she said, picking her up and holding her tight. "Let's get you away from all this, shall we?"

Thanking the two women who'd given her the water, she started down the street, hurrying away from the dragons and the noise. But as she turned off of Kam Avenue onto Haili Street, she saw a familiar figure standing underneath the marquee of the Palace Theater. He was facing away from her, staring at a poster advertising an upcoming movie, but her body tensed as she recognized the man.

It was Larry Kaimana.

"Dere's dat cop again," said Jun that night at the Speckled Gecko. Valerie looked up from crushing mint, sugar, and lime in a pitcher to see Amy take a seat at the far end of the bar. Valerie waved, then finished mixing her batch of Mojitos and delivered it to a table next to the dolphin fountain in the center of the restaurant's outdoor lānai. Returning to the bar, she wiped her hands on a side towel and walked over to where her neighbor was sitting. "Come here often?"

"More often than I used to," said Amy with a laugh. "I think I might be on the verge of becoming a regular. But, hey, what can I say? It's fun hanging out at a place where your friend tends bar."

"Ah, so it's free drinks you're after?"

"Nah." Amy slapped a twenty on the counter. "Just information."

Valerie stared at the money for a moment, unsure how to respond, until Amy let out a laugh as she picked up the bill and shoved it back into her khaki slacks. "Just messin' with ya, girl. It's actually I who have info for you. But not until you mix me up whatever's your drink special for the evening."

"That would be what I'm calling the 'Lemongrass Blast.'" Valerie set about mixing Amy's drink, then set the cocktail glass down in front of her. "Hold on a minute while I get out an order for the dining room, and then I'll be all ears for this new intel you have."

After shaking up a pair of Cosmos, pouring a glass of Chardonnay, and popping the cap on a bottle of Longboard Lager, Valerie returned to the end of the bar, where Amy was stirring her drink with its lemongrass swizzle stick.

"This is mighty tasty," she said. "What's in it?"

"Vodka, lemongrass-infused simple syrup, lime juice, and a splash of ginger beer. I've only sold a few so far tonight, so I'm glad you like it." Valerie glanced down the bar and, seeing that Jun was tending to the few customers they had at the moment, leaned over toward Amy. "So, what's up?"

"It's not actually all that exciting, but I thought you'd want to know that the vanilla I took from Sue Ikeda's house came up clean—no arsenic."

Valerie stood back up and stretched her back. "Well, I can't say I'm too surprised. It would be pretty darn creepy if it had in fact been tampered with. But I've got some info for you."

She told the cop what she'd learned over the past few days: Don's accusations about George stealing his hybrids, how Irene and Hugo Souza had been upset about George refusing to trim his tree, and the arsenic in Larry's garage. "Oh, and someone may have tried to blow me up with an M-150 today at the dragon dance for the Lunar New Year."

"They *what*?"

"Well, it's possible it was just an accident, but the fact that the thing exploded right at my feet—or where my feet *would* have been had Pua not luckily tugged me away at the last moment—suggests otherwise. And right after that happened, I saw Larry loitering just a block away at the Palace Theater."

"Dang, girl, are you okay?"

"Just a flesh wound," said Valerie with a grin. "I'll be fine."

Amy frowned as she sipped her drink. "I have to think it was just an accident. I know how crazy folks around here can get with setting off fireworks an' stuff. Did you by any chance talk to Larry when you saw him?"

"Huh-uh. He was doing his best to avoid my gaze. Plus, it's not like we're on very good terms . . ."

"Right. Well, it's interesting what you said about that guy who claims George stole his orchids. But as for the other stuff, if we suspected everyone of murder who was angry about a blocked view, half of Hilo would be on the list. And simply having arsenic at your house doesn't get us very far, since that's probably true of the other half of the town."

"But couldn't you at least question Irene and Larry about those things?"

Amy shrugged. "Maybe. But I'm not going to at this point. And from what it sounds like, it probably wouldn't be the best thing if Larry found out you were snooping around his garage. Though I may have a talk with this Don character." She pulled a small notepad from her bag and scribbled a note in it, then set it on the bar. "So, is there any more?"

"Uh . . ." Valerie was torn. She wanted to tell her about the arsenic at the ceramics studio, but the thought of Sean's face last night when he'd overheard what she'd said about Tammy—as well as what Kristen would say if she knew she'd been talking to her cop friend about it all—kept her mum. Plus, she reasoned, since Amy hadn't been that interested in the arsenic at Larry's house, she'd likely be similarly unimpressed with it being at a potters' studio, where the substance had a real—and legal—use.

And, she reasoned, there was no point in telling Amy about Emily having been a part of the Mo'o Ceramics studio if she didn't also tell her about seeing the arsenic there.

"No, not that I can think of," Valerie said. "But I'll certainly keep you posted if I learn anything else."

"Sounds good." Amy drained her glass, then stood up from her stool. "I should get home; I have the early watch tomorrow. But it's always nice to come in after work for a drink. Thanks." She paid for her cocktail—this time pulling out a credit card, rather than a twenty-dollar bill—then flashed Valerie the shaka and took her leave.

The next day, Valerie was awakened by Pua's insistent barking. Slowly coming to consciousness, she realized the high-pitched yips were accompanied by a rapping at the front door. *Who could be coming by so early on a Sunday morning?*

"Just a second!" she called out and slid out of bed. She pulled on the blue-and-white cotton yukata she'd recently bought at a Japanese clothing store downtown and hurried to see who her early morning visitor might be. *And why had neither Kristen nor Sean answered the door?* But then she noticed the clock on the kitchen wall and saw that it was actually nine fifteen.

Opening the front door, Valerie was surprised to see Sue Ikeda standing on the front porch. "Oh, hi," said Valerie. "Sorry about my tousled appearance, but I worked late last night."

Sue flushed. "Oh, dear. I'm so sorry to come by so early. I—"

"No, it's fine. I was already up," Valerie lied. "I just haven't gotten into my daytime clothes yet. Would you care to come in?"

"No, that's okay. I only came by to say that I've decided to give away George's orchids to any members of the orchid society who would like them and wondered if perhaps you'd like to have first pick. Since you've been so helpful with . . ." She stared down at her hands. "You know."

"That's so sweet of you. And I'd be honored to take a few of his plants. Though I'm quite new to the world of orchids, so I'd best choose ones that are easy to care for." And then Valerie had a thought. "Do you think Don would be willing to advise me on that?"

"I don't see why not? He said he'd be coming by tomorrow morning, if you'd like to stop by then."

"Perfect. I'll do that. And thanks so much for your generous offer."

Sue blinked a few times, then nodded. "I think it's what George would have wanted. He loved the orchid society, and I know they'll take good care of all his beloved plants."

Valerie watched Sue make her way across the front lawn and then up the street back to her house. *And what better way to get Don talking about those hybrids*, was her thought.

THIRTEEN

Returning indoors, Valerie went in search of her wife and nephew, but neither was to be found, and both Valerie and Kristen's RAV4 as well as Sean's mountain bike were gone. But then, as she passed through the kitchen on her way from the lānai back into her bedroom, she saw a note on the counter: "Paddling with the gals. Pua's been fed."

Right. Kristen had mentioned the day before that they'd switched their workout to Sunday this week.

"Guess it's just you and me," Valerie said to the dog, who'd been following her as she wandered from room to room in the house. "But if you're hoping for more food, no such luck, because we humans unfortunately have this thing called 'writing,' whereby we can communicate to each other, and so I happen to know you've already had your breakfast."

The dog's ears perked up at this last word, only to fall back down as Valerie headed to the bedroom, rather than the cupboard where the dog food was stored. Once dressed, she poured herself a cup of coffee—the early risers had been kind enough to leave some in the pot they'd brewed earlier—and headed out to the lānai. Settling down onto the rattan couch, she immediately jumped up again.

"Oh, the paper. Wanna come with me?"

Pua trotted after Valerie as she went through the house once more, out the front door, and across the lawn to the mailbox with the green *Hawai'i Tribune Herald* newspaper box attached to it. Pulling out the paper—slightly soggy from the overnight rain—she unfolded it and scanned the headlines: the Patriots were favored against the Rams in the Super Bowl, and the Hawai'i House Committee had passed a bill to raise the minimum wage.

A high-pitched shriek made her start, and as she turned toward the sound, she saw Pua, who'd been sniffing the hibiscus bushes along the edge of the yard, come careening toward her.

"What's up, little one?" she asked, and then started as she saw a large brown-and-white blur racing after Pua. It was Larry's dog, Akoni, and he did not look to be playing.

Valerie reached down and swept Pua up into her arms. The dog's eyes were wide, and she was shaking in fear. As Akoni reached the spot where the two of them stood, Valerie shouted in as loud and stern a voice as possible, "No!"

This caused the dog to pause, but only for a moment, after which he began to jump up onto Valerie, his large jaws snapping in an effort to take a bite out of the terrified Pua, who was squirming in her arms. Valerie turned around and butted Akoni with her backside, but the dog continued to growl and snap, managing to take hold of Valerie's T-shirt and tug on it as if she were a pull toy.

Only this was no game.

"No, stop!" she screamed as the dog released the fabric and began once again to take swipes at Pua. Valerie continued to swivel around, trying to avoid the dog's jaws, but she could feel his hot breath on her arms and was starting to feel woozy from all the spinning she was doing—not to mention the adrenaline now coursing through her body.

She tried kneeing Akoni in the chest, but the dog was too big and muscular for this to make any difference. Turning away from him once more, she started across the lawn toward her front door. This only served to excite him even more, however, as the chase instinct kicked in.

"Help!" she cried again, the tears starting to come.

"Akoni!" a deep male voice called out. "No make—dass enough!"

The dog stopped its jumping and turned toward the sound as Larry came running across the lawn and grabbed him by the collar.

"You okay?" Larry asked, and Valerie nodded dumbly, unable to speak just yet. "I saw your dog come onto my property just now, and I guess Akoni must-a seen it, too, an' was bein' protective."

This was enough to give Valerie back her tongue. "Pua was

not on your property," she said, still cradling the small dog in her arms. "And even if she had been, that'd be no excuse for your dog charging onto our property to attack us."

"Eh—you jus' said you was okay, so no can be one 'attack,' yah?"

Valerie stared at Larry a moment, then shook her head. "Whatever. Just keep him away from Pua—and from everyone else in our house—or I'll have to call animal control."

"An' *I'll* be callin' 'um next time I see your dog runnin' around on my property, as well. And dat goes for you, too," he added with a sharp look in her direction. "C'mon, Akoni." Releasing the dog, he nudged him forward, and the two quickly strode away.

Once she was sure they'd gone, Valerie set Pua down. The dog took a few tentative steps toward the house, then turned to make sure Akoni was no longer in sight before dashing up the steps to the front door. As she followed after her dog, Valerie too looked across the lawn toward Larry's property. He and Akoni were nowhere to be seen.

Could that have all been on purpose? Valerie thought about what Larry had just said about "that going for her, too." Was it possible he'd seen her snooping in his garage—or that someone had told him about it—and this was his way of retaliating?

"There's one!" Sachiko pointed across the lagoon to a lone white heron flying close to the water. They were seated at the window of a seafood restaurant owned by some cousins of Sachiko's, and although the food was tasty indeed, she'd told Valerie and Kristen on the drive over that one of the best perks of the eatery was its location next to a series of ancient Hawaiian fish ponds. "The white herons roost for the night in the trees around the ponds," she'd said, "and starting around dusk, huge flocks of them come flying in. I've seen hundreds at a time."

"They're actually Great Egrets," biology teacher Isaac put in. "And they're an invasive species who eat the chicks of the native Hawaiian water birds."

"Party pooper," Sachiko had responded, sticking out her tongue at him.

But now that they were seated at the restaurant, cocktails in hand, gazing at the serene panorama outside the picture windows, Isaac was smiling along with the rest of them. The still water was tinged with a yellow hue, and across the lagoon the grove of ironwood trees had become skeletal silhouettes in the waning sunlight.

"Oh, look, five more!" said Kristen. "No, make it more like ten, 'cause there's another group coming in right behind them."

They watched as the egrets flapped their way across the fish ponds and settled into the greenery, where their white forms could barely be made out as bright splotches high in the branches of the trees.

Isaac took a sip of his gin and tonic, then smacked his lips. "Ahhh . . . I needed this after grading tests all afternoon. Thanks for the invitation. So," he said, "what's new with you two?"

Kristen glanced at Valerie, whose forehead furrowed into a frown.

"What?" asked Isaac and Sachiko in unison.

"Val had a little run-in with a neighbor's dog earlier today."

"Oh, no!" Sachiko's eyes went from Valerie's face to her arms, as if looking for signs of injury. "Are you okay?"

"I'm fine. Just a bit shaken up, is all—but not as much as Pua. The poor thing was scared out of her wits by Akoni jumping up and snapping at her in my arms." A shudder passed over Valerie as she momentarily relived the experience.

"You gotta call da cops," was Isaac's immediate response. "No can let dangerous dogs run loose li' dat. I wen' hear a pack of dogs attacked a woman down Ka'u side a few months back an' killed her."

"Ugh. Well, this was only one dog, and he wasn't after me, thank goodness. I guess Pua had been sniffing around in his yard and he didn't take too kindly to it."

Isaac snorted. "No excuse."

"I agree," said Kristen, turning to her wife. "You should at least tell Amy."

Valerie gazed out the window at another flock of egrets flying low, their wingtips almost touching the water, then let out a sigh. "The problem is, we already have a sort of running conflict with this neighbor, and I really don't want to make it worse. But I'm thinking we do need to make sure Pua's on a leash when she goes out front from now on."

Kristen looked about to say something further, but the server arrived with their food at this point, and once their plates had been set down—steamed opakapaka for Valerie and Sachiko, miso butterfish for Kristen, and New York steak for Isaac—they dug into their food, putting a pause on the conversation.

"Wow," said Valerie after a bit. "This is amazing. It's what—a kind of snapper, right?"

Sachiko nodded, her mouth full. "Uh-huh," she said once she'd swallowed. "Hawaiian pink snapper, I think is its other name. We serve it sometimes at the Gecko when we can get it."

"Right, I thought I remembered it. Maybe we should do it this way some time. That hot peanut oil with the cilantro and shoyu is like crack."

"True dat," agreed Sachiko. "It's my favorite thing here."

They continued to eat and comment on their food as they watched the egrets make their way to their roosting spots. The flocks had grown in size, numbering in the tens and twenties now, and they kept on coming, no end in sight. Dusk had settled upon the peaceful lagoon, and in the darkening evening the white birds seemed like so many ghosts gliding across the water toward their place of rest.

After a few minutes, Sachiko looked up at Kristen and broke the silence. "So, I was hoping Sean would be here tonight. We haven't had much of a chance to get to know him since he's been on-island."

"Yeah . . ." Kristen set down her fork and leaned back, letting the word trail off. But when the others kept watching her, waiting for her to go on, she finally cleared her throat. "The thing is, he seems to have gone AWOL. I'm not sure where he is."

"Oh, no, that's not good," said Sachiko. "When's the last time you saw him?"

"Yesterday morning—after a bit of a tiff with . . ."

"With me," Valerie cut in. "He's mad 'cause of something I said about his new girlfriend."

"What'd you say?" asked Issac.

She told them about the conversation her nephew had overheard, along with the backstory so it would make sense, after which Sachiko and Isaac were momentarily silent. "So . . ." Isaac finally said, "are you saying you think this Tammy person might-a poisoned that neighbor of yours who died?"

"No. I mean . . . I have no idea." Valerie let out a groan. "I don't know what to think at this point. But I feel just awful about Sean."

Isaac slapped the table. "Ho, da guy's probably with his girlfriend, yah? No worry, beef curry."

"Yeah, I bet you're right," said Kristen. "And the little jerk won't even answer any of my texts or voicemails, so I gotta say I'm getting to the point where I'm about as pissed off at the guy as I am worried."

"Sounds like a healthy reaction to me," said Isaac. "So, who wants dessert?"

Don's car—a dark blue SUV—was in the driveway when Valerie arrived at Sue's house the next morning. Coming down the pathway alongside the carport, she stopped before stepping into the back yard to watch as he made his way down the rows of orchids, checking a spike here, snipping off a brown leaf there.

After a minute, though, Don seemed to sense her presence and turned to look in her direction.

"Aloha!" she said brightly, making her way to where he stood underneath the black shade cloth strung over the yard. "Did Sue mention that I was coming over?" From his wide eyes and the sudden stiffness of his body, Valerie guessed not. "She told me yesterday to stop by this morning and pick out a few of George's orchids if I wanted, and I thought it would be a good idea to get your expert advice, since I don't know a whole lot about them—you know, being such a newbie to the group an' all . . ."

Don's face relaxed and he broke into a smile—just as she'd intended. Amazing what a little flattery will do. "Sure, I can help you with that. So, she's decided to give them all away, yah?" A flicker of excitement flashed in his eyes.

"Uh-huh. And I guess she wanted me—and you, too, I'm sure—to have first dibs." Valerie started down the row where they stood, leaning over to examine the various plants in their black plastic pots. But, she quickly realized, she had no idea what she was looking at, as few of the orchids were in bloom.

"You have good instinct," he said with a chuckle. "This area is mostly Paphs—Paphiopedilums, or slipper orchids—which tend to be on the more expensive side. Check out this amazing specimen." He lifted from the back of the row a pot which had been hidden by other taller plants. It had a delicate white-and-lavender bloom, with what looked like a tiny pitcher dangling from the bottom part of the flower.

"Cool!" Valerie exclaimed. "Are they hard to grow?"

"Not here, but on the Mainland they can be tricky unless you get the humidity just right in your greenhouse. Here, I'll show you some of the others that are currently in bloom." Don led her around to the next row and pointed to a robust plant with a spike that must have contained twenty pink-and-yellow flowers.

"Oooooh, they look like tiny ballerinas!" exclaimed Valerie.

"You're not the first person to make that observation," he said with a grin. "It's an Oncidium, and they're quite easy to grow." He led her further down the row. "And these are Dendrobiums."

"Oh, right. George showed this one to me," Valerie said, pointing to the papery white bloom she'd seen before with the egg-yolk-colored center. "Oh, and look at these two next to it," she added, indicating the two hybrids George had shown her whose spikes now each bore a single bloom. "They're so pretty. Maybe they're the ones I should take . . ." Valerie trailed off, glancing Don's way to see if this triggered any reaction.

But he seemed to be studiously avoiding her eye, leaning over to pull out some errant weeds from another pot. After a moment, he stood back up, saying, "Those two? Yeah, they might not be super appropriate for a beginner like you. And, well . . . actually, I was hoping that Sue would let me have them."

"Oh? Is there something special about them?" Valerie asked, knowing damn well why he was so interested in those particular orchids.

When Don didn't immediately answer, she snapped her fingers. "Right, I just remembered. Didn't someone at the benefit dinner say something about some hybrids George supposedly took from someone else? Are these by any chance those plants?" And then, in response to his curling lip and narrowed eyes, "Wait—are they *yours*?"

He stared at her a moment, then slowly nodded.

"Are you sure?" she asked. "That these are the ones you hybridized?"

"I'm sure. I'd know them anywhere." His eyes betrayed a combination of adoration, longing, and . . . what? Anger was definitely there, Valerie decided.

She took in the orchids. One had two spikes, the other just one, each bearing a single large bloom with a yellow center and pink tips to its petals. They were indeed exquisite, she had to admit, in an other-worldly, ethereal way—like something out of a fantastical dream.

How could such flowers even exist?

But she couldn't help wondering as she gazed at the delicate blooms, *could George truly have stolen them from Don?* It didn't make any sense to Valerie that he would do such a thing—if for no other reason than he would have been sure to be caught out if he ever tried to show them anywhere. *Could you do a DNA test or some such thing with an orchid?*

"How about the parent orchids?" she asked, eyeing the plant in front of her with the yellow center. "Did he take those from you, too? Are they around here somewhere?"

Before Don could answer, the slamming of a screen door made them both turn. "Oh, hi, Sue," said Valerie. *Had she heard what they'd been talking about?*

Apparently not, for she had a smile on her face—as well as a plate of baked goods in her hand. "I thought you might be interested in a little breakfast. I didn't make them, but I can tell you they're quite tasty—they're chocolate banana muffins."

"Thanks," said Don, reaching for one. "Don't mind if I do."

Valerie helped herself to a muffin and took a bite. As she chewed, she pondered Sue's demeanor. How could she be so friendly to someone she now knew to have accused her husband of stealing his orchids? Was it an act?

Valerie listened as Sue chatted about the weather and thanked Don for tending to George's plants. There was no sign of the anger she'd demonstrated the previous Thursday when Valerie had told her about Don's accusations.

Watching Sue laugh and smile at Don, Valerie had another thought: *Could she be suffering from dementia?* If so, maybe it had been *both* of their health conditions that had prompted George to consider stepping back from the orchid society.

Or maybe she was in fact some kind of lush and drank a lot more than she'd let on, which was causing a memory problem of some sort.

"So, Valerie tells me that you've decided to give away George's orchids to the members of the society," Don was saying.

Sue stared at him a moment before saying, "Yes, that's right."

"Would you like me to email everyone to let them know?"

"That would be great," said Sue. "Since I don't have their addresses. I mean, I suppose I could find them on George's computer, but . . ."

Don waved a hand. "No need. I'm happy to do it. Do you want to set a time for them to come?"

"Uh . . ."

"Don't worry," Valerie cut in. "Don and I can arrange everything—and be here to organize the pickups, too. Right?" She glanced at Don for approval.

"Sure," he said.

"Which brings up another question. If you don't mind talking about it, that is." When Sue merely shrugged, Valerie went on. "I was wondering if there was going to be some sort of memorial or celebration of life for George. 'Cause I'm sure that many people from the orchid society would like to pay their respects."

Sue let out a sigh. "Yeah, I know I should do something, but . . ."

"Do you have any children?" asked Valerie. "Or close friends who could take that on?"

"No, we never had kids. And truly, the orchid society was George's main focus for the past ten years, so we didn't have a lot of other friends . . ." She trailed off, her brows furrowed.

"I've got an idea," said Valerie. "How about we have a little informal celebration of life here, at the same time folks come to take his orchids?"

The frown disappeared. "Oh, that would be lovely. George would have loved that."

"Does this Saturday morning work for the both of you?" Valerie glanced from Sue to Don, who both nodded.

"Sounds good," said Don. "Shall we say ten a.m.? I can send out an announcement to the group email for the society."

"And I'll tell anyone I happen to run into on the street about it, as well," Valerie added.

"Perfect." Sue smiled. "And thank you—the both of you."

"You're so welcome. Happy to be able to help in any way I can." *And this way I'll get a chance to see all the suspects together at the same time*, was Valerie's unspoken thought. *Just like in a TV mystery.*

FOURTEEN

When Sue went back inside, Valerie was hoping to continue the conversation she'd been having with Don before being interrupted. But as soon as Sue took her leave, he pulled out his phone to check the time and said, "Look, I'd love to stay and chat, but I've gotta be someplace in a bit and need to finish up here before I go. So . . ."

Valerie took the not-so-subtle hint. "Sure, no worries. But maybe you can help me pick out some orchids this Saturday?"

"Absolutely," he said. "Happy to." Then, retrieving his pruning shears, he headed quickly for the next row of orchids.

Well, he's certainly not eager to talk any more about those hybrids, Valerie mused as she turned to go. *Since we could easily have carried on the conversation while he worked.* With a last look at Don, who was studiously facing the other way, she made her way back down the path along the side of the carport.

As she emerged onto the driveway, she glanced uphill at the house next door and saw a woman on the front porch, also wielding a pair of clippers. *Could that be the mysterious Irene Souza?*

Only one way to find out.

Striding across Sue's front yard, Valerie waved at the woman when she looked up to see who was approaching. She had on a pair of loose gray palazzo pants and a floral-print V-neck top, her long hair pulled back into a pony tail. Valerie guessed her age to be in the forties, but with her blond hair—which could be flecked with gray, or even be dyed—it wasn't easy to tell for sure.

"Aloha!" said Valerie, coming to a stop at the base of the stairs. "You must be Irene, yes?"

Holding up a hand to block the sun's glare, she squinted down at Valerie. "I am. And you are . . .?"

"Valerie Corbin. I live down the street. I'm the one who ended up helping Emily with the orchid society dinner when you couldn't make it."

"Ah, right. I thought I recognized you. You have that little white dog that you walk around the neighborhood." But then she frowned. "I'm so sorry about all that happened—and that my absence got you sucked into it all. It's horrible about poor Mr. Ikeda."

"Yeah, so awful. I was actually at Sue's house just now, and when I saw you up here, I thought I should introduce myself."

"I'm glad you did." Irene took a seat on the bench on her front porch and patted the spot next to her. "Would you care to sit for a bit?"

"Sure." Valerie climbed the stairs and sat down.

"So, how's Sue doing?" asked Irene.

"Okay, I guess . . . all things considered. But it's been quite the shock for her—not just his death, but *how* it happened." Valerie studied Irene's face, trying to detect any unusual reaction to this remark from Sue's neighbor. But all she saw was what looked to be empathy and sadness.

"Yeah, that police detective who lives at the end of the block came to talk to me the other day. I still can't believe they found *arsenic* in George's vanilla. How could such a thing happen?"

"That's what they're trying to figure out," said Valerie with a sigh. "But I gotta say, I can't help feeling a little to blame—you know, since I'm the one who actually added the vanilla to that whipped cream."

Irene laid a hand on her shoulder. "No. You shouldn't think that. You were a lifesaver to step in like . . ." She stopped, perhaps realizing the irony of what she'd just said, then shook her head. "If anyone should feel guilty, it's me, since I wasn't even here to . . . I don't know . . ."

"I don't think there's anything anyone could have done to prevent it happening. Anyone other than whoever tampered with the vanilla, that is."

"Right." Irene stared at the row of orchids on her porch, each bearing a large bloom, their black plastic pots hidden inside brightly colored ceramic containers. "I don't suppose you have any information about who . . .?"

"No. And if Amy—you know, our neighbor who's the cop—if she knows anything, she's not telling me. But I did want to let you know that Sue's going to have a get-together this coming Saturday morning to give away George's orchids to any of the members of the society who want some. And there's going to be an informal celebration of his life at the same time, so hopefully you can come to that."

Irene picked up the cell phone sitting on a small table next to her and punched it to life. "Saturday . . . Good, that works. Here, lemme add it to my calendar." Setting the device down, she leaned back with a sigh and gazed down the street. A man in a Green Bay Packers jersey, board shorts, and slippahs was walking a fluffy white Maltese, and Valerie and Irene watched as he encouraged the small dog to step up the pace and continue on uphill.

"You've got a lovely view from up here," said Valerie after a moment. "You can't see the ocean like this from our house."

"Well, it used to be a lot better," Irene replied with a snort. "When we first moved in here, it was an actual ocean view, unlike the barely peekaboo one we've got now 'cause of how much that tree's grown over the past few years. I asked if they could prune it back some—all you'd have to do is cut off that one big branch there for us to get back at least a little of our view." She pointed to the right side of the pua kenikeni tree. "But no, they've refused to trim it even the tiniest bit."

"Yeah, that's gotta be frustrating," said Valerie. "But I know the tree held a special value to George." She explained how he'd planted it in honor of his mother, who used to sell pua kenikeni leis as a young girl down at the port, but Irene didn't seem much affected by the story.

"Whatever," was her only response.

At the sound of a screen door slamming, Valerie looked down the driveway to see a couple emerge from a door along the side of the house.

"Aloha! We're off to explore," said the woman with a wave Irene's way. She had on pink shorts, a white tank top, a wide-brimmed straw hat, and sturdy walking sandals. The man with her wore an aloha shirt with blue-and-white stylized turtles, khaki shorts, tennis shoes with white socks, and a Yankees ball cap.

Definitely tourists.

"Great," said Irene. "Do you have an umbrella? 'Cause it's supposed to rain later on."

The man pointed to his daypack. "No worries; we've read the guidebooks," he said with a grin. "The rainiest city in America! But it's gorgeous this morning, all right."

As the two strode off downhill, Valerie asked Irene, "So I take it you have a vacation rental downstairs in your 'ohana unit?"

"We do. It's just a small studio apartment, but it's comfy and 'well-appointed,' as they say."

"Well, that's good to know in case we have friends visit the island, since our guest room's currently occupied by our nephew for a few months."

"Sure, we'd be happy to host any friends of yours. The rental's not yet listed on any official sites—it's all just word of mouth at this point—but if you let me know, I can save any dates you might ever need." Irene leaned over to pick at an errant thread on her palazzo pants, then cleared her throat. "And if I could ask a little favor, please don't spread it around the neighborhood too much about the rental. 'Cause, well, we haven't completed the process to make the unit completely legal, and I don't want to get busted by anyone who might be a stickler for that kind of red tape."

"Ah. Got it. No problem. Though I can't be the only one who's figured it out from seeing people like that come out of your house."

Irene shrugged. "Yeah, well, nothing I can do about that."

Kristen was on the phone when Valerie returned home, and from her still-damp board shorts and Lycra tank top, Valerie guessed she'd only just got back from surfing.

"I don't need to know his schedule," Kristen was saying, "I just want to find out if he's missed any of his recent shifts.

He's my nephew and hasn't been home for a couple days, so I'm worried about him." She listened a moment before rolling her eyes at Valerie. "Okay, fine. I understand. Thanks. Damn privacy laws," she muttered as she ended the call.

Valerie leaned against the kitchen counter. "I take it he's still not responding to your texts?"

"Nope. And now I'm living in fear that my brother will call and ask how his darling son is doing under my care, and I'll have to tell him I have no friggin' idea."

"Do you have Tammy's number?" asked Valerie. "'Cause I bet that's where he's been staying."

"No doubt. But no, I don't have her number—or even remember her last name, for that matter. Oh, but wait. I bet one of your orchid society cronies would have her contact info."

"I have a better idea," said Valerie, typing a query into her phone. "Good. They open at eleven. I say we go straight to the horse's—or rather, the mo'o's—mouth, and drive down to the ceramics gallery to talk to Tammy in person. We'll learn a lot more by actually seeing how she reacts when we talk to her than if we just called or texted."

"Good plan. Lemme go shower and then I'll be ready to go."

Thirty minutes later, they pulled up in front of the Mo'o Ceramics gallery. "Don't mention anything about the arsenic or what I said about her when we talk to Tammy," Valerie said as Kristen switched off the engine. "Maybe just tell her something vague, like we had a misunderstanding with Sean and he got upset."

Kristen turned to face Valerie. "I think we've maybe gone past the point where I care a whole lot about your investigation. The fact that my nephew is missing—solely because of your little sleuthing game, I might add—seems far more important at this point. But don't worry," she said before Valerie could respond, "I won't tell Tammy that you suspect her of poisoning the orchid society with arsenic from her studio. Though I wouldn't be surprised if Sean already has."

"I'm sorry," said Valerie. "I didn't mean to downplay Sean's disappearance. That's obviously the most important thing here." Nevertheless, as she followed her wife into the studio, she couldn't help but also think, *though I sure hope he hasn't told Tammy what I said.*

She'd expected the studio to be quiet on a Monday morning, so Valerie was surprised to see a group of six people at the table in the middle of the room working with clay and two others seated at the potters' wheels. Tammy was leaning over the table, flattening out a wedge of clay with a rolling pin as she talked to the group, but at the sound of a tinkling bell, she looked up with a smile and waved at Valerie and Kristen as they came inside.

I guess not. Good. Valerie waved back. "Are we interrupting a class?"

"No worries," said Tammy. "You're welcome to sit in, if you want. And we're always looking for new students."

Valerie watched her roll out the clay out as if it were a rectangular pie crust, then use a pizza cutter to slice it into strips. Maybe she should take up ceramics—since it sure looked like her culinary experience would be helpful.

After showing her students how to wet the strips with water, then weave them together into a mat, Tammy left them to it and turned toward the newcomers. "So what brings you in today? Have you decided to buy one of the dragons?"

"Ha—I wish!" said Valerie before Kristen had a chance to answer. "No, we were just passing by and decided to come in and say hey. Oh, and I wanted to tell you that this coming Saturday at ten in the morning, Sue Ikeda is having the orchid society come to her house for an informal celebration of George's life, and to also give away his orchids to anyone who wants them."

"Wow, that's awful generous of her. He has some amazing orchids, I know. And sure, I can come. I have a class to teach at noon, but that should be fine."

"Oh, and speaking of orchid society members, I just found out from my neighbor Emily Higa that she's the one who made those amazing dragon sculptures and co-founded the studio. What a shame about her allergy or whatever it is that's giving her rashes."

"Totally," said Tammy. "She was kind of my mentor here—such a talented potter. I feel so bad for her to have to give it up." She glanced at her students, who were busy fashioning their clay creations, then motioned for the two women to move with her farther away from the group. "So, I was wondering if you knew what was going on with Sean. Is he upset with me for some reason?"

"No, I don't think so," said Kristen. "But that's actually another reason we stopped by. To find out if you knew where he might be, 'cause he hasn't been home since Saturday morning."

"Really? Well, the last time I saw him was that same afternoon when he came to the studio, but he was acting kind of strange."

"Strange how?" asked Kristen.

She shook her head. "It's hard to describe. He seemed really upset about something, but when I asked him what was wrong, he said it was nothing—that he just needed to 'chill,' I think was his word. Though 'chill' was not at all how I'd describe him. More like pissed off. You have any idea what's going on with the guy?"

Kristen looked toward Valerie and nodded for her to take the lead. "He and I, uh . . . had a bit of a misunderstanding about something on Friday night, and I haven't seen him since. And I think he must be mad at Kristen too—by association with me—since he won't answer any of her texts. So, he didn't mention anything to you about what happened?"

"Huh-uh. But I'm glad to hear it wasn't about me. Not that it's good that you two have had a falling out," she quickly added. "But I was worried I'd done something to upset him, given how weird he was being with me."

"No, he definitely wasn't mad at you," said Kristen with another glance Valerie's way. "But if you hear from him, could you let me know? 'Cause I'm starting to get kind of worried about the guy."

"Absolutely. And you can do the same for me." Tammy pulled out her phone and the two of them shared contacts.

They bid goodbye to Tammy and returned to their car, where

Kristen sat for a minute before switching on the ignition. “Do you mind if we swing by the hospital on the way home? I’d like to see if maybe Sean’s bike is locked outside somewhere. I know it’s a long shot, but you never know.”

“Sure, no problem.”

Kristen really was worried about her nephew. And it was all her fault. Valerie closed her eyes as they made their way up Waiānuenue Avenue toward the medical center. *Please let his bike be there. Or let him answer her texts—or better yet, be home when we return.*

But there was no sign of Sean’s mountain bike. They walked the entire perimeter of the large building, but the only bicycles they saw were a couple of rusty junkers that looked to have been abandoned by their owners long ago.

“Maybe he takes it inside with him,” said Valerie as they examined an old ten-speed with a missing saddle, its frame locked to a post in the parking lot. “I would, if I had a nice bike like his.”

“Maybe,” was all Kristen had to say in response.

FIFTEEN

Tuesdays aren't one of the traditionally "big" days at the Hilo farmers market—those would be Wednesdays and Saturdays—but because of the cruise ship docked in town, there was plenty of action that morning when Valerie headed out to do some shopping.

She stopped first at the KTA grocery store for staples such as milk, cottage cheese—which was finally in stock—eggs, tortillas, and rice. Then, after swinging by her car to place them in a cooler, she walked over to the outdoor market. It had rained overnight, which meant lots of puddles to dodge, but in her rubber slippahs it didn't matter much if she missed one and got her feet a little wet. This was Hilo, after all, and it was already quite warm outdoors.

First on her list was a bunch of tart, citrusy apple bananas, which she stowed carefully in her cloth bag. Next, she went in search of some veggies for a stir-fry: bok choy, Japanese eggplant, sweet Maui onions, carrots, ginger, and garlic. Then, smiling at the scene—the heady scent of tropical fruit, the cries of the vendors hawking their wares, the vibrant shades of red, yellow, orange, and green all about her—she made her way to the stand at the very end, which she knew had papayas for three for a dollar. Valerie had learned from past experience to buy these last, as it was no fun lugging the heavy fruit around the market as she searched for other items.

But as she passed by a man offering free samples of Kona coffee, she stopped and set down her bags—checking first to see if she was standing in a puddle. Accepting the small cup, she inhaled the enticing aroma of the fragrant brew.

"Are you the coffee grower?" she asked.

"I am, indeed. My wife and I have a farm in Honaunau, up on the slopes of Mauna Loa at about fifteen hundred feet. It's just five acres, but we hand-pick all the cherries—you know, the coffee beans—only when they're fully ripe."

"Well, it's delicious. I get notes of dark chocolate and some kind of nut—almond, maybe. And it's really smooth. Not a hint of acidity."

The farmer beamed. "So true. And this particular blend has hints of vanilla, too, don't you think?"

"Right," Valerie agreed. But at the mention of vanilla, she shivered and set down the cup. "Thanks for the sample. I don't need any coffee at the moment, but I know where to find you."

"Sure thing." This sale now dead in the water, the man turned to another potential customer and held out a cup to her.

Valerie picked up her bags and made her way to the papaya seller, her previous light mood now gone. Would she ever be able to think about vanilla again without it conjuring up a feeling of dread?

No, that was ridiculous. The whole thing really had nothing to do with vanilla. Whoever tampered with that extract could have put the arsenic in virtually anything. Was she really never going to be able to order white cake again? Or vanilla ice cream, or God forbid, crème brûlée?

"Valerie!"

Startled out of her pity party, she looked up to see her down-the-street neighbor, Shirley. "Oh, hi!"

"You had such a serious expression I was almost afraid to interrupt you from your deep thoughts."

Valerie waved a dismissive hand. "Not deep, I assure you. So, how have you been? I haven't seen you since—has it really been since the night of the orchid society dinner?"

Shirley nodded. "And we didn't really even talk much that night, you were so busy with the meal prep. And since then, well . . ." She shifted her bag from one shoulder to the other. "I was going to treat myself to a shave ice, if you'd care to join me, and we could catch up a bit."

"Sounds perfect. I could go for something fruity and cold right about now."

Valerie followed Shirley across the street, where they stood in line and studied the list of offerings posted next to the order window. "I think I'm going to have the liliko'i, with mac nut ice cream and sweetened condensed milk," said Shirley.

"Oof. That sounds heavenly, but maybe a little much for this gal before noon. I'm gonna go for a half and half, coconut and dragon fruit—no extras."

Treats in hand, they found a spot at one of the picnic benches and dug in.

"Ohmygod," said Valerie after her first taste. "I can never get over how much better these are than the snow cones I grew up with in Southern California. The texture is so fine and powdery, it's like eating a cloud."

"A cloud flavored with tropical goodness," added Shirley with a grin.

They ate in silence, watching the passing parade—locals and tourists alike—as they savored their late-morning pick-me-up.

"So, did you get the email from Don about the get-together this Saturday morning at Sue Ikeda's house?" Valerie said after a bit. "There's going to be a little memorial—or celebration of life, more like—for George, and then Sue's asking folks to take home any of his orchids that they want."

Shirley wiped her mouth with a napkin, then nodded. "I saw that last night. I'm glad she's doing something for George, because last time I talked to her, she was too distraught to even think about it."

"Yeah, they seemed pretty close. It's clearly been super hard on her to lose him—and so suddenly."

"It has," said Shirley. She scooped up the last of the melted ice and liliko'i juice at the bottom of her bowl, then pushed it aside. "They've been like that since they got involved—almost inseparable."

"Right. He told me they'd known each other since they were kids. Did they get together in high school?"

"Huh-uh. He was all about Emily Higa back then."

Valerie almost choked on her bamboo spoon. "He and Emily were once an item?"

"Oh, yes," said Shirley, who'd turned to admire a toy poodle in the arms of a woman who'd just sat down at their table, thus missing Valerie's reaction. "Back in high school, we all thought they were a forever couple—that once George graduated from college and returned to Hilo, he and Emily would marry and settle down. But then he ended up getting together with Sue after he got back home, and that was that."

"Huh. I wonder what happened."

Shirley shook her head. "I don't know who broke it off—Emily or George. Or when, for that matter. It could have happened anytime during his four years at university. I seem to remember he came home for the first summer, but I'm not sure if he did again after that. He was studying some science-y thing—botany, maybe?—before he switched to accounting. That would explain his interest in orchids. So he might have stayed summers in Michigan to work in a lab or something. I was on O'ahu at UH Mānoa at that time and wasn't paying too much attention to what was going on with folks back in Hilo."

"What were you studying?"

"English. And then afterwards I got a teaching credential and taught at Hilo High for thirty-two years."

"Oh, do you know Isaac Pinheiro? He teaches biology there."

"Isaac? Oh yes; he's a love. He started teaching about five years before I left. Is he still there? I hope so, because the kids just loved him."

"Yep. He's a youngster—still in his forties—so he's got a ways to go till retirement."

"Nothing like retirement," said Shirley. "Every day is Saturday! And now I'd better get going. I have a yoga class I need to get to. Hope I didn't eat too much to be able to do a downward dog," she added with a laugh. "But it was good catching up, and I hope I didn't bore you too much with neighborhood gossip."

Not boring in the least, thought Valerie as she watched Shirley cross the road, then head down the block. *Fascinating, as a matter of fact.*

Did George break Emily's heart back in—what, the 1970s?—when he went off to university on the Mainland? Because Valerie seriously doubted it was Emily who'd broken off the relationship. Not based on the way she'd talked about George the other day—and how bereft she'd seemed by his death.

Which made a lot of sense, now.

But could Emily at the same time have held a grudge against him all those years? And could the breakup have festered inside her until it finally reached the point where she decided that if she couldn't have him, no one could?

God knows, many men over the years have come to that ugly conclusion and acted upon it.

And then she thought about the arsenic at the Moʻo Ceramics studio. A studio that Emily co-founded. Could the grudge have been strong enough for her to put some of that arsenic into George's vanilla?

Kristen was standing in the kitchen staring at her phone when Valerie returned from her trip downtown. Setting down her groceries, Valerie stooped to let Pua give her some welcome home kisses, then stood back up and watched her wife scroll through whatever was on her screen. After a moment, Kristen shook her head and shoved the device into her shorts pocket.

"Still nothing?" Valerie asked.

"Not a peep. I was hoping if I just ignored it all and went back to my normal life, he'd text while I was out paddling, but no such luck." Kristen stared out the window, where a pair of mynah birds were squabbling atop the carport.

"Dang," said Valerie, pulling the papayas from her bag and setting them in a large ceramic bowl on the kitchen counter. "I wish there were something I could do to help."

Kristen turned to face her. "There is, actually."

"Oh yeah?"

"Well, I was about to call in a missing persons report this morning, but then it occurred to me that you could ask Amy to look into it. You know, since she has a personal relationship with us, I figure she'd care more about the fact that he's missing than some random cop would."

"Ah, good idea." Busying herself with stowing her stir-fry veggies in the fridge, Valerie considered what Kristen was asking. She had no problem with the general idea of talking to Amy about Sean's disappearance. But the problem was, the cop would surely want to know *why* he'd left and was now incommunicado—which Valerie was a little loath to do.

But this was Kristen's nephew—her nephew, as well—they were talking about. And she owed it to her wife, not to mention Sean, to do whatever she could to make sure he was okay. Besides, she had to admit to herself, she too was starting to get pretty worried about the guy.

"Sure," she said. "I can talk to Amy. But rather than bug her today while she's no doubt working, is it okay if I just wait and see if she shows up at the bar tonight? I'm thinking she likely will; she's become pretty much a regular these past few weeks."

From her pinched expression, Valerie could tell Kristen would have preferred more instantaneous action. Nevertheless, with a shrug she said, "That'll work."

And as Valerie had predicted, Amy did show up at the Speckled Gecko that night. But what she didn't expect was the other woman tagging along with her.

"Evening," said Amy, taking a stool at the bar. "This is Maile. I thought I'd introduce her to the wonders of the drink specials you concoct for this lovely watering hole."

"Pleased to meet you," said Valerie, shaking the woman's hand. Her grip was strong and her hand calloused. As she eyed Maile, taking in her short-cropped hair and pale blue chambray shirt, she wondered what the relationship between the two might be. A fellow cop? Or perhaps a date?

Probably not both, Valerie mused, since that would no doubt be frowned upon by the powers-that-be in the police force.

"Maile's an EMT," said Amy, answering one of the questions for her. "And she's had a pretty crazy day, so I'm guessing she's ready for a stiff drink."

"Well, you came to the right place for that. If you're interested, tonight's special is basically a gin gimlet, but with the addition of celery juice along with the lime." At Amy's exaggerated shudder, she added, "I know it sounds weird, but it's quite delicious, I promise you. The celery adds a bump of je ne sais quoi to the mix."

Maile glanced at Kristen, then grinned. "Okay, I'm game."

"Me, too," said Amy. "You have yet to steer me wrong. What're you calling the concoction?"

"I haven't decided yet. 'Celery Gimlet' doesn't have much of a ring to it."

"True. That's more likely to put people off than anything." Amy furrowed her brow. "Hmmm. Gimme a minute while you whip them up and maybe I'll come up with something better."

Valerie left to take another couple's order—no drink specials for them; just a beer and a glass of Chardonnay—then set about preparing the gimlets for Amy and Maile. Wetting the rims of two coupe glasses with lime, she next dipped them in celery salt. Then, as she poured gin, lime, celery juice, and simple syrup over a metal shaker of ice, she watched the pair. The ease with which they chatted and laughed suggested this wasn't their first time hanging out together. But then again, you never knew. *Could it be a date?*

Valerie hoped so. She'd often wondered about the fact that Amy appeared to be single. At least she'd never mentioned anyone she was seeing—or had been involved with in the past. Yet she seemed like a great catch: a good-looking woman with a steady job and fun sense of humor.

Heck, if I weren't already in a relationship—and were twenty years younger—I'd *be interested in Amy*, Valerie thought with a wry smile.

"Well?" she said as she set the cocktails down in front of the pair.

"Well, what?" asked Amy, seeming to force her gaze from Maile's face.

Yes, quite likely a date.

"A drink name. I'm counting on you, girl."

"Oh, sorry. I completely forgot."

"Uh-huh." Valerie gave Amy a knowing smile. "So, did you two meet on the job? Though I suppose if that's the case, the meeting probably wasn't all that pleasant . . ." She trailed off, imagining what morbid scenario might bring together a cop and an EMT.

But Maile merely laughed. “No, nothing as exciting as that. We met online.”

“Ah, right.” *Of course they did.* That’s how folks hooked up these days. Not like when she was young, when you met through family and friends, or at work, church, softball games, bars, or the like. She and Kristen, for instance, had met at a mutual friend’s birthday party at a bowling alley. Kristen had kicked her butt with three strikes and two spares, to Valerie’s pathetic showing, which included a pair of gutter balls.

“This is our second date,” Maile went on. “It’s been tough, ’cause I’ve been working nights the past few weeks, but my schedule finally changed, thank goodness. And when Amy suggested coming here, I was all in. Matt’s a good friend of my brother’s, so I actually come to the Gecko to eat fairly often. Matt’s a cook here,” she said, turning to Amy, “and does the most ’ono lau lau on the island.” Maile raised her glass and took a sip, then smacked her lips. “My, that is indeed tasty. The celery gives it a depth that’s lacking in most gimlets.”

“Sounds like you’re an aficionado,” said Valerie.

“Well, I do enjoy a good cocktail. And my dad used to be a barkeep up at the Volcano House, so I guess it runs in the family.” She took another sip and swished it around her mouth. “How about calling it a ‘Madam’s Rib’—you know, ’cause of the celery rib and ’cause you invented it?” Valerie shook her head with a laugh. “No? Okay, how ’bout a ‘Celery Celebration’?”

“I like that. Better than ‘Val’s Special Gimlet,’ which is all I could think of,” she said. “You two want something to eat?”

“Sure, I could go for some dinner,” said Amy.

Valerie fetched them menus, and as Maile busied herself with studying the offerings, she leaned over and said to Amy, “There’s something I need to talk to you about. Could you text me when you’ve got a minute tomorrow?”

“Something about . . . the vanilla?”

“No, not about that. Or not directly, in any case. But I don’t want to bug you about it tonight. Tomorrow’s good.”

"So mysterious," Amy said, giving her a curious look. "But sure, I'll give you a buzz tomorrow. Though I'm not too sure what time that might be," she added with a glance Maile's way.

"No worries. I get it." With a smile, she left the couple to it and went to check on the other three patrons at the bar. She was happy for Amy. Maile seemed like a great gal. *I hope it works out for them. She deserves to find someone special.*

SIXTEEN

Kristen was sitting at the kitchen table when Valerie got home from work, flipping through the *Hana Hou* magazine Sean had brought from the last leg of his flight to the Big Island from Arkansas.

"Well?" she said as soon as Valerie opened the back door.

"Hello to you, too," said Valerie, leaning over to give her wife a peck on the cheek. "You're up late."

When Kristen didn't respond to this small talk, Valerie sighed. "Okay, I know why you're still up. And I'm sorry to say I won't be able to talk to Amy till tomorrow. She did come in as I predicted, but get this—she came in with a date."

"Oh?"

"A gal she met online who's an EMT. Maile is her name, and I got a good hit off her."

"That's nice for Amy. Glad to hear it." But Valerie could tell Kristen's heart wasn't in this particular conversation at this particular time.

"Anyway, Amy says she'll text me tomorrow when she has time to talk."

"Did you at least tell her what you want to talk about?"

"Huh-uh. It would've been too weird to bring it up, given that she was on a date an' all. But it's not like she could've done anything about Sean tonight, in any case, so waiting till tomorrow to tell her won't make any difference."

"I guess." With a sigh, Kristen closed the magazine and stood. "Well, I'm gonna go get some shut-eye—assuming I'm able to get to sleep, that is."

Valerie gave her a hug. "I hope so. I'm still too buzzed from work to go to bed just yet, but I'll be there in a while."

Watching her wife trudge toward the bedroom, shoulders slack and head down, Valerie shook her head. *Assuming that*

Sean is indeed fine and simply hiding out from us, boy does he ever deserve a tongue-lashing when he finally does show up.

But Amy did not write the next morning. It was now past noon, and although Valerie continually checked her phone, there was still no text from the cop. And it didn't help that Kristen would come out to the lānai every fifteen minutes to ask if she'd yet heard from her friend.

Valerie considered sending her own text. After all, there was every possibility that Amy had simply forgotten her promise to write, given the fact that she'd been otherwise preoccupied last night. But she decided to give it a couple more hours. No doubt Amy was simply tied up at work.

As she was checking her messages one more time, she was startled by a rap at the front door followed immediately by a high-pitched yip from Pua.

Setting down the phone, Valerie headed into the living room and was surprised to see Irene standing on the front porch. "Hi," she said, opening the screen door. "What's up? Would you like to come in?"

"No need. I'll just be a moment. I don't have your number, or I would have written, but I was wondering if you'd like to help me with refreshments on Saturday for George Ikeda's celebration of life. I know Sue's far too stressed right now to even think about things like that, so I offered to take it on. But then it occurred to me that you might be willing to help out—you know, with setting up and helping serve the food and drink at the memorial. I'm gonna get already-prepared items, so there won't be any advance cooking needed."

"Sure, I'm happy to do what I can. You need help with shopping?"

Irene shook her head. "No, I can do that by myself. But if you could show up about forty-five minutes early on Saturday, that would be great."

"No problem at all."

"Awesome. Thanks so much. And see you then."

Valerie watched her neighbor make her way across the lawn

and up the street back to her house. *Now, that was interesting.* Why didn't she ask Emily, like she had for the orchid society dinner? *Is there a reason she particularly wants my help?*

Letting the screen door slam shut, she retreated indoors, where she heard Kristen talking on the phone in the kitchen. "I just want to find out if he's been admitted in the past three—no, four days. His name is Sean Nilsen. Right, S-E-A-N. And Nilsen is N-I-L-S-E-N. Okay, thanks, I'll hold."

There was a minute's silence, after which Kristen said, "Okay, that's good to know. Thanks for checking."

Valerie came into the kitchen and leaned against the counter. "He's not at the hospital, I gather?"

"No. Which is good. Though he could be out there lying in a ditch somewhere after being hit by a car on his bike, for all I know." Staring briefly at her phone, Kristen shoved it into her pocket.

"Look," said Valerie, "if Amy doesn't contact me in the next few hours, I say we go ahead and call in a missing persons report with the police."

"Agreed." Kristen frowned, then shook her head. "Okay, well I'm gonna go out and do some weeding. I don't think I have the ability to do anything that requires much more concentration right about now."

Amy finally wrote at three thirty, and Valerie immediately called her back.

"Sorry I didn't text earlier," said Amy, "but I ended up being in a training for most of the day. A guy came over from O'ahu to teach us how to use this new computer program that was just installed."

"No worries." *Not.* But she wasn't going to say how anxious she'd been, waiting for the cop to contact her. "You do have a job to do, after all. So how was your date?"

Amy laughed. "Maile's a hoot. We had a great time. And she's cooking dinner for me at her place tomorrow night: grilled mahimahi with green papaya chutney, is what she said she's gonna make."

"Dang, that sounds amazing. And for what it's worth, I

really liked her. She seems like a great gal. So here's hoping it continues to work out."

"Glad to hear that. And thanks. But, hey, I know that's not what you wanted to talk about. So what's up?"

"Well, first off, I wanted to let you know that there's going to be a celebration of life for George Ikeda this Saturday morning at Sue's house, where she's also going to give away his orchids to the members of the society. So I thought you might want to go, to, you know, scope out the suspects an' all."

"Right. Like the detectives do on TV," said Amy with a laugh. "So I take it this is a gathering for the orchid society?"

"I guess so. But you are a part of the neighborhood."

"But not a member of the society. And I'm also a cop. I don't think people would be too happy with me showing up at a private memorial at a private home. It'd be obvious the only reason I was there, since I barely knew Mr. Ikeda. But hey, feel free to let me know about anything you might learn."

"Will do. But that wasn't the main reason I wanted to talk to you. So here's the deal. You know Sean—Kristen's nephew, who's been living with us the past few weeks?"

"Uh-huh."

"Well, he's gone missing, and we're both pretty worried about him."

"Missing . . . how? Did he not show up at home when he was supposed to, or what?"

"Well . . ." said Valerie, not eager to share this information with her cop friend. "He actually stormed out after . . . I guess you'd call it an argument, and hasn't been back since."

"How long ago was this?"

"Last Saturday, so it's been four days now. Kristen keeps texting and calling him, but no answer."

"Huh. I bet he's just staying with a friend. Is he by any chance involved with anyone on-island?"

"Yeah, actually. This woman Tammy, but she says she doesn't know where he is, either. So I was wondering if there was anything you could do in an official capacity, like maybe contact his work or something? He's a visiting nurse at the hospital, but they won't tell us whether he's shown up over the past few days, for privacy reasons."

"Well, he is a grown man and has the right to do as he pleases, so I'm not sure reporting him as missing is appropriate at this point—especially given the circumstances. You know, leaving after an argument as opposed to simply not showing up when he was expected. For all we know, he might simply have gone to Kona or Waikīkī for a few days to cool off. So what was this argument about?"

Valerie let out a sigh. "I was afraid you'd ask me that."

"Okay, what's going on?"

"The whole thing's all because of me. And it has to do with the vanilla, actually. I didn't want to bother you about it, 'cause Kristen thinks I'm being way too suspicious of folks, but . . ."

It was Amy's turn to sigh. "Right. Spill, girl. Now."

So Valerie told her everything. About seeing the arsenic at the Moʻo Ceramics studio and how she thought Tammy might have used it to poison the vanilla, and how Sean had overheard her saying this to Kristen and had gotten angry and then left the house in a huff the next day. "Kristen said she thought he just needed time to 'process' it all, but then he didn't come home and has refused to answer any of her texts for the past four days, so now I'm worried it might be something more than that."

"Like what?"

"Okay, I haven't even said this to Kristen yet." Valerie glanced out the window. Assured that her wife was still out in the flower bed, unable to hear their conversation, she went on. "It's just that I'm afraid that maybe Sean told Tammy what he'd heard—that I suspected her of putting arsenic in the vanilla. And that maybe she did something . . . I dunno, drastic, in response."

"Drastic? Whoa, girl. That's a gigantic conclusion to jump to here. On so many levels. You don't know what Sean might or might not have told this Tammy person, and you certainly don't have any evidence that she was in any way connected to the arsenic poisoning. And to suggest she might have something to do with Sean's going missing is pretty over the top."

"Yeah, you're right," said Valerie, but not meaning it.

"Look, why don't we give it another day or two, and if he's still AWOL, I'll file a missing persons report on him. But in the meantime, I can go ahead and contact his work to see if he's shown up for his shifts. What's his full name?"

"Oh, that's great—I really appreciate it. It's Sean Nilsen. And hopefully he'll decide to contact us soon—like in the next few hours. Thanks so much for listening, and have fun tomorrow."

But having finally spoken aloud the thoughts that had been haunting her as she lay awake last night in bed, Valerie couldn't help but let those ideas take the bit in their teeth and race away, like a horse spooked by a mountain lion. Who knew what could have happened to Sean? Drawing a deep breath to calm her now-pounding heart, she set down her phone and stared out the window at her wife pulling weeds in the garden.

As if sensing her look, Kristen stood up, dropped her trowel and gloves on the ground, and headed indoors. "It's hot out there," she said, filling a glass with ice water and taking a long drink. Then, turning to face Valerie, she asked, "What's up? Why are you just sitting here in the kitchen with that weird look on your face? Wait." Her eyes widened. "Did you hear something about Sean?"

"No, nothing. But I did finally talk to Amy. She says it doesn't make sense for the cops to file a missing persons report at this point, but she did agree to call and see if he's shown up for his shifts."

"Well, that's something. But why not report him as missing?"

Valerie shrugged. "She said that since he's an adult and because we know he left in a huff—you know, as opposed to simply not coming home when he'd been expected—that there isn't much they can really do right now. But she did say that if we haven't heard anything in a couple days—"

"By which time he could have been lying dead in a ditch for a week."

"Sorry," said Valerie. "But maybe she'll find out something from the hospital."

"Maybe." Refilling her glass, Kristen drank it down, then headed back outside to continue with her weeding.

After another restless night stewing about Sean and fretting that Tammy might have something to do with his disappearance, Valerie decided she had to act.

She'd woken up to a text from Amy saying that without a warrant, the hospital wouldn't tell her, either, whether Sean had been at work or not. "I'm gonna give it one more day, then file a missing persons report if he still hasn't contacted you," the cop wrote.

Kristen had left early to go paddling, so Valerie didn't have to worry about whether or not to tell her what she was doing. Which was a good thing, as Valerie didn't relish the thought of sharing her fears about Tammy with her wife, nor did she want to lie to her by omission.

Checking online, she confirmed that the Moʻo Ceramics studio opened that day at ten, which gave her an hour to kill—just enough time for a breakfast of coffee and yogurt with granola and papaya, and then a walk to Reed's Island with Pua.

At 10:05, she pulled up in front of the studio. Through the window, she could see two people standing at the worktable, both of whom looked up at the chiming of the bell as she came through the door.

"Oh, hi," said Tammy, giving her a questioning look. "Here, let me just finish up with this and I'll be with you in a minute."

The potter conferred with the other—Doris, Valerie remembered her name was—about the scheduling for a class, and then Doris retreated to a small office in the back that Valerie hadn't noticed on her previous visit.

"So." Tammy took a seat at the table and gestured for Valerie to do the same. "Do you have any news about Sean?"

"Not really. But I did want to ask you something about that."

"Okay . . .?" Tammy picked up a pencil lying on the table and flipped it between her fingers. Was she nervous?

"I'm just thinking that maybe Sean did tell you something

about what he was upset about when he came down here last Saturday—right before he disappeared."

Tammy cocked her head. "No, like I said before, he didn't say anything. Just that he needed to chill, but he wouldn't tell me what it was about. Why?" The pencil flipping ceased. "Does it have to do with me?"

"Uh, yeah, actually, it does." Valerie shifted in her seat as she cleared her throat. "So, do you know exactly what it was that made all those people sick at the orchid society dinner?"

"No, but I just assumed it was some kind of food poisoning. Why, was it something else?"

"Yeah, it was. They found arsenic in the vanilla that was used in the whipped cream for the dessert."

"Arsenic?" Tammy's grip on the pencil tightened. "Is that why you asked about that glaze when you were here? But like I said, it doesn't have any arsenic in it."

"I know. But later on I couldn't help noticing that you have a bottle of actual arsenic back there." Valerie nodded toward the locked cabinet behind them.

"Right. We have lots of heavy metals that we use in our glazes, but we keep the cupboard locked, so no one could have come in here and stolen it."

When Valerie didn't immediately respond to this, Tammy leaned back in her chair, eyes wide. "Whoa. You think one of *us* could have put arsenic in that vanilla?" And then she blinked a few times. "Is that what Sean was upset about? Does he think I poisoned the vanilla?"

She was either telling the truth or was a very good liar. "No," said Valerie. "He defended you when I suggested the possibility. And I admit that it's a far-fetched idea, especially since I can't think of any reason why you'd want to do such a thing."

Tammy was glaring at her. "Yeah?"

"I know, I know. I guess I've just been grasping at straws trying to figure out who could've done it. But I think Sean was so upset by what I said that he didn't want to even be around me—or Kristen, even though this has nothing to do with her. 'Cause it was after he overheard me talking to her about the arsenic I saw here at the studio that he took off and went AWOL."

"If that's the case, then why hasn't he responded to any of *my* texts?" asked Tammy. "He has no reason to be upset with me, right?"

Valerie shrugged. "Good question. I have no idea why he's gone radio silent for all of us. And the hospital won't tell us if he's been showing up for work—you know, 'cause of the privacy laws."

"Dang, that sucks." Tammy recommenced the pencil flipping. "I haven't been on shift with him since last week, since he's been doing days and I've been on nights. Oh, but I can text some folks at the hospital to see if anyone's seen him."

"That would be awesome," said Valerie. "Just to know he's okay would be huge." For the first time in days, she felt a relaxation of the tension in her shoulders. Leaning back in her chair, her eyes settled on the large dragon sculptures in the front window, and she had a thought. "So, I know Emily Higa isn't a member of the studio anymore, but does she ever come by and hang out here?"

"Not often, but once in a while she does," said Tammy. "I think it makes her kind of sad to stop by, to tell you the truth. Why do you ask?" And then she frowned. "Wait. Does this have something to do with the arsenic we use for our glazes?"

"I know it sounds off the wall, but did you know that Emily and Mr. Ikeda were involved back in high school? I have no idea why they broke up, but what if she's been carrying a grudge against him all these years because of the split and finally decided to act on it?"

"By spiking his vanilla with arsenic from our studio? And risking everyone in the orchid society in the process? That's just too bizarre to even consider."

"People have done worse things for far less," said Valerie.

Tammy shook her head. "Well, not in this case. Because we only bought that arsenic a couple months ago, so there's no reason Emily would even know we have it. And she doesn't have a key to the cabinet anymore, so she couldn't have seen what was inside—not that she'd have any reason to want to look inside it."

"Ah. Okay. Well, it was just a long-shot idea."

Of course, she could have used arsenic from somewhere else, was Valerie's thought. After all, Emily herself had said she might have some in the garage left over from when her parents owned the place.

But Valerie didn't voice this thought to Tammy. Because, she realized, it applied to every single person in the orchid society.

SEVENTEEN

Valerie was startled awake the next morning by a piercing scream.

Jumping out of bed and scrambling to pull on a pair of shorts to go with the Dodgers T-shirt she used as a night-shirt, she tore out of the bedroom toward the sound. As she skidded to a halt in the kitchen, she saw through the window Kristen wrestling with a man out on the lānai. Pua stood by, barking like crazy.

"No!" Valerie shouted, pushing open the screen door. "Let her go!"

The two figures separated and turned her way. Kristen wore a broad smile and the other, a sheepish grin.

Ah. Kristen hadn't been wrestling, she now saw, but rather, hugging the man.

"Sean," she said. "You're back."

"Yeah." He dipped his head and flashed a hesitant smile. "The prodigal nephew has returned."

Valerie strode forward and took him in her arms. But after holding him tightly for some time, she stepped back and stared him in the eye. "I'm thrilled to have you back safe and sound, but do you have *any* idea how much pain and anguish you've caused us over the past five days?"

Sean glanced at Kristen but didn't respond.

"No text, no phone call? What the heck, Sean?"

Kristen laid a hand on Valerie's arm. "Okay, hon, I think he gets it. Let's give him a chance to explain."

"Sorry," said Valerie. "I've just been pretty pent-up of late, is all." She gave Sean another quick hug. "So, are you hungry?"

"Starving, actually. I haven't eaten since last night, and it was just a Spam musubi I picked up at 7-Eleven."

"How 'bout we go to Kekoa's to celebrate your return?" said

Kristen. "I could use some of their awesome pancakes and Portuguese sausage right about now."

Sean grinned. "Sounds good to me. Lemme just put this stuff away." Grabbing his bike, which was leaning against the railing of the lānai, along with the daypack that sat at his feet, he wheeled the bike inside. After he stowed his belongings in his bedroom, Kristen drove them downtown to the 1970s-era diner.

They were seated quickly at one of the faux-leather booths, handed enormous six-page menus, and served coffee. Valerie, who always had a hard time deciding what to order at restaurants, had planned ahead and made up her mind on the way down. "The crab omelet for me," she told the server—a woman who looked to be in her sixties with red-dyed hair and bright red lipstick to match—when she returned to take their orders. "With sourdough toast and home fries."

"You got it, hon. And what can I get you two?"

Kristen ordered her beloved pancakes and Portuguese sausage, while Sean went for the Kekoa Diner's famous saimin.

That done, they sipped their coffee a moment before Sean broke the silence. "Okay," he drawled with a sigh. "I'm sorry I made you both worry. I was pretty darn angry, I gotta admit, but it still wasn't right for me to do that."

"And are you still angry?" Valerie asked.

He thought a moment before answering. "Not angry, I guess, but the whole thing is still pretty upsetting. And it's really messed with my brain."

Kristen leaned across the table toward him. "What do you mean?"

"So, after sleeping on it—you know, what you said about Tammy and that arsenic you saw at her studio," Sean said with a glance Valerie's way, "I went over there to see her the next morning. I was super pissed off that you could even think such a thing, and I'd planned on telling her all about it. But then when I got there and said I was really upset, she started acting all weird. Almost like she knew that I knew something, but I could tell she didn't want to talk about it." He paused his story to take a drink from his heavy mug.

Valerie was about to ask a follow-up question when the waitress returned, bearing three kinds of syrup for Kristen's pancakes: maple, guava, and coconut.

"Anyway," Sean went on after she'd topped off their coffee and moved to the next table, "so after that, I wasn't keen on telling her what you'd said. All of a sudden it occurred to me that maybe you were right." He lowered his voice. "Maybe she did poison that vanilla. Remember how she said she was lactose-intolerant and so couldn't eat the dessert at the dinner?"

"Wait," said Valerie. "Are you saying you've seen her eat milk products since then?"

"No, I haven't." He shook his head, then frowned. "Well, I'm not actually sure, now that I think about it. She may have, but it's not something I was paying attention to. But no matter what, she definitely didn't eat any of that poisoned whipped cream. So at that point—when she started acting all weird in response to my telling her I was upset about something—I got really confused and made some excuse that I had to get going. Luckily I was working days all last week and she was on nights, 'cause I didn't know what I'd say if I ran into her. But I didn't want to come back here, 'cause I needed some time to process it all, so I asked this guy at work if I could crash at his place."

"You needed six days to process it?" asked Kristen, eyebrows raised.

"Okay, so it didn't take that long. But the longer I stayed away, the harder it got for me to come back and admit it all to you. That, well, maybe you were right. I mean, I don't know what to think. I'm not sure of anything anymore." Sean shook his head, then turned to Valerie. "Do you still think Tammy might have done it? Put arsenic in that vanilla?"

"I don't know. I actually went to talk to her yesterday."

"You did?" said Sean and Kristen simultaneously.

"Uh, yeah. We still hadn't heard anything from you, so I was hoping maybe she'd have some info about where you might be. She said she'd text some of your co-workers to find out if they'd seen you, but I never heard anything back about that." Valerie frowned. "Which is kinda odd, come to think of it, given how worried she knew I was."

"But why would Tammy even want to poison the orchid society?" asked Kristen. "Do you have any motive for her to do so?"

Valerie nodded. "Yeah, I know. That's what's kept me from taking her super seriously as a suspect up to this point. And if you'd only answered our texts," she said to Sean, "I'd have told you that."

Her nephew shrugged. "Sorry."

"But now I'm thinking back to how Tammy and Emily acted when we all sat together during dessert at the dinner," Valerie went on. "Remember how they were kind of cool with each other? I mean, they sure didn't seem close—not like people who'd been members of the same pottery studio for several years. At the time I didn't think anything of it. I just assumed they were merely acquaintances from the orchid society. But now I'm wondering if there's something going on between the two of them that we don't know about. Maybe something to do with why Emily quit the studio—you know, as opposed to it being an allergy to clay, like she told me."

"Huh." Sean leaned back in his booth and stared at a man at the next table chowing down on a massive bowl of ox tail soup.

"Oh, no," said Valerie.

Sean turned toward her. "What?"

"When Tammy asked me yesterday why you were upset, I told her about seeing the arsenic in her studio and also . . ."

"What I overheard you say about her," Sean finished. "That you thought she might have put some in the vanilla."

"Uh . . . yeah. Though by the end of our conversation, I'm pretty sure she thought I'd let that idea go."

"But the bottom line is, if she *did* do it, the fact that she knows you saw that arsenic in her studio and considered her a suspect—at least for a while—means you really need to watch your back," said Kristen, reaching into her pocket for her phone. "I think we need to call Amy and let her know about all this."

"Wait." Valerie laid a hand on her wife's arm. "Let's talk this through more before we do anything just yet. I mean, if

Tammy and Emily did have some kind of falling out, then that gives Emily just as much reason to do something rash as it does Tammy, right?"

Kristen set the phone on the table. "So you think Emily might have been trying to poison Tammy?"

The woman sitting at the booth behind them swiveled around at this point and stared wide-eyed at Kristen, who said with a smile, "Don't worry. We're just talking about a TV show we've been watching."

With a shrug, the woman turned back around and, after saying something to her companion, dug back into her breakfast.

"I don't think anything at this point," Valerie answered Kristen in a now-lowered voice. "I'm just brainstorming. Though when I said the same thing to Tammy yesterday—positing that Emily might have used the arsenic at the Mo'o studio to poison Mr. Ikeda in retaliation for him breaking up with her all those years ago—Tammy told me they only got the arsenic a couple months ago, well after Emily stopped being a member of the studio."

"Hold on." Kristen made a T with her hands like a football referee. "Emily and George Ikeda were an item? Did I know that?"

"Huh-uh. I only just learned it a couple days ago, and what with all the worry about . . ." Valerie nodded toward Sean. "You know, it kinda slipped my mind." She explained to Kristen and Sean what Shirley had told her over shave ice on Tuesday, and how learning this had made her wonder if maybe Emily could have been angry enough at her old flame to finally decide to do him in.

"But if she did poison the vanilla, it likely wasn't with the arsenic from the studio," she finished, "since she wouldn't have even known they bought it, and the cupboard it's kept in is locked, in any case." Valerie tapped a finger on the table as she thought back to her conversations with Emily. "And besides," she said, "it's obvious from how she talks about him that Emily really cared for George. She seems truly gutted by his death. It could all be an act, I suppose, but I just don't see her wanting to harm the guy."

"So, what about your neighbor, Larry?" Sean asked. "Do you consider him a suspect?" And then, seeing the look Valerie gave to Kristen, he said, "What? Has he given you more grief about Pua?"

Valerie told him what happened to her at the dragon dance downtown and how she'd seen Larry right afterwards, and also how Akoni had tried to attack Pua the very next day. "So, yeah, you could definitely say the guy's on my list. He's clearly super angry at me and Kristen. Who knows if that anger is enough to try to get me blamed for poisoning the orchid society or something crazy like that. He did for sure have access to the whipped cream when he delivered the wine to the Buddhist hall for the dinner that afternoon."

"Dang, that's creepy," said Sean.

The server approached bearing their orders, and the trio fell silent as they set about doctoring their food. While Valerie shook Hawaiian hot sauce onto her omelet, Kristen spread butter on her pancakes, then slathered them with guava syrup.

Valerie looked up to see Sean staring in awe at the bowl before him. "This is ginormous," he said. A mass of noodles swam in an aromatic broth, upon which floated slices of hot pink fish cake and roasted pork, chopped green onions, and two soft-boiled egg halves.

"Yup," replied Kristen, her mouth full of sausage. "They don't call it the sumo bowl for nothing."

Valerie tasted her omelet. "And this is amazing. It's even real crab." She took another bite, then set down her fork. "Oh, and I haven't told you yet, Sean. There's going to be a celebration of Mr. Ikeda's life tomorrow morning at his house. And his wife, Sue, is going to give away all his orchids to folks in the orchid society."

"Val's hoping it'll be like in one of those TV shows where all the suspects are brought together and one shows his hand and proves his guilt," said Kristen. "But I'm more concerned that one will decide she's been a bit too much of a busy-body and try to do something about it."

Valerie waved a hand. "With all those people there? It'll be fine. But, hey, you can come along to protect me if you like, hon," she said with a pat to her wife's shoulder.

"I think I might," said Kristen. "I have paddling in the morning, but we should be back in time for me to go with you. Not only can I be your bodyguard, but it could prove fascinating to see so many of your suspects in one place like that."

They continued to eat without talking, and then Sean pushed back his half-eaten bowl of saimin. "Oof, I don't think I can manage any more right now, but it'll make for a good snack later this afternoon. So, who all will be there tomorrow that you suspect of putting that arsenic in the vanilla?" he asked Valerie.

"All of them, I think. I can't imagine anyone passing up the free orchids. Let's see . . ." Valerie held up her fingers as she ticked off names. "We've already talked about Tammy, Emily, and Larry, so the only others I can think of are Don and Irene."

"Don's the guy who accused Mr. Ikeda of stealing his hybrids, right?" said Kristen.

"Right. And he didn't take kindly to either that or the fact that Mr. Ikeda claimed he simply made the whole thing up. Which, of course, could well be true. At least that's the opinion of several people in the orchid society I talked to about it."

Sean pulled his bowl back toward him. "Could he have poisoned the vanilla to get back at them as a whole—you know, for not believing him?" he asked, then took another spoonful of the rich broth.

"Absolutely," said Valerie. "I gather the guy's not too well liked by the group. Emily refers to him as a 'pill.' Plus, he definitely benefited from Mr. Ikeda's death. He now has unfettered access to all of his orchids, since he's the one who's been tending them since the death."

"Huh." Sean set his spoon back in the bowl.

"And then there's Irene. She's the mauka—uphill—neighbor of the Ikedas, who was supposed to do the food for the dinner with Emily but conveniently ended up having to go to Oʻahu to take care of an ailing mother."

"Conveniently?" asked Sean.

Valerie shrugged as she swallowed a bite of sourdough toast. "I know. It probably sounds kind of paranoid, me suspecting just about everyone in the neighborhood. But Irene definitely has to be in the mix." She told Sean about the spat between George and the Souzas regarding his tree blocking their view. "I know it's not much to go on, but the bottom line is, someone did in fact poison that vanilla. And it's almost surely someone from the orchid society."

"Or related to someone in the society," said Kristen, causing Valerie to turn toward her.

"Who do you have in mind?"

"Sue Ikeda," said Kristen. "The wife is always the prime suspect in cases such as these."

Valerie frowned. "True. And it's funny you should suggest her, because I've actually been starting to wonder if maybe she has some kind of dementia, or some other sort of memory loss." She explained how Sue had acted so friendly to Don, even though Valerie had told her earlier that he'd accused George of stealing orchids from him and how upset Sue had initially been on learning this information. "But maybe it's all just an act," she said. "Maybe she's pretending to be ditzy for some reason."

"It is a little odd that she's giving away all her dead husband's prized orchids so soon after his death," observed Sean, picking up his spoon once more.

"I wonder . . ." said Valerie. Sitting back against the banquette, she gazed out the window and chewed her lip.

"Wonder what?" asked Kristen impatiently when she failed to finish this thought.

"Sorry." Valerie leaned forward and laid her arms on the table. "I just remembered something. When I asked Sue who could maybe help her out with a memorial of some sort, she said that George's whole life had been his orchids for like the past ten years, and that they didn't have many friends. They pretty much only socialized with the orchid society folks, according to her. And Sue isn't even interested in orchids."

"Okay . . ." said Kristen.

"So, what if she resented him for that? Or resented the orchid society as a whole? I can imagine she might have felt like he cared more about his orchid people than her." Valerie paused a moment, brow furrowed. "I did see them acting all lovey-dovey at the dinner that night, which made me assume they were still deeply in love. But now when I think back, it was really more her than him who was acting all romantic. So maybe she was just trying to get his attention."

Sean nodded. "Could be."

"And if she was jealous of the orchid society—and resentful of George for caring so much about it—that would explain why she wasn't super keen on doing a celebration of life for the guy."

"But wait. Why then would she agree to have them host the memorial?" asked Sean.

Valerie shrugged. "What else could she say when I suggested it? No, I don't want a memorial for my dead husband? And part of her no doubt does want it. He was her husband for, what, forty years?"

"Maybe not," said Kristen. "Not if she's the one who killed him."

"You're really set on the wife-as-killer solution, huh?" said Sean with a chuckle.

"Yeah . . . I dunno . . ." Valerie poked at the remnants of her omelet with her fork. "Sue seemed awful upset about his death when I went to see her that first time. And truly surprised when I said that someone had intentionally put something into the vanilla, as opposed to it being an accidental contamination."

Kristen snorted. "Of course she'd act that way if she was the one who did it."

"But she also told me how guilty she felt about giving him her whipped cream that night, which meant he got a double dose of the poison. Why would she admit that if she were the culprit?" But then Valerie shook her head. "Duh. Because she knew the cops already knew she'd done that."

"And there's another possibility, too," said Kristen. "Maybe it wasn't just George she was going after. Maybe she was trying to poison the orchid society at large."

"Yeah, good point." Valerie let out a sigh. "So many suspects;

so little proof that any of them might have actually done it. But in any case, it's gonna be interesting tomorrow, seeing how everyone acts. I wonder if any of them will in fact somehow show their hand."

EIGHTEEN

Valerie headed up to Sue Ikeda's house the next morning at nine fifteen. It had rained overnight, but the sky was clear of clouds at the moment, and the temperature was already close to eighty degrees.

Wiping off the sweat that was already beading up on her forehead, she walked around the side of the house to the back yard, where she found Irene and Sue struggling to set up a large folding table. The table was old and—this being damp and rainy Hilo—rather rusted, so the legs were refusing to unfold. Valerie grabbed hold of the metal supports on Sue's side and gave them a good tug. Nothing budged.

"Here, let's try it together," she said to Sue. "Okay, one, two, *three*!" Still no movement. Valerie stared at the stubborn legs a moment, hands on hips. "Do you have a single jack?" she asked, eliciting a blank look from both women. "Sorry. It's a small sledge hammer—I only know the name 'cause my wife was a construction worker. But any size hammer would be a help."

"There may be one in here," said Sue, heading for the carport.

Valerie followed after her and looked where she was pointing. Above a shelf covered with a variety of clutter—an old VCR player, several old plastic bottles, a stack of paper plates, a box of tangled cords, and various other odds and ends—hung a dozen or so tools which, from their well-worn looks, had to date from the 1950s or even earlier. George had clearly been far more into his orchids and gardening than house maintenance.

But there was a hefty hammer, which Valerie took from its peg on the wall. "This should work. Oh, and we can use some of that, too," she said, spying a can of WD-40 among the clutter on the shelf.

Back outside, Valerie sprayed a stream from the can's nozzle onto the moving parts of the table, then whacked the legs with the hammer, succeeding in finally popping them out into place. "Voilà! Nothing like the right tools to get a job done."

Applying the same technique to the other pair of legs, they managed to get the long table set up along the side of the house, where it would be protected from the rain should the weather change. Next they placed eight chairs that Sue had brought from inside her house next to the table—not many, but hopefully enough for those unable to stand for the entire ceremony.

"Oh, and I'd best go get a tablecloth," said Sue, eyeing the stains that covered the plastic tabletop, and she headed indoors.

Irene showed Valerie the items she'd brought for the celebration of life: a coffee maker, along with ground coffee and filters; an electric kettle and a variety of different kinds of tea bags; half-and-half, milk, and sugar; and a selection of pastries.

"Oooh," said Valerie examining the croissants, bear claws, Danishes, and donuts. "These look amazing. Is it bad to be impatient for a memorial service to get started so I can eat?"

"Not at all. In fact, I already ate one of the blueberry Danishes, I have to admit. Have one, if you want."

"Nah, I'll wait." Valerie glanced toward the back door to make sure Sue hadn't yet emerged, then said in a low voice, "So, I gotta say I'm a little surprised you volunteered to do this—bring the breakfast today. You know, given your history with George and that tree an' all . . ."

Irene shrugged. "Well, I did end up bailing on that dinner, so it seemed like the right thing to do. But also . . ."

"What? You trying to make nice with Sue because of the tree?" Valerie said with a chuckle.

Before Irene could answer, they were interrupted by the reappearance of Sue, shaking out a pale blue tablecloth. "Sorry I was so long, but it took me a while to find one that would be big enough. How's this look? It's been sitting for years in my linen closet, so I wouldn't be surprised if it has some mold on it."

"It's perfect," said Valerie, helping her spread it out. There were indeed a few dark stains on the linen fabric, which Valerie pooh-poohed. "No worries; we can cover these up with the plate of pastries and other things."

"Are there any electrical outlets nearby?" asked Irene, holding up the coffee maker. Sue pointed out a socket on the wall beneath the table, and while Irene got busy setting up the coffee and tea station, Valerie helped Sue arrange all the other items on the table.

"Should we set some orchids out with the food as table decorations?" Valerie asked.

"Sure," said Sue. "Good idea."

"I think Don put some of the most spectacular ones in bloom up on the lānai." Valerie started toward the covered outdoor area, then abruptly stopped. "Oh, speak of the devil."

"Not sure the devil is someone you should be invoking today," said Don with a grin, striding toward them.

Valerie put a hand to her mouth. "Oh, sorry."

But Sue appeared not to have heard—or if she had, not to care. "Aloha, Don," she said. "Good to see you."

"Yeah, well, I thought I should be here early to help with the orchid giveaway. Are we doing that first, or after the . . . uh . . ."

"Celebration," filled in Valerie. "We're going to celebrate the wonderful man that George was."

This was met, not by immediate hearty agreement, as Valerie had expected, but by mere nods from the other three.

"That's right," said Sue after a moment, as if realizing a more enthusiastic response was in order. "And thank you all so much for helping to make it happen. I do truly appreciate it. And as for when we'll do the giveaway, I'm not sure. What do you think would be best?"

"Well, if we do it first," Irene said, "then everyone will have to put their orchids somewhere, and I'm not sure having them sit in hot cars is such a good idea."

Don nodded. "True. So after the ceremony—whatever that might be . . ." He glanced around at the others. "Do we know how we're going to run this?"

"I had the not-so-great fortune to host a celebration of life last year after my brother died," said Valerie, "and we just asked if anyone wanted to stand up and say something. It was all pretty informal, but ended up being quite moving, actually. Once folks started sharing memories about Charlie, it inspired others to tell their own stories."

"Should we have someone start it all out with a sort of introduction or something?" asked Irene, looking to the others.

Sue shook her head. "I don't think I could say anything."

"No, no one will expect you to," said Valerie. "It's often too hard for the loved one. But perhaps someone else? Someone who knew him better than I did?"

"I can do it."

Valerie turned at this new voice to see Emily standing by the back of the carport. Whereas the others were all dressed in your typical island wear—aloha-print shirts and blouses with light-colored skirts or slacks—she was clad in somber tones of brown and slate gray.

"I'd be happy to say something about George at the start of the memorial," Emily said, stepping into the back yard.

Irene smiled. "Okay, good. Thanks. And then after everyone is finished speaking, we can enjoy the pastries while people take whatever orchids they want. Though I think we should offer the beverages beforehand, yes?"

"Agreed. I could go for some coffee right now, as a matter of fact," said Valerie. "Oh, and good timing, as it looks like folks are starting to arrive."

Many of the attendees were unknown to Valerie, though she recognized some of the faces from the orchid society meeting and dinner. As she was showing a group of four newcomers where the hot water and tea bags were, she spied Kristen come into the back yard. Waving, she flagged her over.

"How was paddling?" Valerie asked, handing her wife a cup of coffee.

"Great! We saw a mamma whale with her baby, and they were breaching and showing off like crazy. It was amazing." Kristen leaned in close to Valerie. "So, anything of note happen yet?"

"No, but most everyone only just got here. We're going to

do the ceremony first—have people say something about George if they want—so I'll be paying close attention to who speaks and what they say."

At the clapping of Irene's hands, the attendees finished fetching their drinks and then gathered around her in the open area between the shade-cloth-covered orchids and the lānai. Valerie studied the group to see who of interest had shown up.

Irene, Don, and Emily, she noticed, were all clustered together next to the long table. Shirley was standing next to Sue, and the two were talking in hushed tones.

Over by the lānai she spied Larry. He too had forgone the typical aloha wear, opting instead for a dark short-sleeved button-down shirt and black slacks. But, she observed with amusement, he wore the ubiquitous local footwear: a pair of rubber slippahs—though they too were black. As she studied her neighbor, Larry met her eye, then quickly looked away.

But where was Tammy? Searching the crowd, Valerie failed to spot the potter.

Once everyone had quieted down, Irene nodded at Emily, who stepped forward into the middle of the circle. Closing her eyes, she waited a moment before speaking.

"I've been asked to start things off, which seems appropriate since I think I may have known George the longest of anyone here." Emily glanced at Sue, who was picking at a thread on her flower-print blouse.

"George and I were in the same kindergarten class," she went on. "He lived just a block and half mauka from me, so he'd stop by my house, and we'd walk to and from school together every day. Then after school, we'd play jacks and hopscotch in my driveway until it was time for him to go home for dinner. George was such a nice boy—polite and always generous. He used to give me half his butter mochi when his mother packed it in his sack lunch, 'cause he knew how much I loved it." Emily blinked several times, then took a deep breath.

"As we got older, we went more our separate ways—he'd play baseball and ride bikes around the neighborhood with the other boys, and I'd jump rope and do somersaults with the girls. But he and I remained friends and, as some of you know, we even dated in high school. And of course we've stayed very close through the orchid society." She blinked several times. "I do miss him."

Valerie watched Sue to gauge her reaction to this part of the story, but George's widow didn't appear to have moved, still focused on the sleeve of her blouse.

"Anyway, George remained gracious and generous for the rest of his life," said Emily after a pause. "And his commitment to the orchid society is an example of that—all the hours he gave to the group and the help he provided to those who didn't have the experience he did."

It was now Don that Valerie turned to watch. Unlike most of the others present who were nodding in agreement, he was shaking his head and rolling his eyes. Not surprising, given his history with George Ikeda, but nevertheless, it seemed like an inappropriate time and place for the reaction.

She glanced around her, wondering if anyone else had noticed Don's reaction. But no, they all seemed to be watching Emily.

All except Tammy, whom she now spotted at the far back of the crowd—and who was looking intently at *her*.

Their eyes met, and Valerie smiled and mouthed "hello." Tammy, perhaps surprised to be caught out staring so obviously at Valerie, took a moment to respond, but then managed a smile in return.

Emily wrapped up her comments. "Okay, that's enough from me. But I invite anyone else who'd like to say something to feel free to speak. Then afterwards, we'll enjoy this delicious food that Irene has provided, and you can pick out any of George's orchids that you wish to take home with you."

Relinquishing her place in the center of the circle, Emily came to stand next to Valerie. There was an awkward moment as folks shuffled their feet and avoided each other's gaze, no one eager to be the next to speak. Valerie was wondering if she should say something—even though she felt as if she barely knew George—when to her surprise Larry stepped forward.

"Aloha," he said, dipping his head self-consciously like a teenage boy called to the front of the class. "I didn't know

George since small kid time like Emily, and I only wen' know him very well aftah I joined the orchid society about ten years ago. But I can say that I truly appreciated all he did for da society, organizing the meetings and orchid sales an' dealin' wit' board members and all kine issues whenever they'd come up. He used to say the orchid society was his 'ohana, and I believe it."

Valerie looked again at Sue, who had stopped picking at her shirt sleeve, her full attention now on Larry. Sue's eyes narrowed at this last comment of his, and Valerie could see a stiffening of her shoulders.

"But even before I got to know him through da orchid society, George was always a good neighbor," Larry went on. "Although he tended to keep to himself, it was obvious how much he cared about da neighborhood—and how much he was truly a part of its history."

Was that directed at Kristen and me? Valerie wondered as Larry's eyes flashed her way.

More people now came forward to say some words about George Ikeda, mostly regarding his work with the orchid society, though a few also spoke about his career as a CPA and his generosity in helping them with their taxes over the years.

The last to talk was the orchid society treasurer. As before at the meeting, she seemed not keen on public speaking, and her voice was so quiet that Valerie had a hard time hearing her. But she got the gist of what she was saying—how Mr. Ikeda had encouraged her to become treasurer even though she knew little about finances, how he'd taught her to cut corners whenever possible to save money for the society (which prompted knowing chuckling from some of the members), and how very patient he'd been teaching her the ropes of basic bookkeeping and accounting.

"Thank you for that, Ana," Emily said when she'd finished speaking. "Anyone else?"

Valerie scanned the crowd to see if any of her people of interest would respond, but neither Irene, Tammy, nor Don took the opportunity to come forward.

When it became clear that everyone who'd wanted to had

now spoken, Emily stepped into the middle of the circle once more. "All right, then. Time to now celebrate George's life with some of his favorite food—donuts and pastries—and we can of course continue to talk story about him as we eat. And it's now also time for anyone who wants any to pick out some of George's orchids to take home. But first, I think we can all join in thanking Sue for so generously offering to give away his beloved plants to members of the society."

This was followed by a round of applause, during which Sue managed a polite smile. But to Valerie's eye, she seemed pretty darn uncomfortable with the whole thing, and as soon as the clapping died down, Sue excused herself to go inside the house.

Emily piped up once more. "And I think Don is available to assist anyone who needs help with choosing their orchids, yes?"

Don raised a hand. "Correct. And I've got cardboard boxes to transport them in for anyone who needs one."

"Okay, great," said Emily. "I'll bow out now. Go ahead and help yourself to treats and orchids, everyone."

There was a general scurrying about, some folks making a beeline for the food and drink, others hurrying over to the shade-cloth-covered area to get first dibs on George's orchids.

But Valerie stayed where she was, watching the others.

Irene headed for the food table, where she picked up the coffee decanter and, seeing it was empty, carried it toward the house to refill with water for a new pot. On her way across the lānai, she passed Sue coming out, and the two exchanged nods.

Valerie's gaze followed Sue as she made her way to where Emily stood next to the pastries. After a moment, Don came over, and Emily moved down the table to allow him to help himself to a bear claw. Sue and Don spoke for a bit, but when Emily returned with a cup of tea for Sue, he gave the widow a quick hug, then headed over to the greenhouse area.

About a dozen people were already over there, and after greeting them, Don began walking down the rows of orchids, pointing to and talking about the various plants as the others trailed behind.

"He must be loving this," Valerie said to Kristen, who still stood by her side. "Being belle of the ball with everyone hanging on his every word. I'm gonna go hear what he has to say." Valerie hurried over and joined the group following Don.

"These are the Dendrobiums," he was saying. "There aren't many in bloom right now, but these two here are your typical pink and white, and those back there will be a more unusual greenish yellow."

"Oooo . . . I'll take one of those green ones," the treasurer said. "They're beautiful."

Don handed her the plant, and the group then continued down the row. But Valerie stayed put, staring at the black plastic pots. Or more accurately, at an empty space where a group of them had once sat.

This was definitely where the hybrids had been, along with their parent plants. But as she'd guessed would be the case, all four orchids were now gone. Don had clearly taken them for himself before the celebration of life.

NINETEEN

Hurrying to catch up, Valerie rejoined the group that was with Don. He was now talking about George's collection of Cattleyas, several of which bore showy blooms: pink and white, lavender, and one spectacular specimen with a riot of orange, yellow, and red petals.

"Cattleyas are relatively easy to grow, especially here in Hawai'i," he was saying, "so for any of you beginners, I'd recommend taking home one of these. Just make sure to give them plenty of bright, indirect light, and make sure not to over-water them."

As he walked around to the other side of the row, several people reached out for the Cattleyas, setting them into the cardboard boxes they held.

Don now stopped at the area with the vanilla plants. "Have any of you grown vanilla before?" he asked.

A man with shaggy gray hair and beard to match raised his hand. "I did, years ago, but never managed to get any beans."

"Well, although it's an easy plant to grow, it's quite difficult to actually produce viable fruit," said Don with a satisfied smile. "It took me several tries before I ended up with usable beans. Once the plant blooms, the flowers need to be hand-pollinated within twelve hours. You have to use a fine brush or chopstick or something similar to take the pollen from the stamen of one flower and place it onto the stigma of another one. You'll be able to tell quickly if it worked, because within a day the flowers that have been successfully pollinated will shrivel up on the vine, and then within a week or so small green pods will start to form."

"I'd like to try," piped up a young woman in a bright yellow blouse. "Should I take a cutting, or what? You know, since they're not in individual pots."

"It's probably best if we dig them up roots and all and give you the whole plant," said Don, "because a cutting can take three to five years to produce any flowers. Anyone who wants a plant, let me know and I can dig them up for you and put them in a pot. And I'm happy to help with the pollination and curing process, if you end up getting any flowers."

"Maybe we could have a workshop with the orchid society," said the yellow-clad woman, and Don nodded agreement.

"Good idea. Oh, and check it out." He bent down and pointed to a trio of beans hanging from several of the plants. "Some of them have already been pollinated by George and have fruit. So, how many of you would like a Vanilla *planifolia*?"

Valerie raised her hand. "I would. Could I have one of the plants with beans?"

"Sure, no problem. And you can have the other one," he said to the woman who'd spoken up first. "Okay, let's move on to the Oncidiums."

At this point, Valerie dropped out of the group. She could choose more orchids later, but right now, she wanted to see what the rest of her suspects were up to.

Spying Larry over at the food table, she walked over and stood next to him. She reached for a plate, then stared at the pastries as if deciding which one to choose, all the while listening in on her neighbor's conversation with the man next to him.

"I got a speeding ticket going over the Saddle Road last week," he was saying, "an' I was only going 'bout five miles over da limit. It's like dey get some kine speed trap goin' on these days, so be careful, brah. Especially when you pass by da army base, yah? I tink—"

A commotion at the end of the food table caused Larry to break off and turn to look. Sue was shouting and shaking a tea towel at something, and people had backed away from where she stood. After a moment, a scrawny black-and-white cat darted from under the table and across the yard.

"Scat!" Sue cried at the fleeing animal, then shook her head in disgust. "They're everywhere, those cats. Pests, they are."

"I know," said the man next to Larry. "And it seems like

they've been multiplying like crazy. I called animal control twice last month, but they have yet to do anything about the problem."

"George and I tried trapping them," said Sue, "but all we ever succeeding in catching was a mongoose."

At the sound of laughter, Valerie turned to see Larry chuckling at Sue's comment. "What you need is a good hunting dog," he said. "Dat'll take care of da feral cats, no worry, beef curry."

This was met with an awkward silence, as even those who'd taken the anti-cat stance appeared taken aback by the image Larry's statement had conjured.

"Well," said Sue after a bit, "I just wish we could at least take them to the shelter to be spayed so they wouldn't reproduce. It really does seem like there are way more in the neighborhood than there used to be."

With a last look in the direction the cat had fled, Sue returned to the table, dunked the bag that sat in her cup a few times before setting it on a plate, then took a long drink of her tea.

Valerie turned from Sue to scan the crowd. Kristen was talking to Shirley over by the coffee machine, and Irene and Emily were standing and chatting near Sue, plates of pastries in their hands. Larry, who remained next to her, was once more talking to his friend about the Saddle Road, and Don was still holding court in the orchid area.

But where was Tammy? Looking about her, she finally spotted the potter over by the lānai, where she stood rigid and unmoving, her eyes steely hard, staring straight at Valerie.

But then Valerie realized it wasn't her Tammy was watching.

It was Larry.

The crowd was now starting to thin out. Don had finished his tour of George's orchid collection, and people were setting down their cardboard boxes full of plants to come say goodbye to Sue. One by one, the orchid society members came to take her hand, as she provided a weak smile and nod in response to their murmured condolences.

She looked haggard, her skin pale and eyes tired, as if she'd aged five years in that one morning. At a break in the line of well-wishers, she took a sip from her cup of tea and glanced back at the house. It was a longing look, to Valerie's eye, as if all she wanted was for this whole thing to be over and done with as quickly as possible so she could retreat back indoors.

Crossing the yard, Valerie came to stand at Sue's side. "Would you like me to get a refill of your tea?" she asked, seeing that the cup—with its pink-tinged lip—was now empty.

"That would be lovely. Thank you."

Valerie headed for the tea station, where she found a new bag of Earl Grey, poured hot water into the cup, and brought it back to Sue.

"How are you holding up?" asked Valerie.

Sue shrugged. "I guess I didn't expect it to be so hard seeing everyone leave with George's orchids. I know I can't take care of them and that they're going to good homes, but it all seems so . . . final."

"Well, if you'd ever like to come visit the plants that I'm taking, you're more than welcome to do so. But you are keeping some of them, right?"

"Oh, yes. Don picked out about a dozen that he said are easy to care for and that have nice flowers. They're up there." Sue gestured to a row of pots sitting on a table on the lānai, many in full bloom. "And he says he can stop by to make sure they're doing okay."

The slamming of car doors caused Sue to peer across the yard toward Irene's house. A couple had just pulled up into the driveway and were taking luggage from the trunk of a Mustang convertible. "More tourists," she said with a shake of the head.

Valerie feigned ignorance. "Oh?"

"Yeah, Irene and Hugo have turned their ʻohana unit into a vacation rental, and the guests can be really loud and inconsiderate—especially late at night."

"Have you ever talked to them about it?"

"Yes," said Sue. "George did, but they didn't do anything about it—or at least nothing changed. And I'm pretty sure it's illegal—that they don't have a permit for short-term rentals. George told them he was going to complain to the planning department about it, but I'm not sure if he ever did. So here we are." She let out a sigh and took another sip of tea.

Valerie watched the couple as they dragged their roller suitcases down the driveway to the 'ohana unit door, punched a number into the lock, and let themselves in. "Well, that's not good," she said with a glance Larry's way. "It's no fun having noisy neighbors." She stood a little bit longer by Sue's side, then, spotting Kristen over by the pastries, said, "Well, I think I'm going to get myself one of those donuts before they're all gone."

"And I think I'll go sit down for a bit. I'm feeling a little weak."

"I'm not surprised," said Valerie. "This must have been a hard morning for you."

"And I haven't been myself lately. The doctor says I have low blood pressure, so I need to take it easy—and drink more fluids," she said with a nod toward her tea. "So thanks for this."

Ah. That would explain her acting so out of it of late.

Walking with Sue over to the line of chairs, she got her settled, then went to join her wife. "C'mere," she said after grabbing a plate and a bear claw. "I just learned something that may be important."

Kristen followed her over to the orchid area. "I saw you talking to Sue just now. I've been watching over you this whole time, just like I promised," she said with a grin and a quick kiss to Valerie's cheek. "So, lemme guess: Did Sue admit to killing her husband because it turned out he was the one feeding the feral cats?"

"Very funny," said Valerie. "Not. But it was something she said. It turns out George was really upset about the vacation rental unit that Irene and Hugo have, which is apparently unpermitted. And get this: not only did George complain to them about it, but he told them he was going to report the illegal unit to the planning department."

"Huh." Kristen swallowed her last bite of Danish, then licked sugar from her thumb. "That is something. Did he ever actually make a complaint, do you know?"

"I'm pretty sure he didn't. I think he was killed before he ever had a chance to do so."

"Ah," said Kristen. "The plot thickens."

They both turned to watch Irene, who was collecting used cups, plates, napkins, and tea bags from the food table, and placing them in a black plastic garbage bag.

"You think she could have done it to keep him from filing the complaint?" asked Kristen. "Or maybe her husband?" She glanced around at the dwindling guests. "Did he come today?"

"Hugo? Huh-uh. He's not a part of the orchid society and he didn't come to that benefit dinner, either. I'm guessing he's not super social, 'cause I've never even met the guy. I've only seen him a couple times out in his yard when I've driven by."

"Unlikely he would have poisoned that vanilla, then. But it certainly could have been her." Kristen nodded toward Irene, who was now packing up the few remaining pastries into one of the large pink boxes they'd come in.

"Right. Even though she wasn't there for the dinner itself, she could have poisoned the vanilla before she went to O'ahu. She is one of the ones who planned the menu, after all."

"As did Emily, right?"

"True," said Valerie. "But other than Tammy, I have yet to come up with anyone in the orchid society Emily might want to poison. And that's based solely on conjecture—you know, that Emily's leaving the ceramics studio may have had something to do with Tammy." Valerie turned to watch Emily, who was now helping Irene clear the table. "But you know, now that I think about it, I didn't see Emily and Tammy interact at all today. Which is kind of weird, given their history."

Kristen followed her gaze. "So maybe the two are at odds."

"Yeah, but enough for one to want to poison the other?" Valerie shrugged. "Well, since I did volunteer to help out with this thing, I guess I should go make myself useful." Walking toward the long table, she looked around to see if Tammy was still there, but didn't spy the potter anywhere.

Only about a dozen people remained, for that matter. Several men were over in the orchid area with Don, picking out plants to take home. Sue was still sitting down, talking to an older couple Valerie didn't know, but recognized from the orchid society meeting and the dinner. Shirley had picked up a trash bag and was wandering around the yard collecting cups and plates that folks had left strewn about.

Typical, thought Valerie. The women are all helping clean up while the men are nowhere to be found. Joining Irene and Emily, she asked what she could do to help.

"You might take this inside and wash it out," said Irene, unplugging the coffee machine and handing the carafe to her.

"Sure, no problem."

Valerie stepped up onto the lānai and was about to open the back door when she was stopped short by the sound of angry voices coming from the open kitchen window. The volume was low, as if the people arguing were trying to keep from being heard, but she could tell it was a man and a woman.

But then, after a moment, the woman's voice rose above the other.

"Murderer!"

Valerie grabbed hold of the coffee carafe, which almost slipped from her grasp, then turned to look out at the back yard. No one else appeared to have heard what was going on indoors. Creeping closer, she knelt down and peered through the bottom of the window.

It was Larry and Tammy. The two were standing about three feet apart, and Larry had his hands out, trying to calm the other down. But she was having none of it. As Valerie watched, she raised an arm as if ready to strike Larry across the face.

"I knew it was you!" she shouted.

Could Larry have killed George? But if so, why would Tammy care so very much?

Larry stepped back two paces. "Chill, sistah. It no like you tink."

"You basically just admitted as much," said Tammy, her arm still raised.

"No way. Jus' joke, is all."

"It sure didn't sound like a joke to me. And the bottom line is he's now gone, and I blame you for it."

Tammy started to advance on Larry. Valerie was caught

between wanting to let them go on so she could learn who they were talking about, or stepping in to stop any violence from occurring. Most likely Tammy would suffer, she figured, as Larry had to outweigh her by at least sixty pounds.

But at that moment Larry glanced toward the window. “Ho,” he yelled, “what you lookin’ at!”

Tammy, dropping her arm, turned as well. “What the hell?”

“Nothing,” said Valerie, jumping back quickly and holding up the carafe. “I was just coming inside to wash this, but didn’t want to interrupt you.”

“Bull,” said Larry, storming out of the house onto the lānai. “You jus’ one pilikia, e’rytime stickin’ your nose where it don’ belong. You bettah watch out, sistah, or you gon’ regret it, garanz.”

Valerie backed up against the wall as he swept past, knocking against her arm as he went.

Tammy joined her outside. “Whoa,” said Valerie. “What was that all about?”

But Tammy simply followed after Larry, a shake of the head the only sign she’d even heard Valerie’s question.

TWENTY

Back at home that afternoon, Valerie took her cardboard box of George's orchids outside and lined them up on the lānai. There were seven, in all: two Dendrobiums with spikes but no flowers yet; the slipper orchid she'd admired with the white-and-lavender bloom; an Oncidium from which over a dozen tiny yellow ballet dancers dangled; the orange, yellow, and red Cattleya she'd seen that morning; and a pair of vanilla orchids, which Don had dug up and put into black plastic pots.

She examined the vanilla plants. As she'd requested, Don had given her one with several beans already ripening, but the other had neither beans nor buds.

As for the other orchids, the ones with flowers needed some nice pots to match their showy blooms. Heading out to the area in the back of the carport where they kept their gardening supplies, Valerie selected three ceramic pots with brightly colored Chinese designs that she'd purchased a few weeks earlier at a garage sale, brought them over to the lānai, and set the plants inside.

"Lovely," she said out loud. Pua looked up at the sound, but sensing no activity indicating either a walk or food, she laid her head back down on the couch where she'd been enjoying an afternoon snooze.

Leaving one of the flowering orchids out on the lānai, Valerie took the other two inside and placed them in spots around the house where they'd get the most attention: on the kitchen table and under the window in the living room. Next, she grabbed her laptop and headed back outdoors.

Time for some research.

Entering a query for how to grow vanilla plants, she clicked on an article entitled "The Ripening and Harvesting of Vanilla Bean Pods." A photograph depicted a vanilla orchid bearing beans at about the same stage as those on her plant, with its tip just starting to change from a pale green to yellow. "This pod is almost ready for harvest," the caption read.

Valerie moved on to the text below the photo, which informed her that once the yellow starts to move up the pod but before it starts to split, "it should be cut from the raceme with sharp shears."

What's a raceme? Valerie wondered and typed in a new query. "A raceme is an inflorescence in which the flowers are borne on short stalks," she read. This prompted her to next type in "inflorescence," which, she learned, was a group of flowers arranged on a floral axis.

Kristen came out onto the lānai at this point with a sandwich and glass of iced tea. "Whatcha doing?" she asked, plopping down next to Valerie and peering at her screen.

"Going down a rabbit hole of botany."

"Well, rabbits do love botany—especially when it involves lettuce or carrots."

"I wonder how they feel about vanilla plants?" said Valerie, clicking back to her original article. She read for a few minutes while Kristen munched on her tuna sandwich—Pua had now risen from her slumber and sat expectantly at Kristen's feet—then let out an "Oof."

"What?" asked Kristen.

"George was right when he said making vanilla was a laborious process. It says here that after you harvest the pods—the beans, that is—you have to scald them in hot water, then wrap them in plastic and put them in a sweating box for two days. What the heck is a sweating box?"

Kristen tossed a chunk of fish to the dog. "Sounds like one of those saunas we went to that time in Santa Cruz."

"And then you remove them from the box and let them dry on a rack so they don't rot. And check it out." Valerie pointed an accusing finger at her computer screen. "You have to do that every day for two weeks—move them from the sweat box to the drying rack and back again. And that's not even the end of the process." Leaning forward, she read from the article: "Once the sweating is complete, the pods must air dry until they reach a moisture level of twenty to thirty percent, which can take from two to six weeks, depending on the size of the pod." Valerie sat back on the couch. "I wonder how you would even measure that."

"It's not like it's an exact science," said Kristen after swallowing a gulp of tea. "I'm sure if you just let them dry for around three or four weeks, they'll come out fine. So what are you going to do with the beans once they're all . . .?"

"Cured? I'm not sure. Probably make some extract, so they'll go further. George told me all he did was put some beans into vodka and let it sit for six months, but here, let's see what other people say." Valerie googled "how to make vanilla extract," and a long list of results popped up. Clicking on the first one that wasn't a paid ad, she scanned the text.

"Yup, that part of the process is pretty darn easy. This person sometimes uses bourbon or rum, but for traditional extract they say vodka is the best, and they recommend going cheap, since the vanilla will mask the taste of any fancy vodka you buy. Oh, but not Everclear, it says, as its high alcohol content can make the extract taste nasty. Good to know. My instinct would have been to use that, since it's what I use when I make limoncello."

Scrolling down, she read on. "And then you just slice open the bean pods—it says to use at least three beans per eight ounces of liquor. Well, three is all I'll have, so that'll have to do. And then you let them soak in the booze for six to twelve months, the longer the better."

Valerie shut the computer. "I guess we won't be having homemade vanilla extract any time soon. But hey, it'll be a fun project."

Valerie was hoping Amy would show up that night at the Speckled Gecko—partly so she could hear about her date with Maile, but mostly so Valerie could fill her in on what she'd learned that morning at George's celebration of life. But when seven o'clock rolled around and the cop still hadn't arrived, she figured she'd be a no-show that night.

Oh, well, Valerie mused as she wiped down the bar top,

sticky from spilled pineapple juice. *I'll just have to give her a call tomorrow.* Hopefully her absence wasn't due to working late, but rather some fun reason such as going out with Maile again. And it had been pretty darn busy all evening, so she probably wouldn't have been able to talk much to Amy in any case.

Greeting the couple who'd just taken seats at the end of the bar, Valerie turned her attention to shaking up a liliko'i Martini and muddling lime, mint, and sugar for a Mojito, then entering an order of Kālua Pork Nachos into the POS machine.

Finally at around seven thirty there was a lull, and she was able to lean against the back counter and drink down a glass of ice water with a splash of Coke from the soda gun. Jun was making drinks for a foursome who'd just been seated in the indoor dining room, so for the moment she had no orders to fill.

A man stood up from his table and made his way across the lānai toward the restrooms, and Valerie did a double take. *Was that Larry?* But no, she realized when he turned her way. Although the two had a passing resemblance, this guy was slimmer than her neighbor, with a bushy mustache to boot.

Nevertheless, the momentary mistake in identity had unnerved her. As she stared blankly at the dolphin fountain splashing water onto the planters of pink ginger and yellow heliconia, she thought back to what she'd witnessed that morning in Sue's kitchen.

What had Tammy meant when she'd accused Larry of being a "murderer"? Could she have reason to believe he was responsible for George's death? And what at the memorial that morning could have triggered her outburst? Valerie frowned as she tried to recall if she'd seen any interaction between the two prior to their ending up in the kitchen together.

And then it clicked: after Larry had made that crack about needing a hunting dog to take care of all the cats in the neighborhood, the look Tammy had given him had been one of pure hatred.

Could Tammy be the one feeding the feral cats? And could Larry have set Akoni on one of those cats—with dire results?

The touch of a hand on Valerie's shoulder made her flinch.

"Pretty jumpy this evening, aren't we?" said Amy with a grin as she took a seat at the barstool in front of Valerie.

"Sorry. I didn't notice you come in."

"I could tell. You seemed awful interested in that couple sitting behind the fountain. Worried they're gonna dine and dash?"

"What?" Valerie glanced at the table she was talking about, then laughed. "No, I was just thinking about something, is all. Though if they do decide to leave without paying, at least there's now a cop here to chase them down."

"Not," said Amy. "I'm off duty, and in sore need of a drink. It's been a long day."

"Yeah, I didn't think you were even coming tonight, it's so late. What's your pleasure drink-wise?"

"I'm thinking a G&T. And a medianoche with a side of fries would be great. I'm starving."

Valerie entered Amy's order for the Cuban-style sandwich, then mixed her drink and handed it over. "So, if you don't mind telling me, inquiring minds want to know: How was your big date on Wednesday night?"

"Awesome. The food was great—Maile really knows how to cook fish—and we just talked and talked until late at night." Amy's grin was infectious, and Valerie couldn't help smiling along with her. "She had to work tonight, or I would have invited her along. But we both have tomorrow off, so we're driving over to Kona for the day."

"Sweet."

Amy took a long drink from her cocktail, then set the glass down and leaned across the bar. "Okay, so fill me in on the celebration of life for George. Did anyone break down and admit to killing him like in the movies?"

"Very funny. I know you think I'm an amateur—and of course you're correct. I very much am one. But I'm also a pretty good observer of detail. And I did in fact witness a few things this morning that might be of interest to you."

Amy leaned in even closer. "Do tell."

"Okay, first off, as I'd hoped, all the usual suspects were there." Valerie glanced down the bar to make sure no one was listening before going on. "My next-door neighbor Larry Kaimana; Irene Souza up the street; Tammy Barker—you know the one at the ceramics studio who Sean is, or was, dating; Emily Higa; Don Ribeiro; and of course Sue Ikeda."

Amy nodded. "I'm pretty sure I interviewed all of them."

"So, when I got there, it was just me, Sue, and Irene, and I helped with setting everything up. The next to arrive was Emily, and we started talking about how we were going to run everything—you know, in what order we should have the talking, the eating, and the orchid giveaway. We all kind of looked at Sue, but she shook her head and said, 'No, I can't do it.' Which wasn't surprising. You often don't see the family talking at a memorial service."

"Right," said Amy. "It's usually a minister or someone like that who runs the thing."

"Well, in this case there was no minister, so Emily volunteered to talk first and kind of run things."

"Interesting."

"Yeah, I thought so too. Though I guess it makes sense, since she's known George since grade school. And she is kind of bossy, as well," Valerie added with a chuckle. "So, at that point, the guests started to arrive, and—"

At the ringing of Amy's phone, Valerie stopped. "You need to get that?"

Amy pulled out the device, then nodded. "Yeah, it's the station," she said, standing up. "Hold that thought." She punched accept, then walked over to the restrooms, where it was quiet enough to hear.

When she returned to the bar, her brow was furrowed. "That was the watch captain. Sue Ikeda's been taken to the hospital, and I need to get over there ASAP."

"What? Do you know what happened?"

"He didn't give any details other than saying she was transported there by ambulance at about five thirty." Amy looked with longing at the remains of her G&T. "Hopefully I can come back later, but don't wait up for me, as they say. These things tend to take a while. Oh, and let me know what I owe for the drink and sandwich; I'll pay you later."

And with that, the cop strode across the lānai toward the front of the restaurant.

As soon as she was gone, Valerie pulled out her own phone and called Kristen. "Did you hear about Sue Ikeda?" she asked when her wife picked up.

"The whole neighborhood's talking about it," she said. "Apparently Sue told Don after everyone else had left her house that she was feeling weak and needed to go lie down. But then a few hours ago, when he came back to check up on her, he found her on the bathroom floor and called an ambulance."

"Uh-oh. On the bathroom floor? Does that mean . . .?"

"Yeah. The same exact symptoms as for all those people after the orchid society dinner."

Valerie could feel the blood drain from her face. "Oh, no."

TWENTY-ONE

By the time Valerie got home from work at the Gecko, Kristen was in bed and, on being awakened by Valerie's arrival, insisted there was nothing either of them could do right then. "Can't we wait till tomorrow to talk about it?" she'd said, groggy from sleep.

So there Valerie was early the next morning, sitting on the lānai, coffee in hand, trying to make sense of this new, ugly development to the case. The rain had returned, again mirroring Valerie's mood. Water streamed off the metal roof onto the grass, and it was chilly enough that she wore leggings and a fleece jacket. Both Kristen and Sean were still in bed—Valerie had been too amped up to sleep in—so she had her morose thoughts all to herself.

No one else who'd attended the celebration of life appeared to have taken ill—at least no one had yet reported any such thing to Valerie. Which was good. But also highly suspicious, to her mind. Did someone specifically target Sue and put something in her food or drink?

She looked up as Kristen joined her outside. "Any news about Sue?"

Valerie shook her head. "The hospital won't tell me anything except that she's a patient there."

"Well, at least that means she's still alive," said Kristen with a grimace.

Valerie slumped in her chair and stared out at the white egret who'd settled onto the far corner of the yard and was pecking at insects in the soggy lawn. Pua, too, was eyeing the large bird, but had yet to jump up and give it chase. They'd learned that, notwithstanding her being a local poi dog, she was none too fond of the rain.

"So, you think it was intentional?" Kristen asked, sitting down next to Valerie on the couch. "As opposed to food poisoning?"

"Given the symptoms, the fact that she's the only one who got sick, the group of people in attendance—not to mention what happened to George—I'd say that's a good bet."

Neither spoke for a bit. The egret, perhaps sensing the little dog shaking in excitement as she watched its every move, finally flapped clumsily off, taking wing over the house to a new, more peaceful spot to pursue its breakfast.

The chiming of Valerie's phone caused them both to start. "Ah, it's Amy," Valerie said. "Hopefully she can tell us something." She punched accept. "Hey, girl. Any news about Sue?"

"Not much. But they say she should be okay. I told them last night to treat it as a possible arsenic poisoning, so I guess they did whatever you do for that. She was already on an IV, and they were about to run a bunch of tests when I finally left last night after midnight. When I called this morning, they said she'd stabilized, but they were going to keep her for a day or two for monitoring, given her age and health history. I'll be going up there later this morning to take her statement, and hopefully by then they'll know if she has arsenic in her system. But that's not actually the main reason I'm calling."

"Oh?"

"Yeah. I'm wondering if you'd be willing to meet me at Sue's house in a few minutes. I want to check out the scene, and since you were helping out yesterday, I figured you'd know where everything was and what I might want to be looking for."

"Sure, I could do that. It'll be good to be doing something instead of just sitting here worrying. But I guess that means so much for your day in Kona with Maile."

Amy sighed. "Yeah, the life of a cop. But if there's any chance of us actually making it as a couple, I guess it's good she finds out now."

"Probably right. Okay, see you in a few."

Valerie filled Kristen in on what Amy had said, then headed indoors for a quick bite to eat—peanut butter and honey on toasted Hawaiian sweet bread—before grabbing an umbrella and heading up to Sue's house.

Amy wasn't yet there when she made her way into the back

yard. The long table was still pushed up against the carport, and two black plastic garbage bags sat next to it. *Best not touch anything till she gets here*, Valerie decided, and walked over to check out what orchids were still left under the makeshift greenhouse.

Not many. The orchid society had clearly been happy to help Sue get rid of George's plants.

But had one of them been happy to try to get rid of Sue, as well?

"Aloha!"

Valerie turned to see Amy standing next to the table, under cover of the carport eave. In her hand was a leather satchel, which she set down under the table.

"Not the greatest weather for searching for clues," said Valerie.

Amy smiled. "Hey, it's Hilo. Nevertheless . . ." She glanced up at the dark sky. "We might as well get out of the rain while we talk. I'd like to hear about what happened at the celebration of life before I start investigating the scene."

Valerie followed the cop onto the covered lānai, which held three rusted patio chairs, as well as a wooden table in great need of refinishing. Upon the table sat the row of orchids with colorful blooms that Don had left for Sue.

"Here," said Valerie, holding out a brown paper bag for Amy.

"What's this? Evidence?"

"No," said Valerie with a laugh. "It's the medianoche sandwich you ordered last night. I didn't want it to go to waste, so had it wrapped up for you to go."

"Wow, great," said Amy, taking the bag. "Thanks. I'll likely need it today, since I may very well not have the chance to get any lunch." She took a seat in one of the rickety metal chairs and pulled out a pen and a small spiral pad of paper. "Not gonna record it this time, since the rain on the metal roof'll drown out anything we say. Okay, so tell me what you remember from yesterday. You know, the logistics of how everything went. I take it there was food and drink?"

"Coffee, tea, pastries, and donuts." Valerie shook the water off her umbrella and set it down. "People helped themselves to drinks when they got there, but before anyone ate anything, we began with folks talking about George—what a great guy he was and all that. Emily started it off, as I said last night, and then others joined in as well."

"Was there anything anyone said—or didn't say, perhaps—that struck you as odd or important in any way?"

"About George, you mean?"

"Right," said Amy. "During the part where people were recounting stories about him and his life."

Valerie chewed her lip as she stared at a faded ti leaf lei hanging from a nail on one of the posts supporting the lānai. "Okay, well, this isn't so much about what people said as how a couple of them reacted to what other people said. When Emily was talking about how generous George was to other orchid society members, Don was totally rolling his eyes. Which makes sense, if he really believed the guy stole those hybrids from him. But it did seem a little odd to be that obvious about it at his memorial."

"Uh-huh," was all Amy had to say, which Valerie didn't know whether to take as meaning she agreed with this sentiment, or simply that she was listening to the story.

Deciding that it likely meant the latter, Valerie continued on. "But that just goes to show he isn't the one who poisoned the vanilla. 'Cause if he did, wouldn't he want to hide the anger he felt for George?"

"Seems like it's a little late for that," said Amy. "Given that he's apparently already told the entire orchid society what he thought George had done."

"True. And I did notice that the hybrids were gone by the time of the orchid giveaway, and I'm sure it was Don who took them."

Amy jotted down a few notes, then sat back in her chair. "So, you said there were two people's reactions you found interesting. Whose was the other one?"

"It was Sue, when Larry was talking about how much George loved the orchid society and how he thought of it as his 'ohana, and I swear Sue was giving Larry the evil eye."

"Oh, yeah?"

"Yeah. She looked really annoyed. I think she was actually pretty jealous of the orchid society—how much time and energy George put into it, as opposed to paying attention to her. I gather they didn't have many friends outside of the society, and she's not even that into orchids." Valerie shook her head. "But making her out to be a suspect doesn't make any sense if we're now thinking that whoever poisoned that vanilla was also the one who tried to poison Sue."

"Are we thinking that?" asked Amy, cocking her head.

"Oh, come on. It has to be the same person, don't you think?"

"We don't even know yet if Sue was intentionally poisoned. But go on. Was there anything else that anyone said or did during the talking part of the memorial that you found of interest?"

Valerie thought a moment. "Just that when Larry was going on about what a good neighbor George was, and about his long history in the neighborhood, I could have sworn he gave me a look. You know, as if to say, 'unlike *you*, haole.' But then again, I could have just imagined it, given my past history with him."

"Right." Amy made a few more notes on her pad, then started to stand. "Well, maybe I should have a look around the yard."

"Wait. I haven't told you the two most important things, which happened later on."

The cop sat back down. "Oh, I thought you were done."

"Well, you asked about what happened during the 'official' talking about George part, and these were both after that. So first of all, I don't know if you know, but the Souzas have a vacation rental in their 'ohana unit, and I don't think it's got a permit."

Amy waved a hand. "We can't go after all of those, or we'd be doing nothing but that all day long."

"No, that's not the point. The point is, Sue told me yesterday that she and George were getting fed up with the noise from the renters, and that when George complained to Irene and

Hugo they just blew him off. So then George told them he was going to make a complaint to the planning department."

"And did he?"

"No, he was killed before he was able to do so." Valerie leaned forward. "And these are the people who were already pissed off about George's tree blocking their ocean view."

"Huh. That is interesting."

Valerie allowed herself a smile. "And that's not all. So, have you noticed all the feral cats in the neighborhood?"

"I have, and it seems to be getting worse of late."

"Kristen and I haven't lived here long enough to know, but that's apparently the consensus of others in the neighborhood. People were talking yesterday at the memorial about how someone's probably been feeding them, hence the increase in the population, and then Sue said that George had been trying to trap the cats but had been unsuccessful. And then get this: Larry next made a comment about how you just needed a good hunting dog to take care of the problem." Valerie paused and gave Amy a meaningful look.

"That's a pretty harsh statement, I agree," said the cop, "but I'm not sure where exactly you're going with this."

"Well, first off, I think I know who's been feeding the cats. It just came to me as I was thinking back on any odd behavior I'd seen yesterday. After Larry made that comment about hunting dogs, I looked around at the people there, and Tammy was totally glaring at him. I mean, it was like she had venom in her eyes. And then later on, I overheard the two of them arguing in Sue's kitchen. And this is the really interesting part. While they were arguing, Tammy called Larry a 'murderer.' At the time, I thought it must mean she thought that he killed George. But now I'm thinking it makes more sense that she was accusing him of having his dog Akoni kill one of the cats she'd been feeding."

"Are you suggesting she might have poisoned the vanilla to get to Larry?" Amy thought a moment, then frowned. "But if Tammy only came to that conclusion yesterday because of what Larry said at the celebration of life, why would she have tried to poison him at the dinner?"

"Good point," said Valerie. "But maybe what he said yesterday was just affirming something she already knew. Or maybe she has a grudge against the neighborhood as a whole for wanting to get rid of her beloved cats. From what I can tell, folks have been complaining about them for quite some time. And there certainly were a lot of people from the neighborhood at that orchid society dinner. That would explain putting the arsenic in something most everyone would eat. And hey, we do know Tammy has ready access to arsenic."

Valerie was becoming more and more excited as she talked all this through. "Oh!" she said with a clap of the hands. "And when Sue said yesterday that she and George had been trying to trap the cats, maybe Tammy just lost it and decided to poison Sue then and there."

"Okay, well, that does sound like one of the better motives I've heard so far." Amy stood up again. "So let's see if I can find something to help prove any of these theories."

They walked back down to the table. "I guess this is where I should start," Amy said, nodding at the trash bags.

"You thinking you'll find traces of arsenic on one of the cups or plates?"

"Who knows. We should have the blood and urine tests back today, which will tell us if that's in fact what made Sue sick, but in the meantime, I'm hoping we might find something here."

The rain had now thankfully tapered off to a drizzle, but Valerie nevertheless opened her umbrella once more. The cop, who didn't seem to even take notice of the rain, bent to pick up the satchel she'd left under the table and pulled out a box of nitrile gloves. Snapping on a pair, she grabbed the first garbage bag, took it up onto the lānai out of the rain, and dumped out its contents.

Amy gazed at all the paper plates and coffee cups, crumpled napkins, pink cardboard boxes, sugar packets, and spent tea bags strewn across the wooden planks. "I don't suppose you happen to know which cup and plate Sue used," she said with a sigh.

Valerie slowly shook her head. But then she spied a cup with bright pink lipstick on its rim. "Oh wait, I actually think I do!"

Reaching down, she was about to pick up the cup when Amy said, "No, don't touch it."

Valerie quickly pulled back her hand. "Sorry. Stupid reflex. But anyway, Sue always wears pink lipstick, and I've noticed it come off on the cups she drinks from. If none of the other ones have lipstick on them, it's a pretty good bet that one was Sue's."

Amy poked around the pile and, discovering no other cup with pink on its rim, fetched the second bag and emptied it out, as well. "There's another one," she said, pointing to a cup with a darker, more brownish shade of lipstick on it.

"No, Sue's shade was definitely lighter—'old lady pink,' I'd call that shade. Not that she's all that much older than me," Valerie added with a snort.

"Well, I'll take them both to be tested, just in case."

They were interrupted by a loud chirp from Amy's pocket. Taking the call, she walked out into the yard—once again ignoring the rain—listened to the person on the other end, then nodded and ended the call.

"That was the lab," she said, returning to the lānai. "It was indeed arsenic."

"Dang," was all Valerie could muster.

Amy bagged and labeled the two cups, then bent to pick through the rest of the trash. "Do you know what Sue drank yesterday, by any chance?"

"I do, as a matter of fact. Earl Grey tea. I even got a refill for her. Oh." Valerie put a hand to her mouth and turned toward Amy, eyes wide.

"What?"

"Which means my prints will be on the cup along with Sue's."

"Well, at least we know in advance to expect that," said Amy as she pawed through the trash looking for used tea bags. There were only a few—this had clearly been more of a coffee crowd—but in the end she came up with two that had Earl Grey labels, which she placed into separate evidence bags.

"Okay, I guess that's it for now. But I should keep all the rest of this for the time being, just in case."

Valerie watched her shove all the trash back into the two bags. "You haven't said anything about it," she said as the cop stood back up and stretched her back, "but I have to think I'm one of your suspects, right? Since I helped out at both the dinner and the memorial yesterday?"

"No more than anyone else," the cop said with a light laugh.

TWENTY-TWO

Back home out on the lānai, Valerie returned to her brooding. It had now been two weeks since George Ikeda's death, and she'd come no closer to figuring out who was responsible. Not only that, but she was clearly still on Amy's list of suspects—not only of his murder, but now of the attempted murder of Sue, as well. For although Amy had tried to make a joke of it when Valerie had asked the question, the bottom line was the cop had responded with a form of "yes."

So, who could have done it—or rather, both of those things? For it seemed likely that the culprit was one and the same for the two poisonings. (There was, of course, always the possibility that the attempt on Sue's life was a copy-cat poisoning, she realized.)

But in either case, *why*? And why go after Sue yesterday?

Could the person have been going after the entire crowd at the celebration of life, but they'd been foiled somehow, so that only Sue was affected? Maybe there was a clue she'd missed—something someone had said or done that would answer her questions.

Closing her eyes, Valerie leaned back on the couch and thought back to what she'd heard and seen at George's memorial:

Emily had talked about knowing George when they were kids, and how kind and generous he'd always been.

Larry had similarly recounted how much George had done for the orchid society and the neighborhood—causing both Don and Sue to have notably negative reactions.

Okay, so, who else had talked?

Several people Valerie didn't know, who'd spoken of his helpfulness as a CPA. *Oh—and then the orchid society treasurer. What had she said?*

How he'd taught her the basics of bookkeeping . . . and something else. Valerie thought a moment. *Right.* It was how George had encouraged her to cut costs to save money for the society. And that wasn't the first time someone had mentioned George's thriftiness, Valerie seemed to recall. But who was the other person?

And then she remembered: Emily had said as much when explaining why they'd chosen the menu they had for the dinner.

But could George's thriftiness somehow be relevant to his murder? Something niggled at her that said it was.

She was interrupted from her thoughts by raucous laughter coming from the kitchen. A minute later, Sean came outside, followed by—to Valerie's great surprise—Tammy. They had drinks in their hands and seemed startled to see her there, sitting on the couch.

"Oh," said Sean. "Sorry. I didn't know you were home. We decided to have an early cocktail hour. Would you like a G&T?"

"Thanks, but three o'clock's a little early for me," said Valerie. "This old lady gets kind of tired when she starts drinking too early."

Tammy giggled. This wasn't likely their first drink of the day, Valerie decided. "You sure?" she said. "I brought over a bottle of Hendrick's."

"Nice—that's a great gin. Much better than the kind we usually keep around the house. Maybe when five o'clock rolls around?"

"If there's any left," said Sean with a grin. "So where's Aunt Kristen?"

"She and her friend Diane went to the movies at the Palace—some Mexican film that's up for an Oscar. It sounded good, but I decided I needed to stay home and chill this afternoon. So . . ." Valerie paused, glancing from Sean to Tammy, unsure how to ask the obvious question.

"So, what's going on with us two?" Sean took a seat and gestured for Tammy to do the same. "Well, I realized I really missed hangin' out with Tammy, so I sent her a text to see if she wanted to meet up. I wasn't sure after what I did last week if she'd want anything to do with me, but lo and behold, here we are."

"Lemme guess: You met up at a bar?"

"Yeah, at the Gecko, actually. Jun says to say hey, by the way. But then we realized if we wanted more to drink, we shouldn't drive, so we stopped at the liquor store and came here." Sean took a slug from his cocktail, then frowned. "Oh shoot, I haven't even asked: What's the news about Sue Ikeda? Is she going to be okay?"

"Yeah, it looks like it—at this point, anyway. They're gonna keep her at the hospital for another day or two for observation, just to make sure."

"Oh, thank goodness," said Tammy. "I'm on the early shift tomorrow, so I'll be sure to stop by and see how she's doing. Do they know yet what made her sick?"

Valerie paused before answering. "Okay, I guess I can tell you, since Amy told me. It was arsenic poisoning, just like at the orchid dinner."

"Oh . . ." Tammy glanced nervously at Sean, who patted her hand.

"It's okay," he said. "I'm over all that. And besides, why on earth would you want to do harm to Sue Ikeda?"

"Yeah, um . . ." Valerie cleared her throat, not sure she should bring up the topic, but feeling she had to do so. "Speaking of wanting to do harm, I need to ask you about yesterday. What you said to Larry . . ."

"Ah." Tammy looked away, then blinked several times, as if trying to control her emotions.

"What is it?" asked Sean. He turned to Valerie. "What the heck happened yesterday?"

"I'll let her answer that."

They both waited as Tammy took several deep breaths, then drank from her gin and tonic. "I'm sorry," she finally said. "I'm still really upset, is all. It's about Rascal—one of the cats I've sort of adopted."

"So you're the one who's been feeding the neighborhood cats?" asked Valerie.

"Right. And one of them—I call him Rascal—has been

missing for about a week now. I know that feral cats tend to wander, but he's never been gone for this long before since I started feeding them."

"What's he look like?" asked Valerie.

"A big orange guy with a torn right ear."

"Oh, I saw him a while back, running across the street in front of Emily's house."

Tammy's face lit up. "Really? How long ago, exactly?"

Valerie thought back to her walk to Coconut Island with Kristen. "Over a week ago—maybe nine or ten days?"

Her shoulders slumped. "No, that was before he went missing. Damn. So anyway, when Larry said what he did yesterday, well—"

Sean interrupted her. "What did he say?"

"That you just need a good hunting dog to take care of the problem. The cats in the neighborhood, he meant. So now I'm sure he had his dog go after Rascal and . . ."

Tammy burst into tears, not able to finish her thought. But Valerie knew from the word she'd hurled at Larry exactly what Tammy believed had happened to the cat.

"So, until yesterday, you didn't suspect Larry or his dog of having anything to do with Rascal's disappearance?" she asked.

"No," said Tammy, wiping her eyes. "Why would I? I mean, I know lots of people in the neighborhood don't like the cats, but I had no reason to think anyone would actually harm them."

Sean was shaking his head. "I knew that guy was trouble. He let Akoni—his hunting dog—out to attack Pua last week, right?" He turned to Valerie for confirmation.

"Well, I don't think Larry actually *set* Akoni on Pua," said Valerie. "Though I have to say he was rather slow in coming to get the dog when he did go after her."

"Same thing," said Sean with a snort. "Or close enough to it."

At the ringing of a cell phone, all three checked their pockets. "Mine," said Valerie, pulling out the device.

Sean shook his glass, now reduced to melted ice cubes. "We'll let you talk in private. Time for another round, in any case."

As Tammy followed him into the kitchen, Valerie punched accept. "Hey, Emily. What's up?"

"Sorry to bother you, but I couldn't help noticing you coming out of Sue's back yard a while back with Amy, and I was just wondering if she gave you any news about how Sue's doing."

"All I know at this point is that it looks like she's gonna be okay. Oh, except—" Valerie paused, not sure if she should tell Emily about the arsenic.

"What?"

I already told Sean and Tammy, Valerie reasoned. Besides, she was interested to hear how Emily would react to the news. "So, the lab tests came back a few hours ago, and it turns out Sue had arsenic in her system."

"No way. That is so creepy."

"You're telling me."

"Wow," said Emily. "I actually had a text from Amy earlier this morning saying she wanted to set up an interview to talk with me tomorrow. Now I know why." She let out a stream of air. "I can't believe it's happening all over again. Was anyone else affected?"

"Not that I know of. So the question is, were they going after Sue specifically, or did she just end up being the unlucky person who ate or drank whatever was poisoned?"

"Yep, that's certainly the question. Too bad I don't have the answer. Oh—" There was a clicking sound, then silence. Valerie was about to hang up when Emily came back on the line. "Sorry. It's Amy calling. Can I call you right back?"

"Sure. No problem." Valerie set the phone on the rattan table. Through the kitchen window, she could see Sean and Tammy making their drinks. Sean held the distinctive black bottle of Hendrick's gin with its white diamond label in one hand while gesturing with the other. Then, as she watched, he leaned over and gave Tammy a kiss.

Turning away to allow them their private moment, she frowned. There it was again—that niggling feeling that she was missing something obvious. It seemed now unlikely it had been Tammy who poisoned Sue's tea, but what could it be that she was missing?

The ringing of her phone made her jump, so caught up in her thoughts was she. "Hey," she said to Emily. "So, what did Amy want?"

"Just to change the time of our interview tomorrow. She's coming by my house at noon."

"Well, she already interviewed me, and I haven't yet been arrested, so I guess I'm off the hook for now." Loud laughter made Valerie look back into the kitchen, where Sean and Tammy were now clinking glasses.

Ah ha! That's what it is.

"So, can I ask you something about George, since you knew him so well?"

"Sure," said Emily. "What would you like to know?"

"It's about what that woman said about him yesterday—the treasurer of the orchid society."

"Ana?"

"Right. She said something about George encouraging her to cut corners to save money, and a bunch of people laughed, which suggests he was known to be . . . thrifty, shall we say. And I seem to recall you saying something similar about him with regard to the menu planning for the benefit dinner. So, was he frugal in his general life?"

Emily chuckled. "Oh, yes. Even as a kid he'd save his pennies when the rest of us would spend our pocket money on crack seed and shave ice. And Sue once told me he was annoyed that she'd bought poke from Sack N Save when they could have made their own for half the price. But why do you ask?"

"It's probably not important. I just have a hunch about something, is all. I'll let you know once I check it out."

"Ooooo . . . very mysterious," said Emily with a laugh. "I'll be anxiously awaiting the results of your investigation."

"Yeah, we'll see if it pans out to anything. Talk to you later."

Valerie ended the call and was about to head into the kitchen when she noticed a shadow through the hibiscus hedge running along Larry's driveway. The form was initially stationary, but as she watched, it moved slowly away.

Had Larry been eavesdropping on her conversation with Emily—or with Sean and Tammy?

She sat for a few more minutes out on the lānai with Sean and Tammy, pretending to listen as they described a trip they were planning to Waikīkī in two weeks' time. "We're gonna stay at the Royal Hawaiian Hotel, visit Diamond Head, eat at Duke's, and hang out on the beach," said Sean, his eyes shining with excitement. "I can't believe I've been in Hawai'i this long and still haven't been to Honolulu."

"Sounds fun," said Valerie. But her mind was elsewhere.

After about fifteen minutes, she excused herself and went inside. Walking into the living room, she peered out the window and looked up and down the street. No one seemed to be out and about in the neighborhood.

Good.

Valerie opened the door, found her rubber slippahs among the jumble of footwear scattered about the front porch, and headed uphill. The rain had now stopped, but a stream of water was flowing down both sides of the road and pooling in people's lawns.

Glancing down Larry's driveway, she saw that his truck was gone. Which meant either that it hadn't been him lurking behind the hibiscus hedge, or he'd left home soon thereafter. Valerie couldn't remember ever seeing her neighbor go anywhere on foot—he always drove away in his enormous red truck.

She continued up the street and, on reaching the Ikeda house, stopped for a moment, taking in the scene. Sue, she knew, was still in the hospital, and Don's SUV was not parked out front. Nor could she see anyone in their yards or peering out their windows, wondering what the heck she was doing standing there in the middle of the road.

Okay, now or never. Taking a deep breath, she walked quickly down the driveway and into George and Sue's carport. She waited a minute to allow her eyes time to adjust to the dark, then scanned the shelves, looking for . . . what?

She'd know it when she saw it.

The table in the middle of the carport held only a few black plastic pots, as well as a bag of potting oil.

On one side of the shed, as she remembered, sat gardening supplies: more potting soil and black plastic pots, orchid mix bark, fertilizer, and rolls of wire and green tape. Behind them on a pegboard hung different size shovels, two rakes, a weed-whacker and leaf blower, as well as various hand tools such as trowels and pruning shears.

Not what she was looking for.

She turned to face the other wall. These shelves held a mishmash of objects. Some were still useful—old cans of paint, wood stain, sealant, and turpentine, as well as boxes of screws and nails and rolls of electrical wire. But a lot of it was junk, in her opinion. Things they no longer needed but weren't yet willing to relegate to the garbage can.

Poking through the items, she discovered an old VCR player, a rotary telephone that must have dated from the 1960s, a bag of tangled cords from outdated electronic equipment, and a box of about two dozen empty spice bottles. Almost hidden behind the box of glass spice bottles stood several larger clear plastic bottles.

She stepped closer to examine them, then froze.

No way.

Her hunch had been correct.

Looking about her, she found what looked to be a clean rag and used it to pull one of the bottles out from behind the box. "Fleischmann's Royal Vodka," the label said. And it was half full.

"Hey, whatcha doin' in there!"

Valerie turned and nearly dropped the bottle when she saw who it was.

TWENTY-THREE

Valerie's eyes went from Larry Kaimana to Akoni, who stood at his side, unleashed. Seeing the dog's bared teeth, Valerie backed up a pace.

"Scoping out someone else's garage now, yah?" said Larry. "Though I didn't think you'd stoop so low as to steal a bottle of liquor."

"It's evidence."

His eyes narrowed. "Is that so?"

Akoni—as if sensing the tension between the two—let out a low growl, then looked up nervously at Larry.

Down the driveway, Valerie could see the big red truck parked out on the street. Had Larry overheard her conversation with Emily and then laid in wait to see what she was up to?

"Let's see this so-called 'evidence' of yours," he said, advancing on her with his hand extended.

Valerie retreated further into the carport. "No," she said, moving the vodka behind her back. "I'm going to give it to Amy."

And no way do I want you making off with and destroying a bottle that may well have your fingerprints on it.

Larry glanced down at Akoni, who was still monitoring his every move, and laughed. "I no tink you'll be much of a match for dis one," he said, then looked back up at Valerie. "You want I let 'um go? It's your choice."

Should she cave and give him the bottle, or stand her ground? The question was whether he was bluffing or if he'd actually go so far as to sic Akoni on her.

The dog was now shaking with excitement, his growls having turned into urgent whines. Terrified he'd lunge at her even if not given the command by Larry, Valerie stood frozen in place, afraid to make any move.

"Hey, what's going on here!" a voice cried out, causing all three to turn and look.

Oh, thank God.

Emily came striding down the driveway, her slippahs slapping loudly on the wet pavement. "Have you let that dog out again, Larry? I've told you before you need to keep him on a leash or I'm going to have to call animal control."

"Eh," said Larry with a snort. "He's completely under my control. Sit, Akoni."

The dog sat.

Emily and Larry stared at each other in a stand-off while Valerie shook out her free arm and released a long breath.

After a bit, Larry finally looked away. "Whatevahs," he said with a wave of the hand. "Akoni, come." Man and dog walked down the driveway and climbed into the truck.

Once it had pulled away, Emily turned to Valerie. "His bark is worse than his bite."

"Whose?" said Valerie. "Larry or Akoni?"

Emily laughed. "Both, I suppose. Though I do wonder what you're doing in Sue's carport."

"Just investigating something, is all."

"Ah, the mysterious hunch you told me about. So did you find what you were looking for? And what, may I ask, does it have to do with all those questions about George being thrifty?" She eyed Valerie—who still held the bottle behind her back—with curiosity. "And I'm also wondering what you might be hiding there."

Valerie shrugged, then showed her the vodka. "I found this over on that shelf," she said with a nod toward the clutter of junk, "and I'm pretty sure Larry wanted to take it from me. I'm thinking it might be important evidence."

"Oh, really? Let's have a look," said Emily, stepping forward.

Valerie retreated a few paces. "No. Like I told Larry, I need to give it to Amy in case it has any fingerprints on it."

She studied Emily's face, which seemed to have tensed on seeing the vodka. *Was that fear?*

"It's okay; I just want to get a better look at that bottle," said Emily. And then, as she continued to advance, now reaching out for the vodka, Valerie had a horrible realization.

"Ohmygod, it was you," she blurted out.

"Whatever do you mean?"

Valerie was now backed up against the carport wall, with no place to go. "Except it was *Sue* that was meant to be poisoned—not George. And not at the orchid society dinner, but much earlier. Six months earlier, to be exact."

Emily had now stopped her forward motion and stood eyeing Valerie cautiously—like a cat stalking its prey. "Okay," she said, "I'm thinking you're going to give that bottle to me right now, and then we can both walk away with no fuss."

But Valerie could tell she had her attention. Curiosity was staying Emily's hand—at least for the moment. Hoping desperately that someone might come down the street whom she could call out to for help, Valerie chattered on.

"One day about six months ago when you came to visit George, you brought along some arsenic. I don't know if it was from your own garage or maybe some you found here in the carport—or perhaps you even stole it from the ceramics studio—it doesn't really matter. But your plan was to put it into a bottle of liquor, since you knew that Sue drank cocktails, but George no longer did.

"And lo and behold, there was a bottle of vodka sitting on the counter when you arrived. What you didn't realize, though, is that Sue had switched to gin once George stopped drinking. And more important, they kept two different kinds of vodka at the house: an expensive brand—the Grey Goose—that was used for cocktails, and the cheap kind that George used for his vanilla extract. Because, as I now know, he would never waste an expensive brand like Grey Goose on making vanilla. But you must have come to the house when he was making the extract, and so that was the vodka that was out on the counter that day."

Holding up the Fleischmann's vodka, Valerie allowed herself a grim smile. "You put the arsenic in the wrong bottle."

Emily's shoulders had slumped, but the look she was giving Valerie was one of pure hatred.

"I bet you were waiting, day after day, for Sue to take ill from the poison," Valerie went on, "and when she never did, you must have been completely confused. Had she quit drinking? Did she switch vodka brands? And I'm guessing that when everyone got sick after the orchid dinner, you were as baffled as the rest of us. But then when George died and they said it was arsenic poisoning, you realized the ugly truth about what had happened.

"I can't even imagine how angry and frustrated you must have been. It had to have tormented you, that you'd been the cause of his death—the love of your life. But then you came up with a crafty plan to try again. At George's celebration of life, you'd finally celebrate the death of his beloved wife by putting arsenic in her tea." Valerie shook her head in disgust. "Ironic, I'll grant you, but sick, very sick."

And then, as she'd hoped, a car drove slowly by the house. "Hey! Stop!" Valerie yelled, waving madly. But whoever was at the wheel didn't appear to notice and instead kept on down the street.

Emily smirked once the car had passed. "That's some story," she said, her lips forming an ugly curl. "Too bad no one else will ever hear it." Then, with a quick glance to her right, she swiveled around, grabbed a shovel from the wall of the carport, and took a swing at Valerie's head.

Ducking, Valerie was able to avoid the blow, which instead came down with a loud *crash* upon the cement floor. But Emily immediately came at her again. Screaming for help, Valerie looked frantically around and, spotting a piece of wood leaning against the wall, dropped the vodka bottle and grabbed hold of it and held it up as a shield when the shovel came at her for a second time.

She succeeded in parrying the blow, but the impact of the shovel was strong enough to knock the two-by-four from her hands and send her sprawling to the ground.

"You'll never understand," said Emily, panting as she stood over Valerie. "Sue and I were *friends* back in high school. But then she does *that*? Woos George away from me as soon as he comes home from college? He was indeed the love of my life—no one could ever take his place. And Sue never even acknowledged what she did, acting as if we were still good buddies all these years—like nothing had ever happened between us."

"But that must have been fifty years ago," said Valerie, praying she could keep Emily talking. "Why try to kill her now, all this time later?"

Emily looked as if she might start to cry—were it not for the hardness to her eyes and the tightening of her grip upon the shovel. "Yes. Fifty years for me to live with it all. Her duplicity. Her utter selfishness. And all that time on the same street, seeing them together every day—the perfect, happy couple, her with that simpering smile?

"But at least I got to still spend time with George at the orchid society—and without *her*, since she never cared to take even the slightest interest in his biggest passion." Emily shook her head in disgust. "But then about six months ago he confided in me that Sue was urging him to step away from the society because of his liver condition. He really didn't want to but was considering doing so solely to appease her.

"And that was the last straw. A few days later when I came across a box of rat poison in my carport, I realized I simply couldn't take it any longer. Sue needed to pay for what she'd done."

"But maybe she didn't know you still loved George," said Valerie, trying to buy more time to do . . . what? She could see nothing within reach as she lay helplessly on the floor of the carport. "Maybe she thought you'd been the one to break it off when he left college on the Mainland."

"And maybe pigs fly," said Emily with a sneer. "Sue knew exactly what she was doing. Just like I did when I put that arsenic in her tea yesterday."

As she raised the shovel once more, Valerie threw out her arms protectively, watching in horror as the blade hovered above her . . .

. . . only to come crashing down behind Emily, who now let out a shriek of her own.

A blur of brown and white was leaping up and snapping at her hands. "Get him off me!" Emily screamed as the dog snarled and tore at her floral blouse.

"Akoni—leave it! Dass enough!"

The dog backed off but continued its frenzied barking as

Larry came charging into the carport and kicked the shovel out of Emily's reach. "You pupule or what, sistah?" he said.

Wrapping her arms about her, all Emily could do was shake her head and stare nervously at Akoni.

Larry offered Valerie a hand to help her off the ground, then motioned for the dog to sit. Once he'd obeyed, Larry turned back to Valerie. "You can thank Akoni for dis. He wen' go lōlō just now, takin' off up da street aftah hearin' you guys makin' some kine racket up here."

"Thanks." Valerie let out a stream of air, then bent to examine her right knee, from which a thin stream of blood ran down her shin. "To the both of you," she added with a nod to Akoni.

The dog sat calmly, gazing up at his caretaker, and Larry gave him a pat on the head. "So," he said to Emily, who hadn't moved and was still eyeing Akoni warily. "What we gonna do wit' you?"

Valerie reached for her phone. "I say it's time for the police to take over." But before she could pull the device from her pocket, Akoni tensed once more, the hair on his back springing up in a stiff line along his spine. Both Valerie and Emily flinched as the dog jumped up and let out a deep growl, his body shaking in excitement.

But then Valerie realized it wasn't them he was focused on. She followed his gaze and saw a cat slinking across the driveway, ears back, its full attention on the quivering dog.

Ha! Valerie's shoulders relaxed. It was a big orange tabby with a torn right ear.

So Akoni hadn't harmed Rascal, after all.

"No make," said Larry, and the dog immediately lay down. They watched as the cat made its cautious way across the Ikedas' front yard, then darted uphill toward Tammy's house.

"See, I told you," said Larry. "He's completely in my control."

Valerie smiled. "Good dog," she said, then pulled the phone from her pocket and called 911.

"Where's Emily now?" asked Kristen three hours later. She, Valerie, Sean, and Tammy were out on the lānai, chowing down on huli-huli chicken, sesame-shoyu poke bowls, and steamed edamame that Kristen had picked up on her way home from the movie.

"Either still down at the police station being booked or already in jail, I imagine." Valerie ripped a wing from the chicken and licked her fingers. "But I have no idea how long these things take. They certainly spent plenty of time interviewing me."

Sean leaned forward to set his lemonade on the table, then stifled a yawn. "Sorry. I'm not used to day drinking, so even with all this excitement I have to admit I'm pretty sleepy. Anyway, you think there's any chance she'll make bail?"

"I doubt it," said Valerie. "Amy called about an hour ago to say that after they found her fingerprints on that vodka bottle, she caved and admitted to putting arsenic in it. So even though she didn't mean to kill George, she did intend to kill *someone*. Which I'm pretty sure is enough to charge her with first degree murder. Oh, and when they searched her house, they found rat poison with arsenic in it in her carport. They also found traces of arsenic in the paper cup Sue drank her tea from yesterday—which also had Emily's prints on it."

Tammy shivered, notwithstanding the eighty-degree temperature outdoors. "It's all so creepy. I mean, Emily? A murderer? I can hardly believe it."

"If you'd seen the look on her face as she tried to wallop me with that shovel, you'd believe it." It was now Valerie's turn to shudder, as she recalled the terror she'd experienced just hours earlier.

"I'll never be able to look at those dragons at the studio the same way again." Tammy turned to gaze out at the plumeria tree, its pink blossoms ablaze in the late afternoon tropical sun. "I suppose we'll have to get rid of them, in any event," she said after a bit. "I mean, it wouldn't be right to sell artwork by a known murderer, right?"

"I don't know about that," said Sean, "but I wouldn't be surprised if it made the dragons even more valuable. People can be kinda sick that way."

No one had a response to this other than to shrug and take another sip from their drinks.

"Oh," said Valerie, leaning forward suddenly. "I forgot to tell you, Tammy, but I saw that orange cat today."

Tammy let out a squeal and clapped her hands. "Rascal? Really? Where?"

"Up at the Ikeda house, and it looked like he was heading up to your place."

"Thank goodness." She let out a long breath and took a drink from her lemonade. "Oh, and just so you know, I'm going to take him—and any of the other cats that I can catch—down to get neutered and spayed. And Sean said he'll help cover the cost," she said, flashing a smile his way.

Sean shrugged. "It seemed like a nice way to give something back to the neighborhood."

"Atta boy," said Kristen, who then turned to Valerie. "So, what about that guy who says George stole his orchids? Do you think it's true?"

"Don? I don't suppose we'll ever know for sure," said Valerie. "But at least we do know he's not responsible for George's death."

Sean shook his head. "It's amazing, though, how passionate people can get over a simple plant like that."

Valerie turned to gaze at her new Oncidium sitting on the table, its troupe of tiny yellow blooms dancing delicately in the warm breeze. "I think I'm beginning to understand that passion," she said.

RECIPES

Lemongrass Blast

(makes 1 cocktail)

This is a refreshing drink similar to a Moscow Mule, but the blast of lemongrass provides alluring, perfumy notes lacking in the other. In addition, this drink contains only a little ginger beer—as well as a splash of soda water—making it less sweet than its cousin.

Note that the recipe here for simple syrup will make enough for about 6 cocktails.

Ingredients

For the Lemongrass Simple Syrup

1 cup water
½ cup white sugar
¼ cup lemongrass, cut into 1-inch chunks (1–2 stalks)

For the Cocktail

2 oz. vodka
1 tablespoon lemongrass simple syrup
1 tablespoon lime juice, preferable fresh-squeezed
2 oz. ginger beer
1 oz. soda water
1 slice lime, slit halfway through, for garnish
1 thin stalk lemongrass (cut as needed to fit the serving glass), for garnish

Directions

Place the water, sugar, and lemongrass chunks in a small saucepan and bring to a boil over medium heat. Turn the heat down to low and let it simmer, stirring occasionally, until reduced by about half—about 10–15 minutes. Turn off the heat and let the lemongrass sit in the syrup until it's cooled, then discard the lemongrass. The syrup will keep, refrigerated in a covered container, for several days.

Fill a rocks/Old Fashioned glass with 6–8 ice cubes. Pour in vodka, simple syrup, and lime juice and stir to mix. Add the ginger beer and soda and stir once more.

Slide the slit lime slice over the lip of the glass and use the lemongrass stalk as a swizzle stick.

Edamame With Furikake And Sweet Chili Sauce

(serves 4–6)

Steamed or boiled edamame (i.e., soybeans in their pods) are a traditional appetizer in Japan, where the dish is typically served merely with salt. This recipe, however, has a more “local,” Hawaiian feel to it, and makes for a flavorful pre-dinner treat. I like to keep several bags of edamame in the freezer, so I can pull one out to make a quick and tasty pupu when friends stop by for cocktail hour.

Both sweet chili sauce and furikake (a Japanese rice seasoning typically made with dried seaweed and sesame seeds) can be found in the Asian food aisle of most grocery stores. There are a variety of different furikakes available (which also include dried fish, egg, wasabi, sugar, or other ingredients), but I like to use the classic “Nori Kori” mixture, which is a simple blend of seaweed, sesame seeds, and salt.

Ingredients

1 14–16 oz. bag edamame in their pods, frozen
2 tablespoons Thai sweet chili sauce
1 tablespoon furikake
1 tablespoon roasted sesame oil
½ teaspoon salt

Directions

Bring a large pot of water to a boil and dump in the frozen edamame. Let the water come back to a boil, then continue to cook the soybeans for one or two more minutes. Drain and pour into a large bowl.

Add the sesame oil, sweet chili sauce, furikake, and salt. Stir well, so all the bean pods are coated evenly with the seasonings.

Serve along with empty bowls for the discarded pods—as well as with napkins for your sticky fingers!

Japanese-Style Potato Salad

(serves 8–10)

What sets this potato salad apart from its American and German counterparts is the inclusion of a variety of unexpected vegetables (peas, carrots, corn, and cucumber), as well as the use of Kewpie mayonnaise. Using this Japanese brand of mayo—made with yolks only, as well as a special blend of vinegar and spices—is a must, as it's what gives the dish its distinct creaminess and strong hit of umami.

Once you try this potato salad, you'll want to make it again and again.

Kewpie mayonnaise can be found in the Asian food aisle of most supermarkets, or online. (Note that there are two varieties of Kewpie mayo—the Japanese one with a hugging baby, a Kewpie doll, on the label, and an American version depicting a sandwich. Make sure to buy the Japanese one.)

The salad is traditionally made with peeled potatoes, but I prefer to keep the skins on—it's your choice. And either Persian or Japanese cucumbers work best, as they have fewer seeds, though any variety will work fine.

Ingredients

3 pounds Yukon Gold or similar potatoes, cut into 1-inch chunks (about 8 cups)
2 medium carrots, peeled and sliced into ¼-inch discs
4 whole garlic cloves, peeled
2 dried bay leaves
1 tablespoon, plus 1 teaspoon salt, divided (plus more to taste)

1 cup corn kernels (canned, fresh, or frozen)
1 cup peas (fresh or frozen—not canned)
2 tablespoons rice wine vinegar
1¼ cup Kewpie mayonnaise
1 teaspoon black pepper (plus more for garnish)
1 medium cucumber, cut lengthwise into quarters, then thinly sliced
4 green onions, coarsely chopped

Directions

Place potatoes, carrots, garlic, bay leaves, and 1 tablespoon salt into a large pot and cover with cold water by at least 1 inch.

Bring to a boil over high heat, then reduce to medium and simmer, uncovered, until a fork can just pierce the potatoes (about 7 minutes). Add the corn and peas and continue to simmer until the potatoes are fork-tender (about 3 more minutes).

Drain the vegetables, discarding the garlic cloves and bay leaves, and transfer while warm to a large bowl.

Add the vinegar and remaining 1 teaspoon of salt and toss to combine. Add the Kewpie mayonnaise and the black pepper and toss again, until everything is evenly coated with the mayo.

Chill, uncovered, stirring occasionally, until cooled (30–60 minutes). Add the cucumber and two-thirds of the green onions and toss. Season to taste with more salt, if necessary.

Garnish with more black pepper and the rest of the onions.

Butter-Shoyu Chicken

(serves 4)

Shoyu Chicken is a popular dish in Hawai'i ("shoyu," the Japanese word for soy sauce, is what the condiment is commonly called in the islands), and is often part of the traditional plate lunch, along with mac or potato salad and steamed rice. But this version, which includes butter, as well, is truly spectacular, as the glaze of salty and savory shoyu along with sweet and creamy butter makes for an especially rich and tasty dish. (Feel free to use low-sodium soy sauce if you're watching your salt intake.)

Serve the chicken with scoops of steamed rice and a green salad—with the excess sauce used as a gravy for the rice—for a simple and luscious meal.

Ingredients

For the Sauce

¼ cup soy sauce
¼ cup sake
3 tablespoons mirin
1½ tablespoons white sugar

For the Chicken

4 large chicken thighs, bone-in with skin, at room temperature
¼ teaspoon salt
½ teaspoon black pepper

2 tablespoons neutral oil, such as canola
½ cup sake
3 tablespoons unsalted butter
2 green onions, roughly chopped, for garnish

Directions

Combine the sauce ingredients (soy sauce, sake, mirin, and sugar) in a bowl and stir until the sugar is dissolved. Set aside.

Season both sides of the chicken with the salt and pepper.

Heat a large, heavy skillet over medium heat and, when hot, add the oil to the pan. Carefully lay the chicken in the pan, skin side down. Cook uncovered until golden brown and crisp on the bottom, about 5 minutes. Turn the chicken over and continue to cook for 3 more minutes, until lightly browned.

Remove the chicken to a plate and pour off any excess oil in the pan, leaving any brown bits that remain.

Return chicken to the pan and add the ½ cup of sake. Cover and continue to cook over medium heat until the liquid has evaporated and the chicken is cooked through, about 7 minutes. (An insta-read thermometer inserted into the thigh—not touching the bone—should read at least 165°F.)

Add the sauce ingredients and the butter to the pan. Once the butter melts, continue cooking uncovered over medium heat for 2–3 minutes, spooning the sauce over the chicken repeatedly until it forms a glaze.

Serve the chicken with a final drizzle of sauce over it and garnished with the chopped green onions. Pour the sauce remaining in the pan into a small pitcher for diners to use on their rice and/or chicken as they wish.

Gochujang Sugar Cookies

(makes 8 large or 24 small cookies)

These cookies were first conceived of by Eric Kim of the *New York Times*, and then quickly became an internet sensation. What makes them so delightful is the addition of gochujang, a fermented red chili paste popular in Korea, whose combination of sweet, savory, and spicy-hot provides the cookies with a delicious and intriguing kick.

They're simple to make and, served with a scoop of creamy vanilla ice cream, would make for a terrific dessert for any dinner party—sure to be a big hit with your guests.

Be careful not to over-mix when adding the gochujang mixture (to ensure that the cookies have distinct streaks of orange-red) and to not over-bake, so they retain their chewy centers.

Gochujang paste can be found in the Asian food aisle of most supermarkets or purchased online.

Ingredients

8 tablespoons (1 stick) unsalted butter, at room temperature
1 cup white sugar
1 large egg at room temperature
1 teaspoon vanilla extract
¼ teaspoon ground cinnamon
½ teaspoon salt
½ teaspoon baking soda
1½ cups flour
2 tablespoons dark brown sugar
1 tablespoon gochujang paste

Directions

Preheat oven to 350°F.

Place 7 tablespoons of the butter into a large bowl (saving the 1 remaining tablespoon for the gochujang mixture). Add the sugar, egg, vanilla, cinnamon, and salt, and mix by hand until smooth. Stir in the baking soda and then the flour, making sure that no dry bits of either remain. A flexible spatula will work well for this task.

Place the bowl in the refrigerator to chill for 15–20 minutes. (Don't leave it in the fridge for longer than 20 minutes, or it will become too stiff to work the gochujang mixture into it.)

In a small bowl, mix until smooth the remaining 1 tablespoon of butter, the brown sugar, and the gochujang paste. Set on the counter at room temperature until ready to use.

Line two large sheet pans with parchment paper or silicone sheet liners.

After 15 minutes, remove the bowl from the refrigerator and spoon all of the gochujang mixture into 3 or 4 separate patches on top of the dough. Using the handle end of a wooden spoon or similar tool, swirl the mixture carefully into the dough, just long enough to see wide, distinctive red streaks throughout. (Over-mixing will cause the cookies to lose some of their visual charm, but they will taste marvelous, nevertheless.)

For 8 large cookies, use a scoop that is equivalent to approximately ¼ cup by volume. For 24 small cookies, scoop with a tablespoon. The cookies do spread when baked, so keep about 3 inches between the bigger ones and 2 inches between the smaller ones.

The large cookies should take about 11–13 minutes to bake, and the smaller ones a few minutes less. Rotating the pans from the top to bottom rack halfway through will give you an opportunity to assess doneness as well as ensure even baking. The cookies are ready when they're a light golden-brown at the edges and just set in the center. Remove from the oven and leave on the pans until cool. *Don't over-bake*: because of carry-over heat from the pans, the cookies will finish the last bit of cooking once out of the oven.

The cookies will keep 2 or 3 days in a sealed container—if there are any left that long. Alternatively, they can be frozen for up to 3 months, wrapped tightly in plastic.

GLOSSARY OF HAWAIIAN AND PIDGIN WORDS AND PHRASES

(Hawaiian words are in italics)

aftah	afterwards
ahi	yellowfin or bigeye tuna
aurite	all right
brah	pal, friend, brother
buggah	guy, dude, annoying creature
coconut wireless	local word-of-mouth, grapevine, gossip
da	the
dass	that's
dat	that
den	then
dere	there
dey	they
dis	this
e'rytime	always
furikake	Japanese rice seasoning made with dried seaweed and other ingredients
garanz	guaranteed
get	have
hālau	school, group, canoe club house
hana hou	to do again, repeat, once more
haole	foreigner, usually of European descent
hāpu'u	tree fern native to Hawai'i
hele on	let's get moving, get out of here
ho!	wow! hey!
huli-huli chicken	rotisserie chicken (from *huli*, to turn, rotate, overturn)

jam	get going
kālua pork	traditional Hawaiian dish of pork steamed in *ti* leaves
kau kau	food
kine	kind, sort
lānai	porch, veranda
lau lau	steamed pork and fish wrapped in *ti* leaves
lei	garland or wreath usually made of flowers, leaves, and other plant materials
li' dat	like that
liliko'i	passion fruit
lōlō	crazy, nuts
mahalo	thank you
malihini	newcomer
mauka	uphill, toward the mountain
mochi	Japanese sweet made from glutinous rice, sugar, and corn starch
mo'	more
mo'o	lizard, dragon, Hawaiian shapeshifter deity
musubi	rice ball with vegetables or meat (often Spam), wrapped in nori seaweed
mu'umu'u	loose dress originally introduced to Hawai'i by Christian missionaries
no make!	stop that! cut it out!
no wayz	no way
no worry, beef curry	don't sweat it
'ohana	family
one	a, an
'ono	delicious
pilikia	nuisance, trouble
pohole	fiddlehead fern, used in cooking
poi dog	mixed breed (from *poi*, a Polynesian staple food made of taro root)

poke	diced raw fish, often made with ahi tuna
pua	flower
pua kenikeni	tropical tree (*Fagraea berteroana*) with highly perfumed blossoms
pupu	appetizer
pupule	crazy, demented
pu'u	cinder cone, hill
saimin	Hawaiian noodle soup, similar to ramen
shaka	friendly hand gesture meaning "hang loose," "thank you," "cheers"
shoots	darn, dang
shoyu	soy sauce
sistah	sister, female friend, pal
slippahs	flip flops, rubber slippers
stay	verb "to be" (e.g., I stay watching—I was watching)
stuffs	things
talk story	chat, share stories
ti	tropical plant (*Cordyline fruticosa*) of great cultural significance to Hawaiians
tink	think
uku	a lot
'um	him, it, them
uncle	term of respect or affection for older man
wen'	used to form past tense of verbs (e.g., he wen' eat—he ate)
wikiwiki	quickly, fast
yah	yeah, right

Acknowledgments

I am enormously indebted to my wife and consistent first reader, Robin McDuff. It's always a little terrifying when I hand over my manuscript to you, but know that your honest and un-sugarcoated comments make me a better writer.

Thanks also to my eagle-eyed beta readers, Nancy Lundblad and Māhealani Jones, and to Shirley Tessler for yet again acting as my marvelous recipe editor.

In addition, my heartfelt thanks go out to Tammy Barker for her generous winning bid on a character naming in this book at the Malice Domestic charity auction to benefit KEEN Greater DC-Baltimore; to Sandra Long, for first teaching me about orchids; and to my late mom, Smiley Cook Karst, who shared with me her love for and knowledge of ceramics.

Being an author is a solitary vocation, but my many pals in the crime-writing community make it far less lonely than it would otherwise be. So thank you to my fellow bloggers at Chicks on the Case (Ellen Byron, Jennifer Chow, Marla Cooper, Vickie Fee, Cynthia Kuhn, Lisa Q. Mathews, and Patricia Sargeant) and at Mystery Lovers' Kitchen (Leslie Budewitz, Lucy Burdette, Valerie Burns, Peg Cochran, Cleo Coyle, Kim Davis, Vicki Delany, Libby Klein, Molly MacRae, Edith Maxwell/Maddy Day, and Ang Pompano), to everyone involved in Sisters and Crime and Mystery Writers of America, and to my beloved readers.

Finally, this book would not exist were it not for the hard work and encouragement provided by my fabulous agent, Erin Niumata of Folio Literary, and by everyone at Severn House, including editors Laurie Johnson, Tina Pietron, Sianna King, Eleanor Smith, managing editor Lianne Slavin, senior brand manager Martin Brown, sales and operations manager Lucy

Page, and cover designer Piers Tilbury. Thank you all for your belief in and support of me and my books!

About the author

The daughter of a law professor and a potter, **Leslie Karst** is the author of the Lefty Award-nominated Orchid Isle and Sally Solari culinary mysteries, as well as the IBPA Ben Franklin and IPPY silver award-winning memoir, *Justice is Served: A Tale of Scallops, the Law, and Cooking for RBG.*

Leslie waited tables and sang in a new wave rock band before deciding she was ready for a "real" job and ending up at Stanford Law School. It was during her career as a research and appellate attorney in Santa Cruz, California that she rediscovered her youthful passion for food and cooking, at which point she once again returned to school—this time to earn a degree in culinary arts.

Now retired from the law, in addition to writing, Leslie spends her days cooking (and eating!), gardening, cycling, and observing cocktail hour promptly at five o'clock. She and her wife and their Jack Russell mix split their time between Hilo, Hawai'i and Santa Cruz, California.

www.lesliekarstauthor.com